FAR FLY THE EAGLES

As he listened to the reports of his scouts Murat heard the sudden discordant pealing of the Kremlin bells ringing for vespers; a cannon pounded the Kutafyev Gate of the Kremlin, where some peasants had barricaded themselves in and were sniping at the invaders as they surrounded the Palace. The noise was a feeble echo in the silence that enveloped Moscow; the shouts of the soldiers who were entering the houses were reedy and unreal; the majestic churches towered above them, shining like buildings in a mirage, and the bells pealed out the prayer of many centuries to a city that was empty except for the stream of invading troops who were pouring into it. Murat spurred his horse forward and rode towards the Kremlin; he was frowning, and shouted angrily to one of his aides to ride ahead and stop the troops despoiling any of the State rooms before the Emperor's arrival.

Messengers went back to the French camp and informed Napoleon that the enemy had abandoned their capital; there would be no deputation, no triumphal entry. Moscow was empty.

**Also by the same author,
and available from Coronet:**

IMPERIAL HIGHNESS
CURSE NOT THE KING

About the author

Evelyn Anthony started writing seriously in
1949 and before turning to spy thrillers,
which include *The Silver Falcon* and *The
Tamarind Seed*, she wrote a succession of
ten highly successful historical novels – all of
which were widely translated. She has six
children, and lives in a beautiful Elizabethan
mansion in Essex. FAR FLY THE EAGLES is
the third volume of Evelyn Anthony's
Romanov Trilogy.

Far Fly the Eagles

Evelyn Anthony

CORONET BOOKS
Hodder and Stoughton

First published in Great Britain in 1955 by Museum Press

Published in 1986 by Century Hutchinson Ltd

Coronet edition 1989

British Library C.I.P.

Anthony, Evelyn, *1928–*
  Far fly the eagles.
  I. Title
  823'.914 [F]

ISBN 0-340-49740-8

Printed and bound in Great Britain for Hodder and Stoughton Paperbacks, a division of Hodder and Stoughton Ltd., Mill Road, Dunton Green, Sevenoaks, Kent TN13 2YA. (Editorial Office: 47 Bedford Square, London WC1B 3DP) by Cox & Wyman Ltd., Reading.

AUTHOR'S NOTE

THERE are places in this story where I have sacrificed strict accuracy to dramatic effect, principally in the case of Talleyrand, whose treason did not become really effective until after Erfurt. Alexander's relationship with his sister will always be in doubt; I have not accepted the view that it was incestuous in practice. The details of the campaign of 1812 are as accurate as possible, except that Barclay de Tolly had withdrawn from Smolensk before the peak of the battle. The Grand Duchess Catherine was already in London when Alexander sailed for the State visit to England. I have discounted the theory that the Empress Josephine became the Czar's mistress, but his affaire with Hortense seems borne out by the fact that Napoleon himself sent her as an emissary to Alexander at a later date. With the above exception, *Far Fly the Eagles* is a true story. The description of the Bolshevik's exhumation of Alexander's coffin is naturally imaginary; though the tomb was opened and found to be empty, there is no way of verifying any details.

LONDON 1955.

CHAPTER ONE

"YOUR Majesty, the Russian Emperor is about to embark." The man seated behind the wide desk looked up at his aide.

"I am aware of that, Henri. I shall be ready in five minutes."

He took up his pen and began writing; the aide bowed and withdrew. Five minutes would ensure that the Russians were inconvenienced, and it was part of his policy to keep them waiting.

He frowned and scratched out a word of what he had written; his face was fine featured, but inclined to fat; portraits and the official stamp on French coins flattered him. He signed and pushed the papers away and withdrew a gold watch out of his pocket. It was nearly time to leave. He had just beaten Austria, Prussia and Russia after a war lasting eighteen months, a war begun by these powers because Napoleon Bonaparte, whose father was a poor lawyer in Corsica, had dared to proclaim himself Emperor of the French.

The young General of the Revolution had become the General of the Directory which followed the fall of Robespierre and the end of the Terror. The shabby young officer who was always at such a social disadvantage in the elegant salons of the new ruling class in Paris had won victory after victory for France. He had made a fool of himself by marrying Josephine Beauharnais, who was years older, and had only agreed to the match because her protector Barras insisted; it was a good way of getting rid of her; he would help the gauche husband with a promising Command. The Command was Italy, and the result—Napoleon, who knew exactly why the Director Barras had smiled on his union with Josephine—Napoleon smiled in his turn when he thought of it.

He had dissolved the Directory after a military *coup d'état* and made himself First Consul. A further series of victories and wholesale annexations of conquered territories had culminated in two things.

The discovery of a Royalist plot to assassinate him—had given him the excuse to have the Bourbon Duc D'Enghien kidnapped out of Germany, tried by court martial for complicity, and shot in Vincennes prison.

That settled any question of re-establishing the old Royal dynasty.

He then made himself Emperor of France.

He had never doubted that he could defeat Austria; the real military question mark was Russia, and though Russian forces took part in the battle of Austerlitz, where the Austrian army was annihilated, the result was less conclusive than Napoleon had hoped. The Russians fought well, but their organization was appalling and their Emperor Alexander had taken Supreme Command. One thing Austerlitz proved, and that was the Czar's lack of military skill. But properly equipped and led by a good general, the Russian soldier might give a very different account of himself.

Napoleon frowned slightly; after Austerlitz the Prussians had come into the war and been hopelessly beaten at Jena and then at Friedland. At Friedland the Russians were defeated for the second time, a defeat which not even their Emperor could deny. The Prussian Army was destroyed, the Russians suffered heavy losses in men and materials, and the Czar led his troops in headlong retreat to Tilsit, and crossed the Niemen into Russia.

Russian emissaries came to Napoleon, hinting at peace without any hope of success. The French had reached Tilsit and were encamped on the opposite bank from the exhausted Russian Army. All Napoleon had to do was cross the river. To everyone's amazement he had agreed to an armistice.

It was the Czar who suggested that a raft be built and moored in the middle of the Niemen so that both rulers could meet in a neutral area; it was a shrewd suggestion because it saved Alexander the indignity of going across the Russian frontier to meet his enemy.

Napoleon saw through it, and his estimation of his opponent rose.

It was a long time since he had been so curious about anyone as he was about the Emperor Alexander; a study of his Ambassador's reports and the facts known about him had presented Napoleon with a puzzle he was determined to solve.

He was gentle, eye-witnesses said, with irresistible charm and a rather shy manner; he professed Liberal sympathies in a country where freedom was unknown, and surrounded himself with young men of similar ideals. He had even talked wistfully of abdicating. If there was any defect in his character it was weakness, the tendency to bend to stronger personalities. Everyone Napoleon questioned agreed on one point. Alexander of Russia was the most handsome man they had ever seen.

Napoleon had then compared this portrait of a good-looking figurehead with the facts; and the facts didn't blend with the portrait. Alexander was the son of Paul I, a madman and a genius whose name was the synonym for terror, and he was the grandson of Catherine the Great.

It was unlikely, Napoleon thought grimly, that such a heredity had produced either a Liberal or a weakling.

It was even more unlikely when one remembered that at the age of twenty-four the gentle humanist of the ambassadorial reports had had his own father brutally murdered and taken the Crown. He had then disposed of the murderers one by one when his position was established.

He was reputed to have had as many women as Napoleon himself, but to have fallen in love with none of them.

And he, the youngest of the three monarchs concerned in the late war, had been the instigator of the whole attempt to smash France and dethrone her new Emperor. He had also been the first to abandon Prussia and sue for Napoleon's friendship as well as for peace.

He had been lucky, Napoleon decided, that peace and friendship were also in French interest at that time. An alliance with Russia and the promise to cease trading with England were what Napoleon hoped to gain from this meeting. In return he would promise Russia a free hand against Turkey; she could attack her hereditary enemy and France would see that no one in Europe dared to interfere. He would resurrect the dream of Paul I, a world divided between France and Russia, as the price of Russian support against England. Once he had beaten England, by strangling her trade and attacking her allies, then he could destroy Russia in his own time.

He never doubted his ability to ensnare the Czar; whether he proved to be a fool or a schemer, Napoleon was quite certain of success. He had matched his wits against the wiliest men in France, seized power and outraged the principals of the Revolution by re-establishing not just the monarchy, but an Empire. The most brilliant diplomats in Europe had failed to stand against his cunning in politics, falling as low as his opponents in the field.

The twenty-nine-year-old ruler of Russia would never succeed where everyone else had failed.

Napoleon looked at his watch again, and rising, called for his valet.

" My hat and my sword."

He stood while his sword-belt was buckled on, a tiny figure of a man, less than five feet four inches tall, in the uniform of the Imperial Old Guard, without any decoration but the red ribbon of the Legion d'Honneur which he had instituted himself. He put on his wide cocked hat; the valet bowed.

"Send for Duroc," Napoleon ordered. "I am ready to leave."

*   *   *

An enormous wooden raft was moored in the middle of

the river, and a pavilion the size of a small floating palace had been erected on it. The June sun was shining that day, glistening on the swelling water, on the gilt, the standards, the coloured tents clustered on the raft, and on the vast encampments on either side of the Niemen, the victorious army of France and the defeated troops of Holy Russia.

In the private sitting-room in an inn on the banks of the Niemen, Alexander of Russia waited with his personal friend and aide, Colonel Novossiltsov.

" Your Majesty, he's late! " the Colonel exclaimed angrily. " This is an insult, it's deliberate! "

Alexander looked down at him and smiled.

" Have patience. I arrived early, if you remember. It is arranged that we land at the same time. A lot depends on appearances, my friend. The King of Prussia has been left to wait on shore."

" I am not concerned with Prussia, Sire. But this is an insult to you! "

Novossiltsov watched his Emperor and frowned; he had learnt at last that Alexander's gentleness was a sign of danger. When he was angry he froze; emotionally touched, he wept; when he was planning something he smiled, as he was doing then.

The Czar's blue eyes turned away from him.·

" This is to be an alliance, you understand," he said quietly. " Not a peace treaty in which we appear the defeated."

Novossiltsov stared at him.

" No, Sire. Of course not."

Alexander knew what he was thinking, knew that he was remembering the battlefield at Austerlitz, the thousands of Russian dead stiffening in the frozen swamps of the Gold-bach, the unforgettable horror of their flight across the Lake of Tollnitz where the ice gave under them and hundreds drowned. Then Friedland, where 40,000 troops had faced a French force of twice that number, and after losing fifteen thousand men, were driven back to Tilsit.

They were not defeated, he had said, and watched the confusion and resentment on Novossiltsov's face as he agreed to the lie. He knew the truth, he and the other members of Alexander's staff who had been engaged in the war, and they were blaming the Czar for having tried to direct the army himself. They were also blaming him for making peace instead of trying to redeem his honour, blinded by anger and pride to the fact that they were practically disarmed, their troops in utter confusion, and that their enemy was the foremost strategist in the world.

They were unused to defeat; the tradition of Catherine the Great and Russian invincibility would not admit it. They wanted to fight, to be annihilated if necessary, rather than return without glory; they would never forgive Alexander for arranging this meeting, and he knew it. The peace party in Russia who had opposed the war in the first place would never forgive him either, for having proved them right.

" Novossiltsov," he said.

The Colonel turned to him. " Sire? "

" I had to make peace while we were still in a position of some strength, do you understand? He would have invaded Russia and no one could have stopped him. He wants peace now, my friend, so whatever his terms I shall be able to safeguard the interests of Russia, you may be certain of that."

" I know that, Sire," the Colonel said quickly. " Believe me, it's just that I resent . . ."

" You resent Austerlitz and Friedland, Novossiltsov. And so do I. I had to ride for my life from the battlefield; do you think I shall ever forget that? "

The Colonel scowled. " None of us will, Sire."

Alexander smiled sadly.

" You will have to trust me, my friend. Trust me to do what is best for Russia."

As he spoke he knew that not even Novossiltsov was really loyal to him any longer. And if he, who had served him devotedly for years, was not to be trusted, then his danger was very great. If failure in war were followed by failure at the Conference, then Alexander knew that he would lose his throne and his life when he returned to Petersburg.

He straightened a jewelled order that hung from his collar. His father had worn it, he remembered; his father had become Napoleon's ally too, but he had been murdered before the alliance could take effect. And that murder had indirectly resulted in the war.

The news of the execution of the Duc D'Enghien had profoundly shocked the Courts of Europe, and not least the Imperial family of St. Petersburg whose record was crimson with murders and Palace revolution. Alexander expressed his horror at the act, and promptly received a reply reminding him that France had not presumed to interfere when the Emperor Paul was murdered. . . .

From that moment he had determined to overthrow Napoleon, and it was for this reason he had persuaded Austria and Prussia to embark on the war which had ruined them. His anger had not abated, it was as bitter on the raft at Tilsit as it was when he first sent his troops into action against the French, but like all his deep emotions, it was hidden. He disguised his hatred for Bonaparte from the moment it became necessary to make peace with him; if the act was to convince his enemy it must also convince everyone else, and all his life Alexander had played different rôles for the benefit of different people. The loving grandson for Catherine, and this was easy because she was the only member of his family for whom he felt the least affection. The dutiful son for his father, but his father was as shrewd in some things as he was mad in others, and his father never believed him for a moment. . . . And the unwilling conspirator in the plot to dethrone Paul; that rôle was followed by the reluctant ruler whose only wish was to reform the abuses of his father's reign and then abdicate. Within six years of his accession he had gained a reputation for Liberalism and personal mildness which practically obliterated the circumstances of Paul's death. The projected reforms were discussed at length, but never put into practice; he would have liked to improve the governmental system to prove to himself and the world that he had justified his means by the end, but he quickly realized the impossibility of abolishing either serfdom or political corruption. While he abandoned the plan he continued to talk, firing the young men who surrounded him with ideals as splendid as they were untenable. His great friend Adam Czartorisky was an enthusiast for the most extreme plans, seeing in every suggestion a chance of securing freedom for his native Poland.

Alexander liked Adam, he admired his courage and unselfishness; he listened to many of his counsels, rejecting the idealistic and accepting the practical, with as little intention of restoring the kingdom of Poland as he had of freeing the serfs.

He found the Poles a fascinating people; Adam was handsome, fierily romantic and quixotic enough to fall in love with the Czarina Elizabeth, Alexander's wife.

And the man who could do that was an idealist indeed, he thought coldly. Thank God for it, thank God for Adam's hot blood and his own quick wits. The scandal of his wife's passion for her own lady-in-waiting was killed by the scandal of her affair with Adam, and the danger of domestic upheaval passed. He had never forgiven Elizabeth for the adolescent abnormality or admitted that his own neglect and coldness were responsible.

And the Czar's sexual indifference which had tormented his young wife was completely cured by a countrywoman of Adam Czartorisky, the beautiful, spirited Marie Naryshkin, wife of one of the wealthiest nobles in Russia.

Oh, God, he thought suddenly, God, how I long to see her, how I long for all this to be over. . . .

"The French are approaching, Sire."

Alexander turned to Novossiltsov. "We will embark at once."

The French boats were tying up at the side and the blast of French trumpets sounded as the Emperor Napoleon landed.

A moment later Alexander stepped on to the raft and

walked towards him. They came within a few paces of each other and then the Czar held out his hand.

" He's so small," he thought, while his brilliant smile greeted Napoleon. " So small and yet not ridiculous. . . . He has terrible eyes."

" I hope we meet as friends, Sire, rather than enemies," he said simply.

Bonaparte looked up at the tall figure of the Czar; his height was accentuated by the brilliant uniform of the Preobrozhensky Guards laced with gold, and the sash of the order of St. Andrew crossed his chest; a Maltese Cross studded with enormous diamonds hung from his collar. His blond head was uncovered and he bowed slightly. Napoleon decided that it was impossible for any man who looked like that to be intelligent as well.

He also smiled, and his grim, sunburnt face relaxed.

" My only enemies are the English, Sire," he answered.

Nominally Russia's ally, England had confined her support to promises and conserved her own strength while the three military powers exhausted themselves in the conflict.

Alexander's face became cold and grave.

" They are Russia's enemies too."

" Then," Napoleon replied firmly, " we are at peace." Side by side they walked to the Pavilion and disappeared inside the room reserved for them. No one else was present at the meeting.

The door closed behind them, and the officers of the Russian Guard looked across the Pavilion at the French. Alexander might shake hands with an upstart who had defeated them in the field; he might smile and show friendship, but they would not. The Russian nobles turned their backs on the members of the French entourage and began to talk among themselves.

" Rabble," Count Ouvarov snapped. " An army of parvenus led by a parvenu. Did you hear what was said about England? He wants us to fight England with him! "

" The Czar will refuse," Novossiltsov said. " You underestimate him."

" I hope so," Ouvarov answered. " I don't like any of this. I don't like this fawning on these French vermin; I don't like this peace. . . . And a lot of others will feel as I do. For his own sake, I hope the Czar knows what he's doing; if Napoleon doesn't take his throne from him his own people might ! "

" You talk treason," Novossiltsov whispered. " Who would replace him, his brother Constantine? Do you want another Paul or worse. . . ."

" I'm no traitor, and you know it. I conspired to put Alexander in power, but I'd not keep him there to make us vassals of France. As for a successor, he has a sister, Novossiltsov, and Russia prospers under women. If he goes too far, there's always the Grand Duchess Catherine."

CHAPTER TWO

THE Imperial family were gathered in the Dowager Empress's apartments in the Summer Palace at St. Petersburg; it was early afternoon and the big salon was bright with sunshine. Sunshine poured through the long windows to the despair of the Dowager Empress Marie Feodorovna, who was sure it would fade her magnificent Aubusson carpet.

She sat in a gilt fauteuil embroidering, wishing that she dared order her daughter Catherine away from the window and have the blinds lowered. Her younger son, the Grand Duke Constantine, paced up and down behind her chair, scowling and muttering to himself. It was quite useless to tell him to sit down; he was always restless and vile-tempered whenever his brother Alexander was near, and Alexander was expected any moment. That was the reason for the unusual family gathering; Alexander was returning from Tilsit, and his mother, his younger brother, his sister and his wife were waiting to welcome him.

The Grand Duchess Catherine stood with her back to them, staring out of the window. She was tall and gracefully built with beautiful hands and perfect shoulders, exposed by the high-waisted white satin dress. Two miniatures surrounded by large diamonds were pinned to her breast, the portraits of her brother the Czar Alexander and of her grandmother the great Empress Catherine. There were pearls in her black hair and round her narrow throat. Catherine the Great had worn them once, and her granddaughter had besought Alexander to give them to her. After all, as Catherine coolly pointed out, the pearls had never suited his wife anyway.

The striking beauty of her face, with its straight features and slanting black eyes was spoilt by an expression of sullen arrogance. She was just eighteen years old.

In a corner of the room the Empress Consort of Russia sat with her hands in her lap, staring into space. She was delicate featured and very fair; her mother-in-law's summons had interrupted the long letter she was writing to her own mother:

" He is coming back to-day, dear Mama, and I'm afraid the situation here is very dangerous. I shall be able to tell you very little because I am not in his confidence as you know. He seldom speaks to me and naturally I cannot approach him. In spite of the pain I have suffered and still suffer from his indifference, and the presence of that creature Naryshkin at Court, I have the most loyal and affectionate feelings towards him. The Court is outraged by this pact with Napoleon Bonaparte, and his sister, of whom I have written before, is the centre of intrigue against him. . . ."

She glanced across at the Dowager Empress who smiled vaguely at her. She had never been unkind to Elizabeth Alexeievna, merely abrupt and inclined to ignore her, which was only natural since her own husband set the example, but she had never been cruel. Unlike the other two. . . .

The young Empress looked towards her brother-in-law Constantine and shuddered. Hideous, a coward, unbelievably cruel and degenerate in his habits, he was more like a wild beast than a man. He was short, thick set, with the flat features of the Czar Paul and the same jerky mannerisms; his own family acknowledged him to be a sadistic maniac.

The Grand Duchess Catherine Pavlovna was as fierce as her brother, but she was cunning, and shrewd. There was an animal quality about her, Elizabeth thought—not the bestiality of Constantine, but a primitive, predatory force allied to a violent temper and an inflexible will. Her whole family were afraid of her, even the monstrous Constantine retreated, snarling and cursing, when she opposed him; only Alexander pandered to her out of love.

Once, years ago, Elizabeth had been jealous of that love, watched Catherine pouting, and wheedling her own way with Alexander, until it suddenly occurred to Elizabeth that she was grown up, beautiful, and that her manner with her brother was almost flirtation. . . .

But the jealousy, with most of her feelings, was quite dead. She dreaded Catherine's vicious tongue, flinched under snubs and mockery, because in spite of everything she was still sensitive. But the hurt was only on the surface. Nothing could really touch her now. The ending of her love affair with Adam Czartorisky had reduced her to a silent shell, listlessly following Alexander from one State residence to another, living and sleeping alone, month after month and year after year, the unwanted, childless wife whom everyone said should be divorced.

He had made her commit adultery with Adam. She could remember his eyes, so cold and deadly with anger as they looked at her, the disgust and implacability in his face when he advised her that her dear friend Countess Golovine would not attend her any more. He preferred her to accommodate Prince Adam Czartorisky instead. The alternative, he told her quietly, was a scandal of such magnitude that the Czar Paul would undoubtedly imprison all of them.

Paul's prudery was notorious, almost as notorious as his

hatred of his son; if the rumours of Elizabeth's strange tendencies reached him, he would certainly blame Alexander. Since it wasn't possible to banish all her ladies-in-waiting to prevent her finding a successor to the Countess, he ordered her to distract herself with Adam.

"The Prince is devoted to me, Madame," he had said. "I have assured him that you are in love with him. His loyalty to me and his chivalry should be sufficient."

She had never forgotten those words, they echoed through the first weeks of her liaison with Adam, until his insistence that he loved her deadened them. He had loved her, and all the frustrated passion of her nature responded to him. They had been intensely happy, oblivious of the upheaval of Paul's murder and Alexander's accession.

The incident with Countess Golovine faded from Elizabeth's memory; now, years afterwards, she wasn't sure what had really happened, what was the motive in the Countess's mind when she comforted the overwrought young wife, and in her own mind when she let herself be comforted.

But it no longer mattered. Nothing mattered, because Alexander had separated Adam from her, giving him posts abroad until the situation changed through absence and despair.

Now she was alone, alone with only the memories of Adam to sustain her and the daily letter to her mother in Germany to look forward to, a woman married to a man who had never loved or wanted her, a woman whose life was over at the age of twenty-eight. Adam's child had died, poor, pretty child, with its father's dark colouring and her fragility.

And there would never be another, for she was not promiscuous; the cynical sensuality of Alexander's sister was revolting to her, and she was sure that after Adam she would never love again.

Nothing remained but a slow ache of unhappiness, a monotony of pain sometimes disturbed by doubt if it was really for Adam or still for the strange man she had married.

He was coming back from Tilsit after signing a peace treaty with Napoleon, coming back to a capital seething with plots and discontent, to be welcomed by the sister whose only ambition was to take the throne for herself. How could he be so blind, she wondered, so blinded by that vixen that he didn't see the envy, the falseness behind her laughter and familiarity? Could he believe she loved him. . . . Or did he see through her, and was this brotherly indulgence a sinister game that he was playing, playing so well that Catherine herself was deceived. . . . 'Whatever it is,' she decided, 'he doesn't need my help. I offended him once, God help me, and I have no excuse for the Golovine, since I don't understand it myself, and he's never forgiven me. But I meant what I said in that letter to Mama. I have loyal feeling for him. Even . . . affectionate feelings. I pray to God he's warned in time. . . .'

"He's coming!" the Grand Duchess Catherine said suddenly. "I can see the head of the procession." She opened the window quickly. "Listen. The people are cheering."

"He's been issuing ukases saying that Tilsit was a victory for Russia!" the Grand Duke Constantine burst out. "These fools out there think we won the war!"

"But we know better," Catherine Pavlovna remarked. "I'm not going to welcome him; defeat is bad enough, but an alliance with that monster! Banquets and reviews every day, embracing and kissing each other. . . ." She laughed harshly. "Can you imagine Alexander kissing that little upstart; he must've had to get down on his knees to reach him. . . ."

"Catherine, for the love of God, don't say anything to anger your brother," the Dowager Empress pleaded nervously, and her daughter smiled.

"I've never understood why you're so frightened of him, Mama," she said. "I'm not. No one could be frightened of Alexander."

The Empress Marie went on sewing and said nothing. No one could be frightened of Alexander. Unless they remembered his father Paul, and the fate of anyone else who stood between him and what he wanted.

What frightened her most was the complete absence of terrorism in his manner; his unfailing courtesy and mildness, even to servants, was somehow more menacing than the furies of his father, and she knew that everyone close to him felt the same after a time.

His wife, that silent, broken woman who was still paying for a crime of which she was never proved guilty, his brother Constantine, his own mother. . . . They knew him and they were all afraid. Only Catherine Pavlovna laughed at him, argued with him, and flouted his authority, insisting that he was only her brother after all, and that he loved her. . . . She was so confident of her hold on him, so sure that when the time came, she'd be able to turn him off his throne, that filial affection wouldn't blind *her* as it did him. The Dowager Empress no longer tried to warn her; she was tired of coping with her savage brood; Constantine was a sadist whose excesses she pretended not to notice; her third son Nicholas seemed quite devoid of sensibility, unfeeling and stupid as a machine; he was still only a boy, and her beautiful wilful daughter Catherine was following the example of her ancestors and trying to engulf them all in family murder.

" He's arrived," Catherine said. " Outside the Palace, there, he's dismounting! "

The Dowager Empress got up and came to the window. " How does he look? " she asked. " I can't see properly."

" Like a god, as usual. Listen to that reception."

Constantine fiddled with his cravat; he was suddenly nervous. For weeks he'd been abusing his brother, and swearing vengeance against the French. Now Alexander had returned, received by his people as a conqueror, and Constantine decided that it might be as well to go down and meet him. It was all very well for Catherine to snub him; he gave her a licence denied to anyone else.

He swallowed and his ugly face contorted in a frightened scowl.

" I'm going down," he announced.

Immediately his mother went to his side. "So am I. I want to welcome my dear son. Elizabeth?" She looked towards her daughter-in-law and the Empress Consort rose obediently.

Catherine Pavlovna looked at them contemptuously.

"I stay here," she said. "You can associate yourselves with what he's done, but I shall not. If he wants to see me, he can come to me!"

She stayed by the window staring out at the crowds massing round the entrance of the Winter Palace, listening to the cheers, and her envy of her brother rose in her till she felt as if she were swallowing gall. Believing him weak, she despised him; she hated him because he toyed with Liberalism, blinded by prejudice to the fact that all he had ever done was talk. And now he was the ally of Napoleon Bonaparte, after plunging into a war for which he wasn't properly prepared. Catherine, steeped in the doctrine of Autocracy, naturally strong-willed and insanely proud, reminded herself of these things and thought furiously that he was not fit to rule. Neither was Constantine of course, and her other brother and young sister Anne were not to be considered. That left herself, the granddaughter and namesake of Catherine the Great, with more intelligence and will-power than the rest of her family combined. Other people thought as she did, she remembered; since Tilsit, some of the most powerful nobles in Russia had hinted openly that Alexander's actions might have to be checked. . . .

In the middle of her reflections she heard the door open behind her, and she smiled contemptuously. He'd given way as usual and come to see her. . . .

But it was not the Emperor; she realized that before she turned round and saw Constantine standing in the room. He stared at her and his little eyes were narrow.

"You should have come down to meet him," he said. "He asked for you."

"What did you say?" Catherine asked. There was a curious, unspoken bond between these two; they were in alliance in spite of themselves.

" Mama said you had a headache," Constantine answered.
" He didn't believe it."

" Mama is a fool."

" Not as great a fool as you! You can't afford to flout
him openly like that. And if he turns on you, don't think
I'll stand by you! " he snarled.

Catherine's lips compressed and her black eyes blazed at
him.

" I don't. I know what a coward you are, my dear brother.
. . . You hate him as much as I do, but you haven't the will
to do anything about it. Well, I have! Now save yourself,
go and tell him what I've said! "

The Grand Duke swore at her, and flung himself into a
chair.

After a moment Catherine walked over to him.

" We're foolish to quarrel. We can help each other," she
said quietly.

" Where has he gone? "

" To the Naryshkin, of course."

" Of course," Catherine smiled unpleasantly. " I hope
he greeted our sister-in-law first."

" He hardly spoke to her," Constantine said. " She infuri-
ates me—whining bitch! I don't know why he doesn't get
rid of her."

" I've noticed how much you hate her, Constantine.
There's something about her that rouses your baser instincts,
little brother. . . ." Catherine laughed. " She asks to be
tormented. Even Alexander enjoys being cruel to her.
Thank God she'll offer no resistance when the time comes."

Constantine looked up at her, scowling.

" In God's name, why should I risk my head to put you on
the throne? " he muttered.

" Because you hate Alexander, and because you don't want
to be Emperor yourself." She came and sat on the arm of
his chair. The mixture of ugliness, naiveté and evil in him
fascinated her; she often felt as if her brother were a distor-
tion of herself. She knew too that in a twisted way he loved
her and looked up to her.

"Do you know why you hate Alexander?" she asked him.

He grimaced. "Because he murdered Papa," he said.

"The devil take Papa! That has nothing to do with it. No, Constán, you hate him because he's so handsome, and all these damned women fawn on him. You hate him because he's head and shoulders taller than you, and you feel like a little ape beside him."

She put her hand on his shoulder and pressed him back in the chair.

"Don't get angry. A lot of other people feel as you do. You envy him for what he is, and I—I envy him for what he's got. And one day I mean to take it from him."

She bent and kissed her brother lightly on the cheek.

"You know that people say he's in love with me, don't you?" she whispered. Constantine's face turned crimson; he caught her arm and twisted it savagely.

"That's not true," he said hoarsely. "You're his sister. . . ."

"No, it's not true," Catherine said slowly. "You're hurting me, Constantine. . . . I only told you so that you need never be jealous, however fond we seem to be at times. I have to be fond, Constan, to make him trust me. . . ."

She slid off the chair and stood looking at him with an extraordinary expression in her slanting black eyes. "Never forget that," she said quietly. Then she walked quickly out of the room.

*   *   *

As Constantine said, Alexander had gone to Marie Naryshkin. She was waiting for him in his rooms, and she ran into his outstretched arms. He lifted her off her feet and kissed her; for several moments they said nothing. He closed his eyes and held her; her smallness, the scent she used, the soft dark hair that always tangled round the buttons on his sleeve, the taste of her mouth, all the familiar things which he had missed so much during the campaign came back to him, bringing an ache of happiness.

She clasped her hands behind his head and kissed him, wanting to cry because he was with her, and knowing that he wouldn't like it, and wouldn't understand.

She had never loved any man before. She was young, very beautiful, and married to a man years older than herself, a solemn, cultured man who didn't know how to make her happy. She had had lovers like everybody else; many lovers, and been contented in a superficial way, until she tried to capture Alexander out of devilment, and fell in love with him herself. Then, for the first time in her life she was uncertain. He was charming, but she discovered that his charm was not reserved for her, he was gentle and courteous, and a passionate lover, but he remained fundamentally aloof. There was a point she had never been able to reach in their relationship, the point where the Czar became the man.

She was a woman of pronounced passions who understood passion and knew how to cope with it; she had learnt very quickly that the key to a man's character was often his weakness, but in Alexander she could find nothing. He eluded her without effort and in seeming ignorance that he was making her unhappy.

The time came when she was forced to admit that the pattern of her previous love affairs had been reversed; she was desperately in love and he was not.

At last he set her down and looked at her.

" Marie, not tears. . . . Aren't you pleased to see me? "

" Pleased! " She laughed unsteadily. " It's been like a lifetime without you, Sire." She came and put her arms round his waist.

" Don't you know that people sometimes cry because they're happy? "

He smiled and stroked her hair. " I've missed you, Marie. My God, I couldn't wait to get back to you. Oh, beloved, I'm so thankful it's all over and we can be together! "

She listened to him and her heart was suddenly beating

very fast. She had never heard that note in his voice before. Almost as if he meant what he said.

She moved away from him. "You must be weary, Sire. Come and sit down and tell me everything. First let me get you some wine."

He watched her as she poured wine into two glasses, and thought how beautiful she was; though much smaller, she reminded him of his sister Catherine. They shared the same dark colouring, the same vitality, but Marie was emotional and gentle where the other reminded him of a prowling panther. . . . He frowned as he thought of her. Her absence was not only a snub but a gesture for the benefit of his resentful Court, a gesture to show that the Grand Duchess Catherine shared their feelings over the new French alliance. She was clever, he knew that; he had always known that once his father was dead he had only one member of his family to reckon with and that was Catherine. At eighteen she was a woman, already a libertine and an intriguer, openly eyeing the throne. Now she thought she saw her opportunity. He was unpopular; he had lost the war and concluded a dishonourable peace. Many Czars had been deposed for less.

'Catherine,' he thought bitterly. 'If I hadn't got one murder on my conscience already I'd know what to do with her. But I can't. I'll have to play the loving brother for the time. I suppose I shall have to go and see her to-morrow. . . .'

"Thank you, Marie." He drank some wine and smiled up at her. It was extraordinary how the sight of her standing there eased him; he hadn't realized how much he'd missed her. "Come and sit with me," he said. She sat on the arm of his chair leaning against his shoulder.

"Tell me about the war," she said.

"It was a disaster," he said moodily. "Austerlitz was the worst. I realized what war really meant for the first time. God knows I'll never forget it."

"You shouldn't go into battle," Marie said. "What would happen if you were killed or captured?"

He smiled cynically. "My sister Catherine would be delighted. Less delighted if she had to deal with Bonaparte, perhaps."

"Tell me about him. . . . What's he like? Handsome? He seems so in his portraits."

"No, he's not handsome, they flatter him. He's very short, Marie, but he's got presence, great presence. He's overpowering when you meet him first. He was very charming to me of course because it suited him, but I could imagine how he would be. . . . He's a bully by nature; I felt him struggling to be amiable and dignified with me, especially when I disagreed with him. He is a brilliant man, Marie, the most brilliant strategist and the most cunning diplomatist you can imagine. He intends to subdue the whole world, and whatever the means he'll use them. He has different methods with different people—silence, blustering, threats and friendship. Friendship is for his most dangerous enemies, and that, my little one, is what he offered me. In return I offered him mine. Which means that one of us will eventually crush the other. There can never be another Austerlitz for us."

She stared at him. "Another? Then you don't really mean to be his ally. . . . You mean it isn't true?"

"What isn't true?" he asked quietly.

"What everyone is saying. That you've abandoned Prussia and Austria to him and promised him help against England."

"It is quite true. Austria and Prussia lost the war, there's nothing I can do for them. My detractors had better try negotiating with Napoleon themselves. As for what I've promised . . ." He paused and lifted her hand to his lips. "Promises are only words. Like peace treaties they can be broken."

"Does he trust you?" she whispered.

"Yes," he answered. "He trusts me. And he thinks I'm a fool. I lost the war, Marie, but I believe I've won the peace. Oh, I know what's being said here! That I'm a coward; that Bonaparte made a fool of me; that I've betrayed

my allies and dishonoured my country. I know that some
of them are measuring Catherine Pavlovna for my crown
. . . I know, Marie, I saw signs of it at Tilsit. Ouvarov,
Novossiltsov, God knows how many others; so stupid they
can't see there's a time for caution as well as courage. Sometimes it's necessary to *play* the coward, and that needs as
much courage as facing death on any battlefield."

" What will you do? " she said at last.

" Go to war again. But not till I'm ready, Marie, not till
I know I can win."

There was silence between them then and the room
began to grow dark. . . . " I'll have the candles lit," she
said.

He turned in the chair and caught her. " No. Leave
them; not now."

He stroked her cheek with his fingers; she stayed very still
while his hand travelled downwards over her throat, then
she began to tremble as she always did when he touched her.
He pulled her down into the chair and kissed her; she knew
that he'd broken her necklace, and the action was immediately symbolic of her own capitulation. Her passion for him
blazed up, mixed with the intolerable pain of her love for
him and the knowledge that he was changed, changed as a
man and as a lover. The room was very dark.

" Marie," she heard him whisper. " Marie, I love you . . .
Marie."

*   *   *

The Emperor Napoleon was sitting in his study in The
Tuilleries, discussing Alexander of Russia with his wife.
Josephine lay back on a gilt sofa and tried to concentrate,
repressing a yawn of boredom.

She was miserably bored with the conversation, most of
which was concerned with politics and Napoleon's military
moves in the war. He spoke quickly, with many gestures, his
dark eyes sparkling, and she thought how unpolished he was
still; one violent gesture menaced a favourite Sèvres vase on

the table at his side, and Josephine winced in anticipation of the crash. She was the personification of elegance herself, mistress of the graceful pose and delicate movement, exquisitely made up and coiffured. The Revolution had destroyed her; she was frivolous, silly and amoral, traits which had been exploited to the utmost, and there was something about the Empress of the French that betrayed a dubious past. But she was naturally kind, with an amiable wit, an enchanting laugh and a snuggling, helpless manner with men. As Napoleon talked, she thought how odd it was that a man of his type should have fallen in love with her; lately she was discovering qualities in him which fascinated other people and used to be invisible to her. His intellectual range and brilliance, his energy, his terrifying ambition, and, above all, his achievements!

Men were always talking, but Bonaparte translated his words into facts. It was a great pity, she decided, that she had never been able to love him. He was a crude and violent lover, and he frightened her by comparison with the other men she had known, mostly aristocrats like herself. She preferred amorous dalliance, he made love like a whirlwind; he was rather a vulgar little man, fond of displaying his emotions, and while she was too good-natured to dislike him, she neglected and deceived him in his absence during the Italian campaign, and was always relieved when his leaves ended and she could continue her life in peace.

In the early days she would have stopped him, explained sweetly that she didn't understand a word of what he said, but now she did not dare. The situation was changed; the rough young Corsican was the ruler of France, conqueror of many countries, and he was no longer in love with her. Her position was precarious and she had many enemies.

She couldn't afford to be bored or selfish with him; she had to sit and pretend to be interested.

"Then everything went well!" she ventured. It was a safe remark, half question and half statement; it wouldn't betray the fact that she hadn't been really listening.

"Excellently," Napoleon answered. "The Czar agreed

to everything including the blockade of English trade; as I was explaining, that's the important factor now. . . . But I was most impressed by Alexander."

" Were you? " Josephine's interest was genuine. She had heard that Alexander was the handsomest man in Europe, and the instincts of the cocotte sharpened with curiosity. Napoleon, who understood her perfectly, noted the changed tone and the large brown eyes turned on him enquiringly.

" I had expected an arrogant blockhead, but he was charming. Quite intelligent too. Once I explained the situation to him and made my proposals he agreed immediately. I promised him a free hand with Turkey, and he was delighted. That was foolish of him, of course. . . . I've no intention of letting Russia extend eastwards. He'll make no difficulties now. I've measured him and I know how to deal with him in future. He's one of those admirable but foolish men who imagine that it's possible to be a diplomat and mean what one says. You would have liked him, my dear."

She smiled and he thought how much older she looked since he had last been in France. There were very fine lines under the make-up, and that revealing pose no longer suited her. She was ageing quickly, and it saddened him. He disliked intelligence in women, considering it out of place, but Josephine's stupidity annoyed him where it had formerly delighted. He found it humiliating to remember that she had once reduced him to a state of crawling servitude, that in those days she considered him boring and ill-bred and was unfaithful to him.

He should have divorced her; returning from Italy to find proof of her adultery he'd nearly done so, but her tears and the pleas of his step-children combined against his better judgment. Though love was dead, sentiment remained; she was silly and somehow defenceless in the ruthless world of his creation, and he couldn't bring himself to abandon her. And in the dark she still awoke in him that tempest of passion which he never experienced with anyone else. But there was one need which Josephine could never satisfy, a new need, growing more urgent every day.

He had climbed to the throne of the Bourbons and founded a dynasty, but he had no heir to succeed him, only his brothers and sisters, none of whom were able enough to keep what he had won.

And Josephine would never bear another child.

She was still smiling at him. " I'm so happy it was such a success, but then I was sure it would be. You're so clever." This time she did yawn, covering her mouth with the tips of her fingers; her hands were lovely, tiny and tapering. The yawn and the look which accompanied it were an invitation.

Napoleon looked at her, remembering the times when he had begged for what she was now offering him, the excuses, the headaches that vanished as soon as he was out of the house, the admonishments to be careful, you're hurting me, you're tearing my dress, oh, Napoleon, not now, *please*. . . .

And no son to follow him.

He stood up, bent over her and kissed her coldly on the cheek.

" I see you're tired, Madame. I'll leave you then, I have a lot of work to do. Good night."

The next morning he sent for his Foreign Minister, Talleyrand, created Prince of Benevento after pillaging Austria by the Treaty of Pressburg, and after discussing the terms of his treaty with Russia, astounded him by suggesting even stronger ties between the two countries.

If he were to divorce Josephine, he said suddenly, he could marry Alexander's sister, Catherine.

* * *

Charles de Talleyrand-Périgord was an aristocrat by birth. An accident in childhood lamed him, and though he was the eldest son, his family deprived him of the right to succeed his father and directed him to enter the Church. But the young seminarist soon adjusted his profession to his personal taste, a process he managed throughout his life; by the beginning of the Revolution, the aristocrat Talleyrand, Bishop of Autun, was a notorious Jacobin and libertine.

His acute mind, completely cynical in its approach to everything, saw that the old régime was not only doomed but deserved to be; he therefore allied himself to the enemies of his class and his Church without hesitation. Immediately his talent for intrigue developed; it was as surprising as his success with some of the loveliest and most important women in France. He was a thin, unhealthy-looking man, with the snub-nose and pale eyes which later reminded his enemies of Robespierre, and a manner of arrogant indifference which affronted everyone he did not consider worth cultivating for his own ends.

His intellect was as cold as his senses were hot; intellect prompted him to make friends with Danton; the savage, passionate Revolutionary and the excommunicated Bishop worked to remove King Louis from the throne and proclaim the Republic. They succeeded, and for his part in justifying the imprisonment of the Royal family, Danton allowed him to escape to America before the massacres of September 1792 began. Danton went to the guillotine, rushed to death by the flood he had loosed, and Talleyrand waited until the fall of Robespierre enabled him to return to France and enter the service of the Directory. His patron was another powerful man, the Director Barras, and Talleyrand adapted himself to the decadence and corruption of the new régime with the ease of a chameleon changing its colour to suit its background.

He was astute, convinced that the violence of change was only equalled by its suddenness; the foppish, amoral trend of the Directory was only a transition from the rags and bloodshed of the Revolution; it must lead to something else, and Talleyrand waited to discover what it was. He was one of the first to recognize that the brilliant young Corsican General was potentially more than just the military fist on the Directory's arm. And after that discovery, he waited, watching very closely.

He saw that Napoleon Bonaparte possessed diplomatic as

well as tactical genius, and that some overwhelming force of personality brought him victory when the muddles of his Government should have ensured defeat.

He recognized immense ambition behind the quiet exterior of the young soldier, already besotted with his silly Creole wife, and noticed his capacity for rousing a blind loyalty in the men who served him.

His name was becoming a talisman to the people, his victories promised them peace as well as glory, and France needed peace above everything else. He made friends with the General, noting how full his receptions always were and that some of the most influential men in France were filtering into the crowd.

But it was a small thing that decided him. During the campaign in Egypt, 3,000 prisoners were herded on to a beach and shot down in cold blood because there was no time to make proper arrangements for guarding them; the order was given by Napoleon himself.

When Talleyrand heard of it, he knew that the last ingredient of invincibility had been added to the man; inhumanity. From that moment he knew that the Directory was doomed; the phase was ending, the era about to begin.

Ambitious, corrupt, incapable of personal loyalty, the man who had sat in Danton's shadow had one immovable passion in life. The traitor and opportunist was a patriot; France held the place in his heart which no man, woman or child had ever occupied. To liberate France from the enfeebled Bourbons and the rule of a despicable aristocracy, Talleyrand had supported the Revolution and all it represented. He loved his country, and he would have embraced the Devil to benefit France. And since he had declared for Napoleon Bonaparte and become Foreign Minister, he sometimes felt as if that was what he had done. Seven years had passed since General Bonaparte had become First Consul and then Emperor of France. Seven years of ceaseless wars, staggering conquest and increasing disillusion. For the first time in his life, Talleyrand realized he had made the wrong choice. But disillusion came slowly, for even he had fallen under Napoleon's spell; it began with the steady influx of Corsican relations into positions of importance they were quite unfitted for; Bonapartes were climbing on to thrones all over Europe, Italy, Naples, Holland, put there by the man who had made himself ruler of France. And the peace which Talleyrand wanted for his country never lasted more than a few months while the Emperor prepared another war.

The success of his arms didn't appease the Minister, still outwardly devoted to him but inwardly hostile; he knew the worth of spectacular conquest without the backing of consolidated power—it disintegrated unless maintained by occupation, and French troops were already stretched across Europe. Napoleon should have been content, as France was content, with the spoils of victory and the international prestige he had won for her. He should have made friends with England, instead of trying to defeat her by building an alliance with the weaker European powers who were only waiting for the chance to break their word if his luck changed.

Talleyrand sat through the conference with the Emperor, occasionally making a suggestion, realizing that if the Czar of Russia had really been duped by all these promises of friendship, he might be persuaded to follow his late father's plan and attack India, while Napoleon invaded England.

'World dominance is what he wants,' Talleyrand thought as he listened to the harsh high voice, and followed the pointed finger as it traced across the map spread out in front of them. Cæsar crowned with golden laurel leaves, visiting the tomb of Charlemagne, placing the Iron Crown of Lombardy on his own head as a sign that he meant to re-establish the Holy Roman Empire as a fact instead of an empty title accorded to Francis of Austria.

'He's gone too far already,' Talleyrand decided, 'and he means to go further. There's no such thing as world domination for one country; what he envisages will mean the ruin of France. . . . He will have to be destroyed.'

The same evening he was present at a reception at The Tuilleries, where he saw a certain member of the Russian Embassy staff standing in the centre of a group of admiring women, and he watched him thoughtfully for some moments. His name was Tchernicheff; he was a Colonel of the Russian Guard and one of the most handsome and popular young men in Paris.

He drank and gambled and spent his time in the fashionable salons; but occasionally he travelled back to Petersburg with a speed that was quite out of character for a frivolous idler, and Talleyrand had long marked him as a particularly clever Czarist spy.

He joined the group, which immediately made way for him, and bowed to the Colonel.

" The ladies always have a monopoly of you, Monsieur Tchernicheff, you shouldn't spoil them for their poor countrymen," he said sourly.

The Russian laughed.

" Ah, no, Monsieur Talleyrand, it is I who am spoilt. . . . So much beauty! It is almost too much—even for a Russian! "

" We must discuss this further, my dear Colonel. Come and have a glass of wine with me. The ladies must dispense with you for a few moments; I assure you, they will appreciate you all the more."

The two men walked away, Talleyrand limping slightly with his hands clasped behind his back.

Over his wineglass Talleyrand looked up at him.

" When do you expect to be in Petersburg next, Colonel? " he asked quietly.

The smile died on Tchernicheff's mouth. " Why . . . some time soon."

The Minister wiped his lips with a lace handkerchief.

" When you do, I would like you to give a personal message to your Emperor. Tell him that I have the greatest admiration for him, and would be happy to serve him in any way I can."

The Colonel's dark eyes were quite expressionless.

"I shall be delighted to deliver your message. And I know the Czar will be glad to receive it."

"I am very anxious that he should," Talleyrand replied. "You like Paris, Monsieur Tchernicheff?" he added.

"It's my second home, Monsieur. I adore it. . . ."

Talleyrand's green eyes were very cold.

"Then I shouldn't delay your visit to Petersburg much longer. The sooner you go, the sooner you can return," he said. "Good evening Monsieur Tchernicheff. I have kept you from the ladies long enough. I fear they may never forgive me."

*   *   *

Within a week Colonel Tchernicheff was on his way across Europe, travelling to Russia with what he believed to be the most valuable information he had ever discovered in his career. On arriving at St. Petersburg, he found that Alexander had gone to Fontanka Castle to stay with his mistress, Princess Naryshkin, and without wasting a night on sleep, Tchernicheff followed him there.

He had his audience in Marie's lavish boudoir, and thought slyly that the setting was not inappropriate; most of his work for Alexander took place in similar rooms, if not actually in bed. . . .

There he informed his Emperor, that for some mysterious reason of his own, Napoleon's Foreign Minister appeared ready to betray his master to the Russians.

CHAPTER THREE

IN the months that followed, Alexander went out of his
way to pay attention to his sister. He went to her apartments every day; took her out riding, dined with her, wrote
her letters and gave her valuable presents. His whole
conduct was an enigma to the Court who knew how
treacherous the Grand Duchess was, and a deep anxiety to
his friends. His Prime Minister Speransky begged him
either to arrest Catherine or marry her off and send her out
of Russia. She was a grave danger and the Czar shouldn't
allow family feeling to influence him. As Speransky
pleaded, he watched Alexander intently, unwilling to
believe the foul gossip which was spreading through the
Court.

Catherine was safe because he was in love with her, it
was whispered. They were always together, shut up alone
for hours in her rooms. . . . The Minister dismissed the
story and supposed Alexander was trying to shame his sister
out of intriguing against him. Speransky shook his head; if
that were so, the Czar was wasting his efforts. That
arrogant, ruthless creature was incapable of feeling; she
would only despise her brother as a fool.

Alexander knew quite well what everyone was saying;
the implication was horrible enough to tickle Catherine's
monstrous vanity and he made the most of it. He understood her nature well, so well that he was sure she wouldn't
be able to resist such a tribute to her charms. Her own
brother had succumbed to her. If the idea kept her at bay
for a little while, he was prepared to act the part.

So he flattered her and spoilt her, watching her become
careless as her contempt for him increased.

He was an adept at concealing his feelings; even as a

child he had lived behind a mask, a gentle, smiling mask, which enabled him to observe other people with absolute objectivity. His grandmother, Catherine the Great, had taught him the technique; he had lived with a doting old woman who delighted to play with him on the nursery floor, and discovered her to be a tyrannical nymphomaniac at the same time.

The paradox fascinated him; he studied her as he studied his father, that unpredictable, gloomy man, and learnt valuable lessons from both. His childhood had been marked by paradox. He was educated by the Swiss Liberal, La Harpe, and learnt principles directly opposed to the system on which Russian society was founded. He was taught to despise religion while outwardly conforming; to hate war and yet be able to drill his troops as efficiently as any Prussian. He was naturally sensitive, and while this was encouraged, he was exposed to a life that outraged sensitivity; he was deeply superstitious, but forbidden to believe in God. Catherine loved him and attempted to fashion his character in the unique mould of her own; as a result she turned her grandson into a highly nervous, deceitful and isolated boy. In spite of it all, he had great courage, an implacable will and natural dignity. And when necessary, he could be ruthless as any of his savage forbears. But one event in his life shackled him. He had taken Paul's life, and the guilt of that crime made it impossible to murder Catherine Pavlovna too. He couldn't put her to death; something warned him that his sanity would never stand it; the humanist teaching of his youth and the muddled superstition inherent in him would not permit another blood murder, whatever anyone advised. So he fought his sister in his own way, pandered to her vanity, and watched her under the pretext of needing her companionship.

One afternoon they were together as usual, playing picquet in her apartments when she lowered her cards and said to him suddenly, "I've heard rumours that Napoleon may divorce his wife and wants to marry me. Is that true?"

She stared at him aggressively over the card-table. Alexander said casually, " Yes, the French Ambassador hinted something of the sort. Needless to say, I would not consider it." He looked down at his cards again as if the subject was closed.

Catherine swallowed. " Why didn't you consult me?" she demanded.

" My dear sister, don't be ridiculous. Marry you to that vulgarian! I knew how angry you'd be at the mere suggestion. It's you to play."

" I'm not playing any more! Why didn't you consult me? Have I no say in the matter of my own marriage?"

She swept her cards to the floor and got up; she was so angry she could scarcely speak. Bonaparte, the vulgarian she had so often denounced, was still the most powerful man in the world. . . . Marriage with Bonaparte . . . it could mean anything to an ambitious woman, a woman with royal blood to back her. . . . She'd heard the rumour and waited for Alexander to say something, till her patience exploded that afternoon. He had been approached and rejected it without a word to her. Damn him, she thought furiously. For what reason? Jealousy—or spite, perhaps. . . . Empress of France, with a claim to the throne of Russia. Oh, God, what an opportunity to miss!

" Alexander." She leant on the table towards him. " I could be useful to you; think of it, your own sister in a position to see and hear everything! But he'd never turn on you again, not if he married me. He needs the royal blood for his dynasty, don't you see that? There'd be a Romanov ruling France one day; and if I did marry him, why Russia and France could rule the world together!"

" That was Father's dream," Alexander said slowly.

" Why not?" she said eagerly. " He meant to achieve it by war, but we could do it through marriage. Alexander, listen to me. I should hate leaving you," she said, " but it needn't be for ever. You could come to Paris, we could see each other. . . . Go to the Ambassador and tell him you've reconsidered."

He smiled up at her. "Very well, my Catherine. If it pleases you."

When he left her he was still smiling, but the smile was not pleasant. How well suited they would be, his sister, and Napoleon of France.

How warmly they would press him to visit them in Paris, as the Spanish Royal family had been invited to Bayonne, where Napoleon had solved their family differences by placing them all under arrest. He could see Catherine planning it, drafting the ukase proclaiming herself Empress of Russia with that terrible little man looking over her shoulder. Two souls united by ambition, and probably by passion too, for he knew Catherine and he had heard reports of Napoleon. He sent for the French Ambassador, Caulaincourt, and discussed details for the meeting which was soon to take place between himself and the French Emperor at Erfurt.

The interview lasted two hours and the Ambassador left it convinced of the sincerity of Alexander's friendship for his master, but no mention was made of any marriage.

*   *   *

Dmitri Naryshkin had given his wife his house on the island in the middle of the Neva. It was a beautiful setting for an idyllic love affair, comparatively small, staffed by servants picked for their self-effacement and discretion, and surrounded by magnificent grounds.

The Czar spent long periods there during the time he was preparing to travel to Erfurt for his second meeting with Napoleon, and he loved the house, isolated on the lovely island. It was completely informal; he lived there with his mistress like any country nobleman, and in the gentle pursuits of the day, he found great happiness.

He hurried to the islands to relax, to lie in bed till noon with Marie by his side, to read and drowse and forget for a few hours that his throne was insecure, his family treacherous and that the greatest war in European history was soon going to be fought. He had determined on war at Tilsit, determined to redeem himself and his country's honour if he lost his life in the attempt, and while the nobility seethed with discontent and trade languished under the embargo on English goods which he had promised Napoleon to enforce, Alexander had begun to build up his army. It was done in the secrecy that his vast country made possible, and so far no whisper of it had reached France. With every month his strength was growing in the field. He had kept his sister from open action, and he was now turning the rumour of Bonaparte's suit to good advantage after the interest she'd been foolish enough to display. He would never have allowed her to marry Napoleon, because such a marriage would mean the end of Russian independence, but he pretended to consider it, dangling the French crown in front of her covetous eyes to divert them from the one he wore himself. She had fallen into the trap, and was besieging him for permission. The story of her ambition to marry her country's deadly enemy had done a great deal to weaken her influence with the malcontents, while it enflamed them still more against the Czar. Not content with an alliance which was ruining the country's trade, he was going to Erfurt to become still more embroiled with France, even to discuss a marriage. . . . It was Marie who came to him one day and broke the unwritten rule that they should never discuss politics during their stay on the island.

He looked up from the book he was reading and held out his hand to her, thinking how fresh and beautiful she looked. She was dressed in white, which suited her dark hair and brilliant complexion, and as usual she wore no jewellery. He found the simplicity entrancing and she knew it; her perfect neck and shoulders needed no diamonds to enhance them; a single red rose pinned to her breast was her best ornament.

"Where have you been, beloved? When I woke up this morning you'd gone."

She came and sat on the arm of his chair and kissed him, but her expression was grave.

"I awoke very early and didn't want to disturb you. Alexander, I've got to tell you something. My husband sent a messenger. I've been with him till a few moments ago. I know how you hate the outside world intruding on us while we're here, but you must let me tell you what Dmitri has heard in Petersburg. It's said that if you go to Erfurt you'll be either assassinated on your return or dethroned in your absence. The country will never permit a marriage between Napoleon and any of your sisters."

"I have only one marriageable sister—Catherine. Anne is still too young. And while I have every intention of finding a husband for Catherine before long, it will never be Napoleon! What else is being said?"

"That your Prime Minister Speransky is a traitor, that he wants peace with France and intends to liberate the serfs."

"Speransky is an honest man, my dear, and an able one. But his policies are not necessarily mine. Go on."

She turned to him quickly. "I could talk like this for hours! But you know it, you must! You have the Secret Police; don't they keep you informed? Alexander, for the love of God, don't test your fate too far. Ever since you met that Corsican devil, your life has been in danger here, and as long as you go on treating with him, making a friend of his Ambassador, spitting in public opinion's face, you'll never be safe. They'll kill you as they killed your father!"

The moment the words were spoken she turned pale with horror. "Forgive me, I didn't mean . . ."

"I killed my father," he said, and his voice was suddenly harsh and strained. "I killed him. There was no 'they'. . . . The responsibility is mine, as it will be my successor's, if anything happens to me. God help me . . . I can never forget it."

"You must protect yourself," she whispered. "What's done is done. Arrest your sister."

"No!" he shouted and sprang up. "No, arrest would

have to mean death. My father and my sister. . . . No, not even I can order that! Even now the shadow follows me; I dream of it, I see them strangling my father, jumping on his body to drive out the soul, the brutes, savages! . . . I hear his footsteps. Oh, Jesus," he muttered, " I've got to rule to justify myself, but I can't kill to do it. But no one knows that. If Catherine or Constantine knew it, even my mother, any of them, if they knew, my life wouldn't be worth a kopeck. But they don't, they think that if they went too far I'd do what has always been done. Only you know that I can't."

He caught her by the shoulders, so tightly that he hurt her.

"And you will never tell, because you love me, Marie Antonovna. I know that."

"I love you," she said. "I love you with all my heart. You can trust me always."

He put his arms round her and held her close.

"I need you," he whispered. "I never thought I should need anyone, but I've learnt at last that I couldn't live without you. We're a cursed family, Marie; warped and cruel and mad. The devil fathered us—my grandmother, my father, and now my brothers and sisters and myself. You'll find that out if you remain with me."

He hid his blond head against her breast and held her with such force that she almost cried out.

"But you must promise to stay with me," he said fiercely. "Do what you like, squeeze the treasury, take lovers, do anything, but don't leave me, never leave me. . . ."

She touched his face with gentle fingers.

"If I can make you happy, Alexander Pavlovitch, then I ask nothing more from life. I don't pretend to understand you. I love you so much that I'd rather you committed any crime than stand in danger, and the death of your father is no reason at all. . . . But two things I beg of you; marry your sister quickly, and be careful when you go to Erfurt."

"I shall be careful," he promised. "I shall have to be.

Because when I return to Russia, we shall go to war with France."

* * *

Colonel Tchernicheff had returned to Paris again, and he frequented every fashionable gathering in the hope of seeing Talleyrand without appearing to seek him out. Ironically, they met most often at The Tuilleries, ostensibly paying homage to the Emperor.

Napoleon's temper was uncertain in those days; events in Spain had upset him, for after dethroning the Spanish Royal family and giving the Crown to his brother Joseph, the Spanish people, so long the poorest and most despised in Europe, had revolted against the French domination and coined a new phrase in international language—guerrilla, the little war. The revolt was not yet suppressed, despite much bloodshed and appalling cruelty on both sides, and the incident rankled, as Talleyrand knew. He knew every mood of the man he had once served so well and was now systematically betraying.

Tchernicheff walked over to Talleyrand and bowed; the Emperor had just passed among them and he was scowling, looking more yellow and drawn than usual.

"His Majesty looks ill," the Colonel remarked. "Perhaps the trip to Erfurt will benefit him."

Talleyrand stared ahead of him. "I doubt it," he said. "Unless he finds a Russian wife there."

Tchernicheff smiled; it was a rather vacuous expression which meant nothing to the onlooker.

"That is something I'm afraid he'll never find," he said cheerfully. "But eventually he may find some Russian soldiers."

The Minister coughed. "I hope so, my dear Colonel. Unlike His Majesty, I feel that Erfurt will be of great benefit to *me*. I hope to renew my acquaintance with the Czar. Unfortunately I was kept very busy at Tilsit."

"The Czar is looking forward to meeting you again, Monsieur. He feels that much more can be gained from a little discussion," Tchernicheff answered. "He asked me to convey his affection for you and his desire for the ultimate good of France."

"Thank him for me," Talleyrand said. "And tell him that in my opinion the Russian soldiers you mentioned will be of greater service to my country than anything else."

*   *   *

In Petersburg a ghost had suddenly appeared in the middle of the new society of the nineteenth century, freezing the drawing-rooms and audience chambers of the Winter Palace with its reminder of the terrible days of the Czar Paul. The ghost was Count Alexei Araktcheief, the most dreaded figure of the previous reign and an intimate friend of the late Czar. His name was a synonym for cruelty, and Alexander's summons caused the first tremor of fear the Imperial Court had felt since the beginning of his reign.

Why Araktcheief, the nobility asked; why that archaic monster whose military sadism was still a byword; what did the Czar want with such a man? The answer was simple, and for those who recognized it, ominous. Araktcheief's record of loyalty to Paul was outstanding from a period when everybody had betrayed him; only his banishment had enabled the murderers to carry out their plan, and now Alexander had sent for him on the eve of his departure for Erfurt.

The thin figure, immaculately uniformed, followed the Czar everywhere, and the grim, flat-featured face bent over Alexander's shoulder at the conference table and smiled up at him in the ball-room. Araktcheief was restored to favour, flattered and deferred to before the men who had once been Alexander's intimates, and the devotion he had shown Paul was soon transferred to his new master. He was a morose, stiff man, with light, piercing eyes and a parade-ground manner that made the trivial conversation of the salons an impossibility in his presence, and the stories of his savagery shocked even the Grand Duke Constantine.

"Why did Alexander have to bring him back?" he demanded of his sister. "God in heaven, he's resurrecting the past and none of us want that! No one dares speak of Father's death in front of him, yet he sends for father's oldest friend and makes a favourite of him!"

Catherine frowned; she disliked Araktcheief; the stare of those green eyes made her uncomfortable. She had been unbearably haughty to him as a result, but for all his reaction the man might have been made of stone.

"He's afraid," she said. "Afraid of a revolution while he's at Erfurt, that must be the reason. And he's chosen the right man, damn him. So much for all this talk of Liberalism! I have a feeling that our gentle brother is about to prove himself a ruler after all. . . ." She shrugged. "But I don't really care now; if I'm to marry Bonaparte I'll be content, and Alexander's promised it."

Constantine scowled at her, wondering why he had ever allowed himself to be caught up in her intrigues. He was a stupid man, incapable of unravelling his own complexes or of resisting the influence of personalities stronger than his own; but nature had endowed him with a little imagination, unlike the robot Nicholas, his younger brother, and he glared at his sister with hatred.

"Trust him if you like, sister. Personally I don't think you'll ever see France. . . ."

She was angry, but she laughed at him and forgot his prophecy, too confident of her hold on Alexander to suppose that he had reversed positions and was deceiving her.

As usual, the most inconspicuous member of the Imperial family was the Czarina Elizabeth; she moved among them like a phantom, accepting the Grand Duchess Catherine's snubs and Alexander's cold neglect with an indifference that roused Constantine's suspicions.

She was cowed, and with the instinct of all sadists, he delighted in adding to her humiliations; at the same time she was the kind of gentle, self-effacing woman that he hated, precisely because she aroused the worst in him. Sullen, stabbed by jealousy of his sister, who no longer seemed to need him, and by physical envy of his brother, the Grand Duke searched for a victim, someone on whom to wreak his disappointment with the others. He watched the defenceless Czarina and his little eyes narrowed. Something told him she was happy, that the monotony of her neglected life had been relieved. He set spies who soon informed him that Elizabeth had at last found a successor to Adam Czartorisky.

The Empress of Russia was the mistress of a young cornet in the Guards named Okhotnikov, and she was also pregnant. There was no doubt that Alexander knew and would accept the child; and this child might live, unlike the bastard born to Czartorisky. A secured succession would not suit any of them, and a frightful plan began to form slowly in Constantine's mind. From the moment of its inception his spirits rose and he began shadowing the unhappy Czarina from room to room, watching her with a half-smile on his ugly mouth.

She bore this strange persecution until the nervous strain and her advanced pregnancy forced her to seek an interview with Alexander.

He received her in his study where he had been signing documents and talking to his Minister Speransky. Speransky had just left him; he had tried to do so sooner when the page announced the Empress, but Alexander waved the boy away and ordered Speransky to stay where he was; the Czarina could wait. The incident puzzled his Minister; he could never understand how Alexander, the gentlest of men, could behave so implacably towards his wife.

Speransky's origins were humble; he was the son of a poor priest and owed his position to a rare mixture of integrity and administrative genius; his policies were peace and liberal reform, two projects which he believed to be equally dear to Alexander. The hatred borne him by the Imperial family and the nobility would have frightened a lesser man out of office, but he ignored it, confident of the Czar's protection, and developed his unpopular plans for trade with France and the abolition of serfdom. He saw the Empress waiting as he passed through the anté-room a little later, and saluted her reverently; she hardly seemed to notice him.

" Good morning, Elizabeth."

Alexander rose politely when she came into the room and she curtsied. " This is an unexpected visit. I'm afraid it may have to be brief, as I'm very busy. What do you want? "

She swallowed nervously, it was a long time since she had approached him privately.

" I came to wish you God speed at Erfurt," she said.

There was a pause while Alexander watched her, impatient and hostile. It was extraordinary, he thought, how the sight of her always annoyed him. She had become a living reminder of his own failure as a young husband and the success of Adam Czartorisky in his place. He had never forgiven her and he had never lived with her since.

" Why did you really come? " he asked her.

She looked down and the colour rushed into her face.

" I am pregnant," she whispered.

" So I see. I believe a certain Monsieur Okhotnikov is to be congratulated."

She walked towards him and then sank down into a chair.

" Are you going to abandon me now? " she asked slowly.

He stared at her and then shook his head. " No," he answered. " Why should I now, when I didn't before? I enjoy my freedom and I permit you yours. As to the child, I shall acknowledge it. The only thing that surprises me is why you should suddenly doubt it."

" Any other man would divorce me," Elizabeth said. " And your brother's been looking at me so strangely that I thought perhaps you were going to do so."

" I'm not responsible for Constantine. You have nothing to fear from me. I've kept to the bargain I made with you all those years ago and I don't intend to break my word.

If I did divorce you, it would only be to make Princess Naryshkin my wife, and I shall never do that as she's a commoner. Is there anything else?"

"No, except to thank you."

She came to him and suddenly kissed his hand. "God go with you at Erfurt, Alexander. And if you could ever find it in your heart to forgive me, I might find happiness again."

She turned and walked quickly out of the room before he had time to reply or to see that the tears were running down her cheeks.

The next moment he had forgotten her, having decided to tell his brother to leave the Czarina alone. If he wanted amusement he must find someone else to torment.

Speransky, he thought, pacing up and down the study. A good man, but a pacifist, humane to the point of folly, with his dream of ending serfdom; no wonder he was hated. And he would never sanction the war with France on which he was determined; he would never see as Alexander did, that it was inevitable and vital to the ultimate peace of the world. He sighed suddenly and swore, which he very seldom did.

God, the intrigues of ruling, the countless factors that had to be weighed and considered before a move was made. Speransky. Already he knew in his heart what had to be done.

*   *   *

Just before her confinement, the Empress Elizabeth was woken at midnight one night by a serving maid, who told her that the cornet Okhotnikov had been murdered as he left the theatre. A few hours afterwards she gave premature birth to a daughter. The child survived for only a few weeks.

*   *   *

In the first days of September, 1808, Alexander left Petersburg and began his journey to meet Napoleon at Erfurt.

CHAPTER FOUR

ERFURT was a lovely old Thuringian town, architecturally quaint with its ancient city walls and narrow, cobbled streets. On the 27th September it shook with the roar of cannon firing salvoes of welcome to the Czar of Russia and the Emperor of France; they rode into Erfurt at the head of a magnificent cavalcade. There were troops of Napoleon's Guard in their splendid uniforms, arrogant veterans of his great campaigns, who swaggered through the streets as they had done in cities all over the world; squadrons of Cossacks in their colourful dress, and soldiers of the Russian Imperial Guard. The orders issued to the Russian forces were strict; no drinking or rioting and as little mixing with French troops as possible; Alexander knew the temper of his men and wanted no incidents. The petty German Princes whom Napoleon had made Kings were crowded into Erfurt to pay homage, a ridiculous, undignified gathering of men who had betrayed their people and were unaware that the treachery was bitterly resented. In spite of the flags, the salutes, the brilliance and colour which flooded the quiet German town, there was an air of unrest among the Thuringians. They viewed Napoleon with hatred and respect, but already two words were being whispered in Erfurt as they were throughout Europe. " Remember Spain."

Spain, poor and degraded before the world, had risen against the tyrant and was still fighting him successfully. Also the English had landed an army in Portugal under General Wellesley; trade with England had been reopened, and the position was so serious that Napoleon himself was rumoured to be going to Spain to direct the war.

The body of Europe, for so long paralysed under the foot of the conqueror, suddenly breathed a deep breath. The strongest rebellious intake came from the principalities of Germany, led by Prussia, who had been stripped of her lands and crippled by a French levy of 140,000,000 francs.

At his first meeting with Napoleon, Alexander was astonished by the change in him. They embraced as usual with protestations of delight, the Czar bent double over his tiny ally, seeing that the stern, not unattractive looking young victor of Tilsit had become fat and so sallow that he was almost jaundiced.

After a State Banquet, the Conference opened the following morning, and one of the first people to bow and kiss Alexander's hand was the crippled Prince of Benevento, Charles Talleyrand.

* * *

The French Ambassador to St. Petersburg was sent for by his master within the first few days. He knew when he entered the room that Napoleon was in a furious temper, for the Emperor was striding up and down, clasping and unclasping his hands behind his back. When he saw Caulaincourt he swung round.

"What in the name of damnation have you been doing at Petersburg?" he demanded. Caulaincourt began to stutter.

"Doing, Sire. . . . I don't understand. . . ."

"Why those reports week after week, telling me how friendly the Czar is to France, how devoted to me, when he's nothing of the kind! " Napoleon shouted. "You idiot, you blockheaded fool, the man's no more my friend than the King of England! "

"But, Sire," Caulaincourt protested, "Sire, he's never ceased to praise you to me. We've talked together for hours, he's shown me every mark of favour from the moment I arrived! I admit Petersburg society is hostile to me, but the Czar is devoted to the alliance with France. Sire, I assure you, he's told me over and over again . . ."

"I don't care what he's told you," Napoleon snapped.

" You're an idiot and he knows it. This isn't the man I dealt with at Tilsit, he agrees to nothing ! "

Caulaincourt made a wise remark. " He's stronger than he was at Tilsit."

Napoleon's eyes gleamed. " An intelligent observation, my dear Caulaincourt. It's a pity you didn't make others while you were in Russia. Do you know he's practically refused my offer of marriage with his sister Catherine ? "

" I know that, Sire, I spoke to him about it yesterday as you ordered, and he said the right to choose husbands for her daughters remained with his mother the Dowager Empress. He could promise nothing without her consent."

" Bah ! That's what he said to me this morning. Very well, I said. If not the Grand Duchess Catherine, then the younger sister Anne. If he's his sister's lover as they say, that might have accounted for the refusal, but by God he practically said no to Anne as well. That's not jealousy, Caulaincourt, that's policy ! He's changed towards me. Still charming, yes, but that means nothing. I've learnt that in two meetings in twelve months while you, you imbecile, couldn't discover it seeing him every day ! "

" Monsieur Talleyrand suggested that he might talk with him," Caulaincourt ventured.

" That snake ? " Napoleon paused. " Well, why not. God knows he's deceitful enough to deal with Satan himself and emerge with the best of the bargain. Talleyrand; very well. Send him to me. And you can go now. I repeat, Caulaincourt, you've proved yourself an idiot ! "

The Ambassador bowed and went out.

That evening Talleyrand paid a visit to the Russian Headquarters. The players of the Comédie Française had been brought to Erfurt to perform before the Emperors, and there was just an hour before Alexander need dress to go to the theatre. He received the French Minister in his private sitting-room, and offered him some wine. In the first few minutes, Talleyrand considered him.

He was, he decided, a very handsome man, with a gentle,

serious expression and immense natural charm. A man who
would draw men to him and hypnotize women, yet a man
with a tortuous brain, as his dealings proved, a man capable
of ruthless action, for he had murdered his own father, and
kept his throne under circumstances of great danger. Courageous, and with a very long memory; it was as well to take
his measure, for if he defeated Napoleon, he would become
the most powerful ruler in the world.

Talleyrand opened the conversation properly by
speaking of his love for France, and Alexander, listening,
nodded. He then said that in his opinion Napoleon
was bringing his country to absolute ruin by his insane
ambition and the wish to conquer the world. As a result,
his servants were in the unhappy position of having to
choose between their personal loyalty and their duty to
France.

" I, Sire, have chosen France," he said quietly.

" I applaud your decision, Monsieur," Alexander answered.
" Why did he send you to me? "

" To try and persuade you to agree to his proposals. His
temper's become very short lately; he's afraid he might lose
it with you if he has to press these points himself."

"And what does he want me to agree to? " Alexander
asked.

" A marriage with one of your sisters, the recognition of
his brother Joseph as King of Spain, and an appeal to the
English to do the same. He also wishes you to put pressure
on Austria who is rearming, as he doesn't want war with
her yet. Also he thinks England will get out of Portugal if
she sees Austria weakening. Should war come, then he
wants an assurance of Russian military assistance against
Austria."

Alexander poured some more wine into his glass and
offered it to Talleyrand.

" What do you advise? "

" I advise that you grant him nothing in respect of any
marriage or of threatening Austria. Those are the two most
important concessions; the others you can afford to make for

appearance's sake. Your recognition of Joseph as King
of Spain will have no effect on either the Spaniards or
the English, as long as they know Austria is about to
go to war. As for the military aid you give the Emperor
in event of war, well, that is a matter for Your Majesty's
discretion."

"I agree, my dear Monsieur Talleyrand, and I shall follow
your excellent advice. France is indeed fortunate in possess-
ing such a patriot as yourself," Alexander said.

Talleyrand smiled coldly.

"My patriotism must appear much like treason to you,
Sire, but believe me, the infamies I have had to commit in
the service of Napoleon Bonaparte have well fitted me for
what I am doing now. It is nearly time for the performance.
May I bid Your Majesty good night."

*   *   *

The conference at Erfurt ended as it had begun, in splen-
dour and apparent amity between the two principals, for the
Czar had agreed to most of Napoleon's proposals. But the
credit was really due to Talleyrand, who had succeeded in
beguiling Alexander where the Emperor had failed; so said
observers who had seen the ruler of France lose his temper
and dignity at one meeting to the extent where he threw his
cap on the floor and jumped on it, under the cold eye of the
Czar, who had snubbed him and prepared to leave the room.
It was an unfortunate incident, for it revealed the vulgar
spirit of the little parvenu from Corsica, still vulgar and a
parvenu in spite of the Royal Purple he had assumed.
Alexander noted it, noted that the proud young diplomat
of Tilsit, whom he had been forced to admire as an adversary
if not as an equal, had become a violent tempered bully,
the prey of rages and impulses of savagery. He threatened
and abused without restraint, but he was polite, even affectionate to Alexander, which was most significant.

"I leave Erfurt and you, Sire, with great sadness," he said
on their last evening. "I have been happy in the peace and

friendship I found here. But I go now to less peaceful duties."

" To Spain? " questioned Alexander sympathetically.

" To Spain," Napoleon replied. " To scatter the rabble that a parcel of incompetents have allowed to make a noise out of all proportion to their importance."

"Success and God speed, my friend," Alexander said to him. " Your interests are always mine."

The next morning the Imperial carriages drove out of Erfurt with their colourful escorts and the cannons fired their last salvoes of farewell. It was over, and the two sovereigns took their different roads, one to Paris and then embarkation for Spain, the other to St. Petersburg.

Dispatches had arrived for Alexander regularly, and he re-read the last as he drove out of Erfurt. It assured him that everything in Petersburg was peaceful; rumours had crept back that he had refused Napoleon's offer of marriage for his sister, the Grand Duchess Catherine, and public opinion was pleased. The Grand Duchess's reactions were less favourable, but the police and administration had maintained absolute calm in his absence. The dispatch was signed Alexei Araktcheief.

Peaceful and calm; Alexander leant back in his carriage and thought of those two words in connection with Araktcheief and his Court. They meant that he must have paralysed them all with fear.

He closed his eyes and immediately thought of Marie Naryshkin; his thoughts were sentimental as well as voluptuous. He had missed her badly, and the casual embraces of one or two German ladies at Erfurt had only increased his loneliness and sharpened his desire for her. He fell asleep with his blond head pillowed against the satin upholstery and dreamt that he held her in his arms.

On his arrival at the Winter Palace, the first person he sent for was his mother. The Dowager Empress went into her son's room and remained shut in alone with him for nearly an hour. Then a page was sent to bring the Grand Duchess to her brother.

Catherine had expected the summons, and she was blazing with anger. He had betrayed his promise at Erfurt; she was to remain in Russia, unmarried and rotting, idling away her youth and beauty with lovers who kept her sensuality at bay but did nothing to satisfy her ambition. She stormed into Alexander's room and stood still abruptly when she saw the mother and son standing side by side.

" My dear sister," he said softly. " How happy I am to see you."

She noticed suddenly that he had made no move towards her, no attempt to kiss her as he always did after a separation. There was something cold and forbidding in his manner, in spite of the gentle greeting, and her mother's face was heavy and blank.

" Rumour has preceded you," she said sharply. " Unless you send for me to contradict it. There is to be no marriage. Is that correct? "

She could see her mother's colour rising and knew that she was frightened, frightened of Alexander. . . . She stood rigid with pride and defiance, fighting a queer sensation of fear that was creeping through her. She had never seen such an impersonal, dead expression in his eyes as he studied her and then answered in the same level voice.

" I'm afraid it's quite correct. There is to be no marriage between you and Napoleon."

" You betrayed me! " she accused. " You promised and you've broken your word! "

It was then that the Empress Dowager spoke. She too was calm, and the effect of the composure of these two people suddenly made Catherine feel she might have hysterics.

" Your brother has done everything and more than he promised. Napoleon wouldn't have you, Catherine Pavlovna. He wants to marry your sister Anne."

" Wouldn't have me . . . it's not possible! For what reason? " She was gasping with surprise and rage.

Alexander explained quietly, " Anne is not yet sixteen and he prefers a very young wife to bear his heirs. I'm sorry,

Catherine, I know how humiliated you must feel, as I do, for your sake."

"As we all do," her mother added.

Catherine stared from one to the other. Napoleon had refused her . . . truth or lies, God only knew. Why was her mother aiding him? Had he deceived her, bullied her, or was it really true that an Italian guttersnipe had refused to marry Catherine Pavlovna Romanov? . . .

"In order to spare you public humiliation, I have decided on another marriage for you," Alexander said. "Mama agrees with me that you must be married before Napoleon makes any other choice. We have selected Prince George of Oldenburg."

"Oldenburg!"

A tiny Duchy, a living grave of ambition, even of life itself. She had seen George of Oldenburg; he was frail and spotty complexioned, a stupid oaf many years her senior.

She stepped back from them. "No," she said. "No, never. You can't do that to me, Alexander. This is you, not mother. You can't. I won't marry him."

"You will, Catherine, you will do exactly as your brother and I tell you. You will marry George of Oldenburg, or you'll stand before the world as the Princess Bonaparte rejected. You have no choice."

Her mother had a vein of implacability in her nature, though she seldom showed it, but Catherine recognized it now.

She turned to Alexander. Her throat constricted so that she could hardly speak.

"Anne," she whispered. "Anne instead of me . . . I can't bear it!"

Alexander came close to her and put his arm round her shoulders; she was beaten and he knew it. "He will never have Anne. I give you my oath on that. Go now, my sister." He kissed her lightly on the forehead and glanced quickly over at his mother.

She knew the truth, but he had forced her to act out the lie for Catherine's benefit, and as usual when he exerted his will, she did what she was told. She came to Catherine's side and led her out of the room.

Within eight days the betrothal of the Grand Duchess Catherine to Prince George of Oldenburg was officially announced, and the unhappy Ambassador to Petersburg had the task of conveying this unprecedented insult to the Emperor of the French.

*   *   *

" You'll never know how much I missed you, Marie," Alexander whispered. He turned his head on the pillow towards her as he spoke, but the brocade bed curtains made a cavern of complete darkness; he could feel her breath on his cheek but he couldn't see her.

" I'm glad, I wanted you to miss me. I was miserable. But not now."

Her lips touched his and lingered. He drew her small body closer within the circle of his arm and caressed her; as he did so, the memory of the other women to whom he had done the same things passed through his mind with amazing clearness while his blood began racing with desire. His grandmother's lady-in-waiting, a middle-aged bawd of incredible coarseness and experience had initiated him with Catherine's approval; afterwards, bewildered and ashamed, he had imagined the Countess telling his grandmother details and the two of them laughing.

Perhaps that was why he had failed with Elizabeth, who was nervous and strangely ardent in spite of her ignorance. He had loathed making love to her, hated the pale hair, the slanted cat's eyes with their unexpectedly sweet expression, the slim body that stiffened with expectancy when he touched it, and never passed the point where sensual rigidity became response. He had fulfilled his marital duties for a time and then abandoned them when his wife remained childless.

His mistresses were women of every class and type; some very young, the lisping daughter of the nobility one night, and a pretty servant girl the next; sophisticates, who began the affair out of vanity and ended by falling in love with him, common whores picked up in gypsy taverns who would have died with fear had they known who he was. Countless women had taught him the power of his own fascination for them without moving him in the least.

And then Marie Antonova Naryshkin, who was dark and beautiful, exactly the type he admired, who laughed up at him and eluded him for a time, till the conquest of her became an obsession. After she had surrendered, her attraction increased, where it had waned with all the others.

As a mistress she combined the qualities he needed, and had never found in one woman before; she was beautiful, a refined companion who knew how to be gay or restful according to his mood, and a lover who roused him and responded herself as no one else had ever done.

He had taken possession of her, installed her as his official mistress, been generous, ardent and kind for three years, and only fallen in love with her after Tilsit.

He had since learnt from experience what his reason had accepted second-hand, that love was painful, unselfish and absorbing, and had far less to do with sensuality than was commonly supposed. He had slept with women at Erfurt, and when Marie was abroad, as he would always sleep with them because he needed them, but his infidelities only increased the aching affection he felt for the woman beside him.

"Alexander, oh, Alexander," she whispered, and he smothered the words with his mouth, his mind suddenly blank as his passion engulfed him and was met by the force of her own.

Afterwards she slept, deeply, like a child, with her head cradled in his arm, and in the darkness he smiled and kissed her gently.

Unlike Elizabeth, Marie had borne him children. She could have given him the heir he would never conceive with his wife, but the happiness they shared could never be regularized by marriage. He knew it and so did she; no Czar had officially married a commoner since Peter the Great, and whether Alexander loved or hated her, Elizabeth Alexeivena was a Princess of the Royal house of Baden.

He knew this to be the reason why Marie, usually so carefree and good-natured, treated the Empress with open rudeness, and always informed her in person when she was pregnant by the Czar; jealousy made her cruel, and like all women in love, whose way is barred by a rival, she was very cruel. Everyone was cruel to Elizabeth. He remembered the murder of the cornet Okhotnikov, and the horror of Constantine sitting at the Imperial table getting drunk that night and grinning like a demon. But she had courage, he admitted, and she was loyal. Nothing could or ever would induce her to intrigue against him, and he knew it. ' If you could ever find it in your heart to forgive me, I might find happiness again,' she had said at the end of their interview before he went to Erfurt, and he thought for a moment that it was an odd remark for her to make . . . and then forgot both the words and the woman as he always did. Marie stirred beside him and murmured something, but she didn't wake. He moved his arm away from her shoulders and raised it behind his head, knowing that sleep was far away for him. In the silence he began to think of Erfurt and Napoleon.

Spain was bleeding him, Austria meant to attack him, but Napoleon was still too strong, far too strong to challenge openly. He would wait as he had had to wait after Tilsit, wait and see what the outcome would be between France and Austria, and hurry the reorganization of his own armies, for this time there would be no margin for mistakes.

He pulled back a corner of the hangings and saw that the room was growing light. He turned slowly and looked down at Marie Naryshkin; she lay in the shadow of her own hair. He let the curtain fall and lay back in the darkness, listening to the twittering of the birds nesting in the trees outside, until a movement told him that Marie was awake beside him, and he leant over and took her in his arms.

*   *   *

In Spain an army of a quarter of a million men, led by Napoleon himself, were fighting the raw Spanish troops who numbered only 90,000. They fought savagely, driving the rebels across the dusty plains and through the ruined towns and villages of Spain, leaving death and desolation behind them, penetrating the mountain districts, where they engaged in a final battle with the patriot forces at the pass over the Somosierra mountain. From the heights, Spanish gunners poured down a hail of grapeshot on the mass of struggling troops; dust, gunsmoke, the screams of the wounded and the pounding of cannon had transformed the peaceful mountain slopes into an inferno of noise; officers were yelling themselves hoarse above the bedlam, urging the French troops forward over the bodies of their comrades, into the blast of the Spanish gunfire.

Napoleon watched from the fringe of the battle, a tiny figure on his white horse, unshaven and covered in dust. Forgotten was the borrowed dignity of kingship; the Emperor had once again become the General, with the roar of the fighting in his ears and the sharp cordite smell drifting on the hot air, the smell of Marengo, of Austerlitz, Jena, the smell of cannon, of victory and death. He stared upwards at the mountain slopes where the batteries were belching down shot on to his army, shielding his eyes from the sun. He remained rigid for a few moments, till some of the Spanish irregulars on the slopes pointed him out and began aiming at him. Bullets whined and ploughed into the ground a few yards away, and his aide-de-camp called to him anxiously.

" They've seen you, Sire! For God's sake ride back! "

Bonaparte turned his horse's head; his sallow face was flushed, and for a moment the aide remembered the young General of the Revolution whom he had loved and followed, and who was often unrecognizable in the Emperor of France.

" Ride to the commander of the Polish Light Horse. Tell him the Emperor orders him to put those cannon out of action! Ride! "

And then he turned again to watch the battlefield. Within minutes of his order, he saw the lines of Polish cavalry moving forward, pennants fluttering, the sun striking light off their breastplates; very faintly the jingling of their harness came to him, and he remembered that the inconsequential sound was the most striking feature of every charge, the tinkling accompaniment of death, more terrible than the roar of cannon which broke out as the first line of horsemen rode up the slope. They were riding recklessly now, their ranks broken by scores of casualties as the shot scorched down on them, men and horses stumbling, slipping on the rocky surface, dead and maimed animals in a hideous confusion while the survivors still rode on, urging forward and up.

The leaders swept down on the first gun emplacements, sabres swinging in the sunshine; the gunners were cut down and trampled before the second wave of Polish cavalry descended on them yelling and slashing.

The Emperor sat very still, till the slackening fire from the mountain ceased altogether and the mass of French infantry heaved forward through the pass like a tide overflowing; he could hear the men cheering, cheering the Poles who were riding slowly back, trying to re-form their scattered survivors into two lines. As they passed him they saluted, and he saw one wounded trooper sway and fall forward over the neck of his horse.

The colour had died out of his face, leaving it sallow and puffed with tiredness; he was feeling the pain in his belly again, the gnawing, indigestible pain that attacked him whatever he ate, and somehow the pain was superimposed on the knowledge that the battle was won. He saluted the remnants of the light cavalry and then turned his horse and rode slowly forward.

On the 10th of December he entered Madrid. He was so

used to the pattern of victory that the refusal of the Spaniards to accept his brother as their King astonished him; after the battle the defeated agreed meekly to his terms and resigned themselves to whatever form of government he chose for them; no nation had ever dared to do otherwise, but neither threats nor bribes could move the Spanish people. They refused allegiance to Joseph Bonaparte and gathered their forces to continue the war. Napoleon left Madrid and marched out to crush the British expeditionary force of 26,000 men who had ventured into the heart of Leon under the command of Sir John Moore. Moore retreated steadily, drawing the French after him, until the two armies met at Corunna. In the ensuing battle, Sir John Moore was mortally wounded in the moment of victory.

Meanwhile news reached Napoleon that Austria was about to declare war on him while he and his armies were engaged in Spain, and abandoning the campaign, which he believed to be practically over, he set sail for France to confront this new danger.

On board ship he was more morose and irritable than usual, and spent hours shut up in his cabin, or walking the quarter-deck alone.

So Austria was hoping to revenge herself for the defeat of Austerlitz, thinking that the rebellion in Spain and the continuous war with the English in Portugal were portents that the power of Bonaparte was weakening. . . . The feeble Hapsburgs, patching the rags of their past glory, were actually going to make war on him! He laughed aloud in anger and contempt. War. They should have war and learn the lesson of defeat as they had never learnt it. He thought of Russia and his mood changed. Russia had promised him men, and she must keep that promise, she dared not do otherwise, he decided, banishing the disquiet that memories of Alexander aroused in him. He had measured his strength against France once and been beaten out of the field; he was strangely obstinate and cold, where he had been admiring and pliable at Tilsit, but Napoleon was confident that he was still afraid. He remembered the

hurried marriage of the Grand Duchess Catherine and
sweated with anger; he would revenge that insult when the
time came. But for the moment he preferred to ignore it,
and his Ambassador Caulaincourt was instructed to continue
negotiating for the hand of Alexander's sister Anne. As
soon as he had defeated Austria, he intended to carry out
his long-term intention of divorcing the Empress Josephine
and founding a dynasty with a new wife.

*   *   *

In December of 1808, the Ambassador Caulaincourt asked
for a private audience with the Czar. He was nervous
and fidgeted while waiting in the ante-room, aware as always
of the hostility of the Russian courtiers and officials who
waited with him. He had become hardened to insults during
his stay in St. Petersburg, able to answer the taunts of the
Grand Duchess Catherine, now Princess of Oldenburg, the
hauteur of the Dowager Empress, with smiles and tact;
but social ostracism still stung him, and for all Frenchmen
who were not *émigrés* from the old régime, Petersburg was a
very lonely place. Caulaincourt's only friend was Alexander,
and the extent of his gratitude was almost treasonable. The
Czar was the kindest and most unassuming of all the
monarchs with whom Caulaincourt had dealt; the impression
of sincerity and friendship which Alexander conveyed to him
at every meeting was far stronger in effect than the bitter
reproaches of his own Emperor at Erfurt. He trusted the
Czar and he genuinely liked him, he almost clung to him,
surrounded as he was by hatred and suspicion from everybody else.

As usual, Alexander did not keep him waiting long, and
he hurried through the double doors; before they closed
behind him, those who remained in the ante-room were able
to see their Emperor rise and come forward to embrace
him.

At the end of an hour he left, bowing to the Russians
grouped outside the Imperial suite, smiling and obviously

satisfied. A few moments later, one of Alexander's pages was sent to summon the Austrian Ambassador Prince Schwarzenberg to an immediate audience.

The Prince was a member of one of the oldest and wealthiest families in the Holy Roman Empire; a shrewd diplomat and an able soldier, he was as popular in Court circles as Caulaincourt was hated. When he entered, Alexander offered him his hand to kiss, and asked him to sit down. Schwarzenberg, who knew that the French Ambassador had only just left, thanked him and waited for Alexander to begin. There was a silence of several minutes, while the Czar fingered the ornaments on his desk, frowning slightly. Then he looked up at the Prince.

" Monsieur Caulaincourt informs me that your country is about to attack France. Is that correct, Prince Schwarzenberg? "

Schwarzenberg's expression did not change.

" It has been many nations' experience that France has a habit of accusing someone else of the aggression she intends to commit herself," he said.

Alexander's blue eyes considered him, and the Prince saw in them a penetrating, stony look which he had never seen before; it occurred to him suddenly that Alexander's magnificent features could become inhumanly hard.

" I am bound by alliance to come to the aid of the French Emperor," he said evenly. " So it would be wiser if you were more truthful and less diplomatic, Prince."

Schwarzenburg bowed slightly; every instinct told him that evasion would gain him nothing.

" It is true," he answered.

" Then I must condemn the proposal . . . officially," Alexander remarked. " At the same time, I assure you of my personal friendship for Austria and for his Majesty the Emperor Francis. Should you undertake this war, you will have nothing to fear from Russian interference."

He looked down as he spoke, and began scribbling a note, then he glanced up at Schwarzenberg and smiled his warm smile.

" I hope I shall see you at the reception this evening. *Au revoir*, my dear Prince."

Bowing low, Schwarzenberg backed out.   Meanwhile Caulaincourt sat in his study in the French Embassy, writing a dispatch assuring Napoleon of Alexander's passionate devotion to him, and to prove it, added that the Czar was at that moment warning the Austrian Ambassador that if his nation moved against France, Russia would immediately attack in defence of her ally.

INTERLUDE

ON the 18th of April, 1809, the Archduke Charles of Austria began the offensive in Bavaria, but within nine days Marshal Davoust had defeated him at Eckmuhl and Napoleon marched on Vienna.   Vienna surrendered on May 13th.

On May 17th he issued a decree annexing the remaining Papal States to the French Empire and reducing the Pope to the position of a Bishop of Rome in receipt of a yearly French stipend.   The world gasped at the action; at that moment the struggle with Austria faded into insignificance as the most powerful temporal ruler on earth turned his strength against the leader of the Catholic Church.

Pius VII was a sick and ageing man, surrounded by enemies, and there were some who said he would submit, that the Papacy's only hope of survival was to bend in obedience to France.

The Pope's answer was to issue a Bull excommunicating Napoleon, and from his headquarters in Austria, the French Emperor sent orders to arrest him and imprison him in Florence.

Then he turned to drive the Archduke Charles from his position at Aspern-Essling, on the northern bank of the

Danube, and there suffered a severe and unexpected defeat, losing 25,000 men.

On the island of Lobau, Napoleon gathered the remnants of his army, and went to Ebersdorf to his faithful servant Marshal Lannes, who was dying after the amputation of both legs. In the makeshift tent where Lannes lay bleeding to death, Napoleon wept for his own defeat as well as for the loss of his most loyal Marshal, and out of his emotion a new resolve was born, a fierce determination to avenge himself on Austria, to crush the treacherous Germans who were already rising in revolt after the news of his defeat.

On the banks of the Danube, in towns and cities all over Austria, the people were rejoicing, hoping that this reverse would end in the ruin of French power and the withdrawal of her armies, and the victorious Archduke Charles was hailed as the saviour of his nation. All this Napoleon knew, and he knew that if the Russian troops promised by Alexander had arrived at Essling, the battle would never have been lost. But no troops came; a token force had been assembled, but the order to march was not given till the 3rd of June, twelve days after the engagement took place.

Reorganizing his troops, Napoleon admitted finally that Alexander had tricked him, that the ally whose protestations of faith and friendship were still arriving by courier, was in fact his enemy.

From the Palace of Schoenbrunn, he dictated a secret letter to Caulaincourt, informing him that the alliance between France and Russia was invalidated by Alexander's treachery, and he was to act accordingly, while pretending that nothing was changed between his master and the Czar. And in Petersburg, Alexander waited for the outcome of the Austrian war, overwhelming the French Ambassador with favour and promises while he withheld the troops Napoleon needed. As usual, a large section of the Court deplored his caution, urging him to throw in his forces with Austria and the German nationalists who were in revolt in the Tyrol and Westphalia, to turn on Napoleon and crush him while he had the chance. But Alexander waited, and on the 5th of July, Napoleon proved him right by winning a decisive victory at Wagram. Within a hundred days, Austria had signed the Treaty of Vienna, the war was over, the revolt in the German states was ruthlessly stamped out, and Napoleon emerged more powerful than ever.

On his return to Paris, he sent for the Empress Josephine and informed her that she was to be divorced; pleas, tears and hysterics availed her nothing; she was retired to her estate at Malmaison, and on the 23rd of February, 1810, Caulaincourt delivered Napoleon's revenge on Alexander. While still negotiating for the hand of the Czar's sister, Anne, the French Emperor had concluded a marriage contract with the Archduchess Marie Louise, daughter of the Emperor of Austria.

Without betraying a sign of his anger and disquiet, Alexander sent his congratulations to Napoleon, and then retired in conference with Araktcheief. He also sent for the two Prussian tacticians Pfühl and Clausewitz, who had been exiles at his court since Tilsit. On April 2nd Marie Louise became Empress of France, and from the following month, Russian troops began arriving battalion by battalion to the Dwina, the Niemen, the Berezina and the Dnieper. The Russian frontiers were fortified, the work being carried out in secret, while the formidable Araktcheief took over the organization of the Russian forces.

Alexander was informed that by 1811 he would have an army of a quarter of a million men, well trained and properly equipped. It only remained for him to inveigle Austria out of her alliance with Napoleon, in spite of her marriage tie, and to bribe the Poles into joining him by promising restoration of the Kingdom of Poland.

At this juncture, he came into real contact with the new Austrian Minister for Foreign Affairs, the former Ambassador to France and the friend of Talleyrand, a man with the same insiduous charm as himself, a genius, a liar, a patriot, the most unscrupulous statesman and enigmatic personality of his age—Count Metternich.

As the long months passed, the rulers of Russia and France played out the last phase of the comedy of friendship, Alexander smiling, exuding charm and massing men and armaments within his boundaries, while Talleyrand kept him informed of Napoleon's position, of the unrest in France, where the blockade of English goods was causing hardship and abuse, of the smouldering nationalism of the German States which only needed a breath to burst into flame, and the endless bloody war with Spain.

Behind the façade of Imperial might, the foundations were beginning to crack under the strain of one man's unbridled autocracy, an autocracy which no longer tolerated advice or forgave criticism. The time was coming, Talleyrand told Tchernicheff, and Tchernicheff repeated his words to the Czar. The Empress Marie Louise was pregnant, the birth of an heir might mean the continuation of this unbearable dynasty from an infamous father onwards, unless Russia gave the signal to Europe and rose up against Napoleon. On March the 20th a son was born to Napoleon, but the event which he had imagined would stabilize his throne now turned to his disadvantage. The Czar congratulated Austria, and the hint followed that should the French Emperor lose his throne, Austrian power might rise to world eminence through the Regency of the Austrian born Empress for her infant son.

Metternich received this intimation without committing himself, but the cleverness of the diplomacy revealed the Czar Alexander in a very different guise to the one Metternich had previously assigned to him. The whole machinery of the conspiracy against Napoleon was conducted directly by Alexander; his Minister Speransky knew nothing, the Ambassador to Paris was the grotesquely incompetent Kurakin, behind whose back men like Tchernicheff and the diplomat-spy Nesselrode were intriguing and making their reports direct to the Czar. His contacts with Austria were made personally, with only his confidential secretary in collaboration. He was at once engaged in deceiving his own Ministers while he out-manœuvred Napoleon, and Metter-

nich hastily amended his opinion of him as a handsome
figurehead.   A review of his achievements decided the
Austrian that Alexander of Russia was a power to be
reckoned with; of all Bonaparte's opponents, he was the only
one who had lost nothing to him but a battle, and gained
time by sheer diplomatic acumen in which to gather his
forces and prepare for war.

Metternich responded cautiously to the Russian overtures,
while the idea of an Austrian Regency for France appealed
to him more and more, as Alexander hoped it would.   It was
understood that should Russia win the coming war, the
Bourbons would never be restored to power.   Alexander
promised this to Austria, assuring her of his friendship as
beguilingly as he had once assured Napoleon; it was Metternich's first error in his dealings with the Czar, that like that
other arch-deceiver Bonaparte, he believed him and was himself deceived.

A less gullible pawn in the political game was Adam
Czartorisky, still lured by Alexander's promises to restore his
native Poland, but with the discovery of the Czar's efforts
to extract an undertaking from Napoleon that Poland should
never be reconstituted to shake his confidence.   He had loved
Alexander, forgiven him his treatment of the Czarina Elizabeth, because he trusted his word and believed him sincere in
his Liberalism.   But that trust was wavering; the calculating,
ruthless monarch was not the gentle humanist of his youth,
the enemy of Bonaparte was revealing himself as a Czar in
the old pattern of autocracy and nationalism, and the fact
that he was as mild mannered and charming as ever could
no longer confuse one who had known him and served him
for so long.

But love of his country urged Adam to place his confidence
in the one man who had the power to carry out the intentions he expressed so convincingly.   This time, if Poland
rallied to Russia and turned on Napoleon, she might be
rewarded with her independence.   So Adam joined the conspiracy, and began urging the Poles to prepare for the day
when they should rise against the French.

In the meantime, Alexander approached the country that had so far withstood Napoleon on land and sea and was surviving the blockade he had enforced throughout Europe.

Russia had a deep and friendly regard for England, and no wish to aid France in her attempt at economic strangulation. Russian ports would be secretly open to English ships, and Russian influence might be exerted in Sweden to secure a similar concession there. The English Prime Minister received the message and read into it the news that within a short time Russia and France would be at war. He hastened to return similar sentiments to Alexander, and the promise of English assistance in any contingency that might arise.

As he had promised, Alexander sent envoys to Sweden, assuring Napoleon that they were to investigate the charge that the new Crown Prince of Sweden, the former French Marshal Bernadotte, was betraying France by relaxing the blockade. In public, they conveyed reproaches, and in private persuaded Bernadotte to give entry to as many English ships as he wished, with Russia's blessing. Bernadotte, the Gascon soldier who had been made heir to the Crown of Sweden, was already breaking free of Napoleon's domination. Ambitious, ruthless and jealous of his own power, he promptly entered the conspiracy against his Emperor, and wrote to the Czar advising him on the best military tactics for defeating him. Avoid the pitched battle at which Napoleon excelled, drag on the war as long as possible. If the plot to attack him simultaneously through Austria, Poland, Germany and Prussia did not materialize, then draw him into Russia.

The rumours of a gigantic movement against him spurred Napoleon to speedy action; to enforce the blockade of English goods he annexed the Hanseatic territories from the Ems to the Weser, including the Duchy of Oldenburg, whose heir Catherine Pavlovna had married. The pretence of friendship was wearing threadbare between the two countries, and as the news of Alexander's gathering army reached Napoleon he began collecting his own forces to meet them.

A volley of threats forced Prussia to send 20,000 men to join the French army, and Francis of Austria dispatched 30,000 more, assured by Metternich that they could reverse their loyalties the moment Napoleon appeared likely to lose the war. Russia understood the plight of nations like Austria and Prussia, and knew that their aid was unwillingly given and unreliable. Besides, they dared do nothing else for the moment.

In the first months of the year 1812 a host of men began moving across Europe and massing on the Russian frontier, while the soldiers of Holy Russia swelled their encampments on the Niemen and stretched to the banks of the Dwina. From every capital in the world statesmen watched these preparations for the greatest conflict ever to be fought, between the invincible Napoleon and the man of whom little was known except that he had been France's ally for the last six years. Europe had felt the power of French arms, it knew and dreaded the genius of the oppressor, but almost nothing was known about Russia.

She was huge and barbarian, hundreds of years behind the other European nations in national development, with an internal record of unparalleled violence and a reigning house composed of a long line of lunatics and tyrants. Alexander's vaunted Liberalism was remembered and treated as an eccentricity; he had ascended the throne by murdering the rightful ruler; he was reputed to be in love with his own sister, to be a weakling who wept at the sight of a battlefield and a few thousand corpses, vain, sensual, devoured by ambition. At the same time he was reported to be noble minded, religious, courageous and wise. A fool rushing to destruction or a cunning, ruthless adversary who had bided his time and duped the most formidable man in the world—no one knew which was his true rôle, and until the armies met in battle, no one would find out. On either side of the Russian frontier, the two great forces faced each other, waiting. Each was composed of half a million men.

CHAPTER FIVE

IN the first months of that year of 1812, Alexander made several journeys to Tver to see his sister Catherine; on her marriage, he had given her a magnificent estate there, and an enormous income. The sight of Prince George of Oldenburg, pimpled and undersized, pricked Alexander's conscience when he thought that he had forced his sister into marriage with him. Conscience had long since ceased to be a word to the Czar; it troubled him violently over many things, and not least for having condemned his sister to the life she hated most, pampered inactivity. The fact that he knew her to be evil and unscrupulous did not excuse his own harshness, and he tried to make amends by lavishing money and favour on her. She had conspired against him, she had no more moral sense than an animal, and her debauches at Tver were already notorious; he knew all this, but her faults faded to insignificance beside the enormity of his own crime.

He had murdered his own father; lain in bed listening while a crowd of drunken traitors battered him to death, and then pretended to be sorry, to be innocent, so that his confederates and not himself should bear the blame. When he thought of that he thanked God for two mercies granted him; he had resisted the temptation to put Catherine Pavlovna to death, and he had been allowed the opportunity of repairing his terrible wrong by freeing the world from the tyranny of Napoleon.

Through the worry and intrigue of the past four years, the agnosticism of his early training had been replaced by the need of religious guidance, and with the admission of God there followed the sense of his own sin. During the long hours when he knelt praying, the feeling of guilt, of unclean-

ness, nearly overwhelmed him, and was followed by the urge
to atone. It was not long before his resolve to humble
Napoleon became inextricably involved with the idea of a
reparation as tremendous as his crime. The first impulses
of hatred, national jealousy and ambition which were the
motivating forces in his pursuit of vengeance became
swamped in a mystical sense of God-given mission. The
approaching conflict filled him with exhilaration; he worked
and planned with the energy of ten men—his pleasures
dwindled as his duties grew. Marie Naryshkin became his
only distraction from the crushing routine he had imposed
on himself.

When he alighted from his gold-painted sledge and entered
the Palace at Tver, his sister came forward to greet him.
He kissed her affectionately, saluted his brother-in-law,
and then asked Catherine to receive him privately in her
apartments.

He had shed the heavy fur-lined greatcoat and was warm-
ing his hands by the fire when she came in.

"You look tired," she said. "Very tired. I'll ring for
some wine and we can have supper up here. I want to hear
every word of news."

"That's why I came," he said. "I have some good news
for you, Catherine, and I wanted to deliver it myself."

He sat down, drawing his chair by the fire.

"What news?" she demanded. "Tell me quickly. You
know I'm dying of boredom in this place."

"Isn't George pleasant to you?"

"The devil take George. You know very well I don't
rely on George for amusement. . . . Tell me the news!"

"It's about Prince Bagration," Alexander said, watching
her; he saw the colour rise in her olive skin.

"Bagration . . ."

"I'm giving him command of the Southern army," he
said.

Bagration was her lover; he spent weeks at Tver under the
complaisant eye of George of Oldenburg, and the stories of
his passion for the Grand Duchess and of hers for him were

circulating through every salon in Petersburg. He was an exceptionally brave and able soldier; his appointment had no bearing on his relationship with Catherine, but Alexander knew how it would please her.

She laughed and swung round with the quick movement so characteristic of her. " Thank you, Alexander. He'll serve you well. Before God I shall miss him, though! "

" Has he made you happy, Catherine? " he asked. She looked down at him, her eyebrows raised in surprise at herself.

"I love him, but I respect him, which is so ridiculous, for I've never cared for anyone before. He's as noble as I'm base, and you can appreciate that, my brother. Tell me, how is our dear family? Mother still writes those irritating letters which I never answer. And how is the charming Marie— still in favour? "

" Everyone is well—they all send messages to you. As for Marie, I don't know what I'd do without her! "

Catherine laughed maliciously. " You'll do well enough. Really, you're so faithful to her it's indecent! "

"You misunderstand me." He was irritated by her coarseness, but he repressed it. Love to Catherine meant only one thing. Bagration's nobility of character was equalled by tremendous virility; the gentler moods were not for Catherine, nor indeed for him.

" Marie gives me affection, loyalty. They're precious things. If you were Czarina you'd appreciate that."

Catherine turned half away from him and stared into the fire. " There was a time when I might have been," she said slowly.

Alexander's expression did not alter, though the confession astonished him. " I know that," he said quietly. " Why do you tell me now? "

" Because Bagration says I was disloyal," she answered. " I told him of it, and he was very angry. I can't bear his anger, Alex."

She gazed at him out of her slanting eyes; bewildered by her own reaction. Alexander thought how beautiful she was, how tremendously alive. Everything about her radiated vitality, her shining black hair, the glowing healthy skin, her magnificent body in the revealing Empire dress. No wonder Bagration loved her; no wonder that any man who came in contact with her must be suspect, even her own brother. Perhaps God had forgotten to give His creation a soul, he thought suddenly; vain, cruel, treacherous and without moral values, the discovery of a fundamental decency in her feeling for Bagration had wrought havoc in her. He wanted to laugh at the irony of his sister falling in love with the most honourable and chivalrous soldier in Russia. And he pitied her, because for the first time she was defenceless, far more so than when he had tricked her and forced her into marriage. He also pitied Bagration, the recipient of such a woman's passion. If he abandoned her she'd kill him.

'Catherine Pavlovna—of us all she is the true Romanov; somewhere, in spite of all the German inter-marriage, the strain of Peter the Great, of the Empresses Anna and Elizabeth Petrovna has come out in her,' he thought. 'She belongs to a past century. A hundred years ago she would have been Empress of All the Russias by now and I would have been dead. . . .'

But aloud he said, "All that's past, Catherine, I spilt our father's blood and let that be the last crime to disgrace the name of Romanov. Everything happens according to God's will; had He wished you to reign instead of me, you'd have been born the eldest son. You've forgotten the wine," he added gently.

She pulled a bell cord and then sat down on the opposite side of the enormous marble grate.

"God's will, eh? Don't tell me it's true that you've become religious!"

"I've discovered the need of Faith, if that's what you mean. If you bore on your conscience what I bear on mine, you would need it too."

She shrugged, and the diamonds circling her throat blazed with the movement. "You shouldn't brood on Father's death, Alex. All that is past, you've just said so yourself. Then let it be. Forget it. We're a bad family; Constantine's a monster, Nicholas a heartless blockhead, I make no excuses for myself, God knows, and as for you, my dear brother, you're probably worse than any of us if the truth were known!"

He stared past her without answering; it was a mannerism that annoyed her because it baffled; it was impossible to deduce from his expression whether he had even heard her last remark.

At that moment a footman entered, and she ordered wine and supper to be brought to her rooms. If anything, her dislike of Alexander had increased during the last four years, but it was now tempered with a grudging respect; she realized at last that the brother she had dismissed as a weakling had outwitted her in the most subtle way.

The idol of the salons, she thought, watching him as he sipped his wine, his fine profile outlined by the firelight; equipped with every fashionable grace of bearing and accomplishment, ready with a soft word even for his enemies. As a result he was always underestimated, and, by God, what a mistake that was. . . .

' No one really knows him,' she decided, ' I least of all. Perhaps Marie Naryshkin does, but even that I doubt. He knows I hate him and hoped to overthrow him, but he's kind and generous to me, and God knows why, for he asks nothing in return.'

She put down her wineglass and said, " What other news have you, brother? "

"We shall be at war with France in a few months," Alexander answered quietly. "And that leads me to the second thing I have to tell you. It will gladden your heart to hear that I intend to dismiss Speransky."

She sat upright. "At last! At last you've listened to me!"

"And to Araktcheief and many others," he reminded her. "I've hesitated because he's a good servant and Russia owes him a great deal."

"He's a Jacobin," she interrupted fiercely. "Low born and treacherous. All he wants is peace with Napoleon, the cur! When are you getting rid of him?"

"Soon now," Alexander said. "When I return to Petersburg. And that's not the only change; I shall appoint your friend Feodor Rostopchine Governor of Moscow."

Catherine's eyes widened. Rostopchine, the fanatical friend of their father, for so long a semi-exile till she welcomed him into her circle at Tver because his hatred of the French reflected her own feelings. Rostopchine and Araktcheief. Two phantoms out of the past instead of one; in some sinister way the influence of Paul the First was creeping back as his son recalled those men most prominent in his terrible reign.

"He's completely loyal," Alexander explained. "I remember the service he gave my father and I hope he will give it to me. He can be trusted with the safety of Moscow before any other man in Russia. Naturally, my dear sister, you won't speak a word of what I've told you, even to Bagration. There's a faction at Court who wants peace with France as much as Speransky, and what I'm going to do must take them by surprise."

"I know," she said. "And Constantine's at the head of it, damn him. The miserable coward, he tells everyone we're going to lose the war; he predicts Napoleon will defeat us in a few months and have your head; it's his own he's worrying about. I shall never forgive him!"

Alexander glanced at her over the rim of his glass.

"Nor shall I," he said.

*   *   *

On the evening of the 29th of March Speransky received a summons from the Emperor. He went to the Winter Palace, carrying his portfolio under his arm; he was quite determined to try and argue the Czar out of this mad project of war with Napoleon.

Speransky shook his head as he walked, lost in his own

reflections as he conducted an imaginary conversation with Alexander. "Why ruin Russia, why pit his army against the greatest military genius in the world when there wasn't one Russian General to compare with him. . . . France had never violated Russian rights; the Duchy of Oldenburg, yes, Napoleon had seized that, but only because his allies were letting English goods flow into their ports in defiance of the agreed Continental System. Was Alexander going to sacrifice his people and lose his throne for the Duchy of Oldenburg?"

It was his sister Catherine, of course, Speransky concluded angrily. An evil troublemaker, anxious to destroy her country to satisfy her own personal spite against Napoleon. What a pity Alexander was too gentle to deal with her. . . . There was something to be said for the old system. . . .

He passed through the ante-room and was admitted to Alexander's private study.

Two hours later he emerged, his face as white as the papers his shaking hands were trying to put back into his portfolio. He walked away and down the long Palace corridors with jerking steps that were almost a run. In those few minutes he reverted to his former background; the Minister was a peasant again, a peasant in Court dress with a shabby dispatch case under his arm, trembling as if he were going to be beaten.

He knew instinctively that the news of his dismissal had preceded him with the uncanny speed that always informed a Court which way the wind of Imperial favour was blowing. No one bowed to him this time as he passed, and many turned their backs; some laughed and he heard them. His grey head shook as another imaginary conversation took place between him and Alexander.

'If you have no further need of me, then I'll retire to my estates. I'll live quietly, Sire, I've had my fill of public service, but if you should ever want me . . .'

He left the Palace and drove home in his own sledge; in its privacy his face suddenly contorted and he wept.

*　　　*　　　*

Alexander sat on in his study. No one dared disturb him as the time passed; when Speransky had left he made a few notes, and then laid down his pen and covered his face with his hands. He could still see Speransky's face when he heard that his trusted Sovereign had had him watched by the Secret Police, when the accusations of partisanship for France and personal criticisms of the Emperor were read out to him.

He had looked so terribly old at that moment, and his clever tongue, which had so often swayed a Council, stumbled and he choked on his excuses. Even his education deserted him and he made mistakes, his accent broadening; he dropped his papers and forgot to pick them up, but remained on his knees, pleading with Alexander not to dismiss him, not to destroy his life's work for the progress of Russia, and all the time Alexander's resolution hardened the more his heart was touched. Speransky angered him by becoming suddenly so pitiful and making his task so much more difficult. So much more difficult than even Speransky knew at that time.

The Emperor folded his papers and arranged the pens on his gold inkstand. The desk was the one Catherine the Great had used; as a youth he had often come to see her and helped her out of the chair he was sitting in at that moment. He thought of her and wondered if she had ever felt as he did, if she had ever known a spasm of loathing for the things she had to do in the name of Authority.

Plump, smiling Grandmère who loved him so dearly; remembering, he realized her calm benevolence was terrifying in its assurance that whatever she did she was above the law. As he was. It was the privilege and the burden of kings.

"I am not cruel by nature," she had said once, and her words came back to him. "But there are times when my position forces me to play the hangman."

He glanced at the clock inset in gold that stood on a corner of the desk. Speransky would have reached his home and found Balachov, the Police Chief, waiting with the last part of Alexander's sentence. By now they would have bundled the old man into a closed troika and driven him off to exile in Siberia.

He rose and went into the ante-room, which he found to be crowded with people; he recognized Araktcheief, who bowed low and smiled; everywhere he saw the faces of Speransky's enemies, the men who wanted war with France and could be relied on for support.

He nodded to them all, smiling and calm, and went to his own rooms. There he sent his valet for Marie Naryshkin. She understood and loved him well enough to know that exhaustion, not comfort, was what he needed, and eventually he fell asleep in her arms.

*   *   *

At the beginning of May the Emperor Napoleon arrived at Dresden, where a great Court had been assembled to pay homage to him. As at Erfurt there were Kings and Princes, a dazzling display of troops, the most beautiful women in Europe, and this time his wife the Empress Marie Louise. Marie Louise was not pretty; her looks were feline, her colouring fair and her figure voluptuous in the style Napoleon admired, but the pointed face and tilted eyes were stupid, far more stupid and less fascinating than the Empress Josephine even in the days of her decline. Marie Louise's success with the Emperor was due to three things, her obedience to his will, an unexpected talent in bed, which delighted him, and the birth of the heir he wanted so desperately. He was unfaithful to her, but always kind, and she submitted to him with sleepy eagerness, confident in any situation where her senses and not her brain came into use. Oddly, he had become quite fond of her, so fond that in a moment of madness he had ordered the doctors to save her life instead of the child when a crisis arose during her confinement. She smiled sweetly and kissed him when she heard of the incident, and despised him in her vague way as a common little man who put his personal feelings before the good of his dynasty. She was as happy with him as she could ever be with anyone.

There were banquets and receptions, reviews and military displays, all calculated to impress the Czar of Russia with the power and resources of the French Emperor. Never had Napoelon appeared more confident and over-bearing; he still persisted in treating the possibility of war with Russia as a mistake Alexander had no real intention of committing. The Czar was a man given to gestures, he declared casually; no one need think he would do more than parade up and down, manœuvring his vast army and then turn back to Petersburg. But when he was alone with Marie Louise, he dropped the pose.

After a strenuous day and an evening reception attended by many hundreds, the Emperor had retired to his wife's rooms. She was already undressed, the gold embroidered gauze dress put away, the fabulous tiara and necklace locked in her jewel case. She sat before her dressing-table, twisting yellow strands of hair round one finger and looking at herself in the mirror.

Bonaparte sat on her chaise-longue, his shoulders hunched, his hands hanging down between his knees.

"The reception went well to-night," Marie Louise remarked.

Napoleon glanced up at her moodily. "It always does," he said. "Thank God it's the last, I leave for the frontier to-morrow."

The Empress pushed her hair over one temple with her fingers and frowned slightly, undecided whether the line suited her.

"I shall miss you dreadfully, dear heart," she said. "Perhaps he'll make peace at the last minute."

"Alexander doesn't mean to make peace. I've suspected that for weeks, though I had to pretend otherwise to all these fools in Dresden. He's determined on war, Marie, and war he shall have now, whatever the consequences."

She turned round and looked at him, surprised by the gloomy tone and hang-dog air. He looked ill, she thought,

suddenly, and very tired; it was so unlike him to be depressed
before a campaign.

"You'll win, dear heart," she said. "You always do."

He was staring at the ground, his hands clasping and
unclasping. "I'll win. Never doubt that. But this is one
war I didn't want to fight. God knows, I trusted him—and
then he turned on me! I should have known better. At
Erfurt I suspected him; if it hadn't been for your father
going to war with me, I'd have attacked him then and beaten
him!"

The Empress's cat's eyes changed colour at his reference
to the Emperor Francis and the campaign which had ended
with her being sent to France as the price of defeat. Then
she turned back to the mirror again; after all the man was
a vulgarian, one had to expect occasional lapses of good
taste.

"Why don't you try and make peace even now?" she
suggested.

He scowled at her back. "And humble myself before
Europe! Where are your brains, Madame?"

"Well, you could say he asked for it," Marie retorted.
She pouted at her reflection.

"I think I shall have my hair dressed higher. . . ."

After a moment Napoleon rose and came behind her.

"I apologize, my dear. That was a very wise suggestion."

His eyes were narrowed and she watched them in the
mirror, thinking that it was odd that such a little man could
look so frightening at times.

"He may also be hampered by pride. If I make a show of
force, cross the frontier and then send an envoy to him . . .
he might be glad to avoid doing battle. The whole problem
might be solved. . . ."

He placed his hands on her shoulders and immediately she
leant against him; he bent and kissed the nape of her neck.
She closed her eyes and enjoyed the sensation; she liked his
hands, they were white and delicate, almost well-bred. . . .
The thought passed through her mind, already hazing with
sensuality, that she had said something really intelligent. . . .

" All is not lost," Napoleon muttered as he held her. "I'll fight if I have to and I'll win for you, my Marie, and for our son. I'll erase Russia off the map if necessary, but I'll win. . . ."

A little later he slept, and she moved cautiously to escape his weight without waking him, wondering why this episode was somehow different from all the others in their married life. The element she sensed but could not identify was new to Bonaparte himself.

It was desperation.

She lay for a few moments puzzling over it and then drifted into a calm sleep.

The next morning Napoleon left Dresden at the head of a great cavalcade to join the Grand Armée on the left bank of the River Niemen.

*   *   *

In the stifling heat of June Alexander and his entourage arrived at Wilna ostensibly to review the troops stationed there and to hold manœuvres, but in fact he travelled to his army as Napoleon left to join his.

The Czar's arrival began a round of fêtes and entertainments given by the local nobility. Every evening there was a ball or a dinner in his honour, and while the armies of France camped a few miles away on the opposite bank of the Niemen, beautiful women danced with him, flirted with him and retained an impression of his charm that lasted for the rest of their lives. In the day-time the factions surrounding him squabbled and intrigued against each other.

In accordance with General Pfühl's strategy, Russia's armies were divided into two mobile forces, the main body commanded by a Lithuanian of Scottish descent, Barclay de Tolly, the other by Prince Bagration. The pivot of the Russian strategy was a huge fortified encampment built by a bend of the River Dwina; it was intended that this bastion at Drissa should bar Napoleon's way, that the decisive battle should be fought close to it by Barclay de Tolly's men, while Bagration and his forces remained separated and harassed the French in the rear or the flank. Alexander had adopted the plan and disposed his forces accordingly, but a threefold campaign was being waged to make him change his mind. Araktcheief and Barclay de Tolly denounced Pfühl's theory as fiercely as the German emigrant tacticians defended it, and Bagration prophesied disaster if the plan was really put into practice.

Still another faction urged Alexander to take over the command of the army himself and direct the war, but the memory of the disasters of Austerlitz and Friedland had not faded from Alexander's mind if it had from his supporters, and he rejected the proposal. The fourth cabal surrounding him demanded that he should make peace with Napoleon as soon as possible, and his brother the Grand Duke Constantine led this chorus. It was the measure of his tact and diplomatic skill that he remained above the bickering and enmities which flared up round him every day; while supporting Pfühl he listened carefully to his detractors; his immunity enabled him to weigh the merits of each argument and to form an unbiased judgment while he sat through one angry conference after another.

He had followed Pfühl, and if necessary he would continue to do so for a time, but it was first necessary to induce Napoleon to commit the aggression which must make him responsible for the war.

The French envoy General de Narbonne had been treated with exquisite courtesy and dispatched with the answer that while the Czar had no wish to shed blood, he would never agree to anything contrary to his country's honour.

"All the bayonets in Europe," he added, "if they were concentrated on my frontier, would not shake my resolution."

After that there was silence, an ominous silence, while the nobility of Wilna vied with each other in their attempts to honour Alexander, and his staff fought with each other about the best method of defeating the French. There were even a few lost voices who declared that Napoleon would never attack at all.

On the evening of June the 24th Alexander attended a ball
at the house of a local landowner; it was a brilliant assembly,
graced by exceptionally lovely women, and the Emperor was
enjoying himself for the first time in weeks. He felt relaxed
and gay, for a few hours the shadow of the war and its
problems receded; even Araktcheief was smiling as he talked
to a group of officers in one corner of the huge supper-room.
The strains of music from the ball-room mingled with talk
and laughter; Alexander listened to it absently while he
paid compliments to an admiring audience of Polish
ladies.

He saw Balachov enter the supper-room, and thought suddenly of Speransky and the night Balachov had arrested him.
Speransky was in Perm, sentenced to the living death of
exile. . . . He was still writing letters begging for mercy,
letters which remained unanswered and would no longer be
followed by others, for his gaolers had been ordered to
remove pen and paper from him. Balachov pushed his way
towards the Czar; at that moment Alexander noticed the
expression on his face. "You will excuse me, just for a
moment." He turned to the woman nearest him, before
he moved quickly forward to meet the Chief of his Police.

"Sire," Balachov bowed and looked round, "I must speak
to you."

"What is it? Speak quietly. We can't be overheard."

Balachov whispered and Alexander bent over him;
when he straightened he was pale. Followed by Balachov
he left the supper-room, and a few minutes afterwards
Araktcheief and Speransky's successor, Admiral Shishkov,
were summoned.

Early that morning the advance guards of the Grand
Armée had crossed the Niemen into Russia.

*   *   *

Pontoon bridges had been thrown over the Niemen, and
three enormous French columns commenced the crossing
near the town of Kovno. There was a sudden roar of cheer-

ing, swelling and rolling like thunder from regiment after regiment drawn up on Russian soil as the figure of the Emperor Napoleon appeared and rode his horse over the bridge. The noise reached a crescendo as his mount stepped on to the bank, and for a moment he waited, one hand raised in salute. Men were pouring in torrents over the bridges, spreading out and blackening the land with their numbers. Heavy waggons bumped and swayed and lurched down on to the river bank, carrying cannon, clothes, medicines, food and supplies of every kind. And there was more equipment on the way. In the meantime, the French troops could supplement their rations by living off the land.

Within a few hours of the invasion two things became clear; there was not a Russian soldier in a radius of several miles, and the country was a sandy waste. The rough cart tracks were obliterated by the passage of men and horses, there was no fit pasture for the animals and no shelter for either the Emperor or his troops.

But the order to march was given, and slowly the host began to move; the objective was Wilna, where the Czar was sure to stand and fight. When they reached Wilna, they found the Russians had withdrawn.

At the village of Rykonty the advance guard brought in a Russian nobleman who claimed to be the Czar's emissary. It was Balachov. He was taken to Napoleon's headquarters where he delivered Alexander's protest against the invasion of his country without even a declaration of war. Napoleon raged at him, abusing and threatening in the most violent terms, but Balachov stared at the floor and appeared not to hear. His silence and the phrasing of Alexander's message roused Napoleon to a climax of rage.

" Which is the road to Moscow? " he shouted suddenly.

Balachov raised his eyes and looked at him blankly.

" Your Majesty's question embarrasses me a little. The Russians have a saying like the French, that all roads lead to Rome. To reach Moscow one takes the road one fancies; Charles XII set out by way of Pultava."

Napoleon swallowed. Pultava, where the Swedish invaders had been annihilated by Peter the Great in 1709. Pultava . . .

He swung round and walked away.

Balachov was escorted beyond the French outposts and rode out to rejoin the Czar.

Alexander was with the main Russian forces commanded by Barclay de Tolly, and the army was withdrawing towards the encampment at Drissa in accordance with the official strategy. Bagration, with a smaller force of 45,000 men, waited in the province of Volhynia. When the French advanced to attack Barclay, Bagration would strike at their flank.

As the Imperial army passed, it burnt crops and villages to the ground on the Czar's order. Nothing was to be left for the invader; he would march into a smouldering desert, abandoned by the people who were driven ahead by their own troops. All possible shelter was razed, the livestock carried off or slaughtered.

In the course of the long march to Drissa, Alexander rode through the ruins of his own countryside, with the smoke of burning villages rising into the summer sky, the golden wheat fields trodden down by his cavalry, the water wells blocked, the carcasses of cattle and horses putrefying under the hot sun.

"A desert," he had promised, "where nothing grows or stirs. The soldiers of Bonaparte will never live off Russian land."

The scenes of desolation did not move him outwardly; he felt nothing because he dared not. He saw devastation and misery with blind eyes, knew that his troops were driving the peasants to starvation and death, that they pillaged and raped like an invader in some cases, but the knowledge made no difference. Nothing mattered. He would destroy Russia if he had to, before he left a grain of wheat or a wall standing for the benefit of the French.

Barclay de Tolly spent long hours conferring with him; he was a dour man, hard-headed and cautious, and he was convinced that the Prussian strategy would mean disaster.

"If we fight Napoleon before Drissa we're lost!" he declared as he rode beside the Emperor. Alexander shifted the reins to one hand and wiped his sweating face with a handkerchief.

"Pfühl has perfect confidence in the plan," he replied. They had been riding for some hours, and for most of the time De Tolly had been warning him not to listen to the Prussian and risk a pitched battle.

"Pfühl's a German, Sire. He's sure he's right, and by God when a German thinks he's right there's no more obstinate fool alive! We're dealing with Bonaparte, not Frederick the Great! Is it likely he'll oblige us by attacking Drissa and letting Bagration encircle him?

"No, Sire, I tell you if I wouldn't fall into that trap, no more will he. He'll wipe out Bagration, that's what he'll do and then come after us. And small use Pfühl's plan will be then. For God's sake, Sire, abandon it, send for Bagration, and link up your armies before it's too late."

"Bagration says the same," Alexander answered. "And my sister writes urging me to listen to him." He turned to Barclay, frowning, and the Commander-in-Chief realized how tired he looked. His face was drawn and lined through lack of sleep.

"If Pfühl's wrong, I'll abandon him. I'll abandon anyone, you, Bagration, Araktcheief, anyone, but I won't lose this war. We'll inspect Drissa as soon as we arrive. There may be some news of Napoleon's movements by the time we get there."

At Drissa Alexander set out to look over the artificial bastion, followed by General Pfühl himself. The General stamped along a few paces behind the Czar, red-faced and scowling; he took the inspection as a personal insult; he had spent years working out his plan, his invincible theory, and now these miserable Russians were trying to alter it. He intended to question the Emperor, but somehow the opportunity did not arise; Alexander seemed suddenly cold and aloof, he walked through the encampment in a silence that no one dared to break. And he returned to his headquarters in silence. There he found a courier waiting with Araktcheief.

"Sire," Araktcheief burst out as soon as he entered. "Sire, Bonaparte's sent Marshal Davoust and his forces out towards Volhynia."

"I knew it." Barclay swung round. "He's going to attack Bagration! God in Heaven, he's splitting us up; if he meets Bagration and defeats him we're lost!"

"Nonsense, nonsense. It's a feint, he'll attack Drissa, he's bound by my theory . . ." Pfühl interrupted, and Barclay turned on him.

"Damn your theory! Now see where it's brought us!"

"Gentlemen. One moment!" Alexander's voice cut through them harshly. He was white and the expression on his face closed even Pfühl's mouth.

He took off his gloves and threw them on to a chair. Then he spoke softly. "Your plan is abandoned, General. You may go."

Pfühl stared at him and seemed about to speak, then he bowed stiffly and went out. There was a moment of dead silence after the door had closed behind him.

"We will march the garrison out of Drissa and join them with your forces," Alexander said to Barclay. "What news is there from Bagration?"

"None, Sire," Araktcheief answered. "He's probably unaware that the French are advancing on him."

"Then send word at once. Order him to avoid contact with them and to retire towards Vitepsk. There the main army will join him. Hurry! Barclay!"

"Sire!" The Commander-in-Chief stepped forward; he was red with delight at Pfühl's dismissal and the prospect of conducting the war in his own way.

"From now on, you are to take what course you think fit. I shall leave the army and go back to St. Petersburg; you are in complete charge. What do you propose to do?"

"I propose to retreat," Barclay said quietly. "I shall draw Napoleon after me for as far as he will come, without ever giving battle. Raiding parties can harass him, cut down the stragglers. I shall carry out your orders and destroy everything so that if he can't supply his troops they'll starve. And the longer his lines of communication, the weaker he will be! It is now July, Sire. If he goes far enough into the heart of Russia, Russia itself will defeat him."

* * *

"The French are there," Alexander said, pointing to a place on the map. "In three days they'll reach Smolensk."

Marie was standing beside him in his study in the Summer Palace, bending over the table on which he had spread the map of Russia; his arm was round her shoulders and she reached up and caught hold of his hand.

"Will it be taken?" she asked.

"If God wills."

She looked up at him, puzzled. He was always talking about the will of God, and he spent hours in the Palace chapel praying before the High Altar; he invoked the aid of the Almighty in every order issued to his army and commanded his people to pray daily for the defeat of the enemy. To Marie it was inexplicable; Alexander the atheist, whose materialism was as honest as her own, Alexander religious, listening to priests, wasting hours in draughty churches when he might have been amusing himself and taking everyone's minds off the danger. . . .

"He's not well," she thought tenderly, and kissed the hand that lay on her shoulder. "He's worried so much and he sleeps so badly now; even I don't seem able to help him. . . ."

The idea that his sudden conversion might be genuine was something she refused to accept; he did nothing by half measure, she knew that; if religion were really to take root in his mind it might be followed by morality, and that would be the end of her. No, she brushed the fear aside, it was all due to anxiety . . . he would come back to her when this miserable war was won; he'd make love to her as often as he used to instead of sitting in her rooms talking about the war.

" Barclay and Bagration are going to make a stand at Smolensk," he was saying. " Bagration insisted; he says the troops' morale is weakening with all this retreating from the enemy. I don't think they'll hold the city, neither does Barclay."

" Why don't you forget it for a moment," Marie pleaded. " You're wearing yourself out. Beloved, you're at Petersburg and they are at Smolensk, there's nothing you can do now. Why don't you let me put all these maps and papers away and come and relax? "

He smiled down at her.

" Have I neglected you so much lately? "

She slipped between him and the table, some instinct of self-preservation urging her.

' This withdrawal I sense in him, it's not just preoccupation with the war. It's the beginning of indifference, it means I'm losing him. . . .'

She reached up and pulled his head down and began to kiss him.

" We never used to talk politics in the old days, do you remember," she murmured. " Now whenever we're together it's nothing but the war, the war, all the time."

He was holding her in his arms and she clung to him. trying to arouse and maintain the warmth of the affection which had existed between them for so long. He rested his chin against her forehead and his lips touched her temple.

" Do you remember that day on the islands? " she asked suddenly. " We were like this then; just before you went to Erfurt, and I'd been warning you about plots in the capital. You told me you couldn't do without me, Alexander. You begged me to stay with you always, and I promised. You were in trouble then and you needed me. . . ."

" Then it was only myself," he answered. " Now it's my people, my country—the whole world. I challenged him, Marie, and if I lose, all Europe is lost, perhaps for ever."

He released her and stepped back.

"Do you know what's happening in Russia? Do you know that our troops are burning every town and village they pass through? From Wilna to Smolensk Russia is a desert, Marie. That's what I promised Napoleon and I've kept my promise. He's conquering a desert. If he takes Smolensk Barclay will blow it to pieces first. His soldiers are nearly starving, dysentery's broken out . . . and my own people are also starving, homeless. I ordered it, Marie, and nothing will make me rescind that order, nothing!"

"He wanted to make peace," she said dully, leaning back against the table, crumpling the map. "Why didn't you, and stop all this?"

Alexander turned and looked at her.

"I will never make peace," he said. "Not until I've driven him out of Russia."

She made a movement with her hand and then stopped.

"You are not in love with me any longer, are you?" was what she said.

He shook his head but his expression was kind.

"I have always loved you, Marie," he said gently. "But I haven't time to think of you now."

He walked to the door and closed it quietly behind him. For some moments Marie stayed by the table, then she turned and swept the map to the floor; she was crying helplessly, heaving books and papers off the table until the mirrored surface suddenly showed her a reflection of herself. She leant forward and stared at her own image, remembering that Alexander had given her the table years ago. It was marble, inlaid with lapiz-lazuli; at that time no one in Petersburg had possessed a table with a looking-glass top. It had become the rage. She wiped the tears away with her fingers and gazed at herself.

"Am I growing old? . . . Is it that? Is that why I almost have to kneel to him now before he consents to make love to me? Am I ugly? . . . Why, why, after all these years! He's changed to me, ever since he came back to Petersburg, since he left that damned army at Drissa. He's gone to other women, in the past, I know that, but he's always come back to me. He loved me! " She cried the words aloud. " But not now, not any more. I've tried everything, everything to please him, but it's no use."

She stood upright away from the looking-glass and instinctively one hand strayed to her tumbled hair. After months of self-deceit she had faced the truth, and the truth suddenly restored her composure. He had begun to grow cold to her; he was affectionate and kind, but the tremendous sexual bond was broken between them and she was experienced enough to know that with a man of his type her principal hold over him had gone.

She moved one of the books aside with her foot and thought that whoever won the war, she had lost everything.

She went to her bedroom and sent for her maid; an hour later she left the Summer Palace, dressed in her most beautiful white dress, wearing the rubies and diamonds round her neck and in her ears that she never wore because the Emperor didn't think jewels suited her. Her coach drove to a magnificent house on the Nevsky Prospect, belonging to a Polish nobleman who had never made any secret of his admiration for her.

" Is it true," her new lover whispered that evening, " is it true that the Czar had you painted like this? "

Marie opened her eyes.

' I have always loved you, but I haven't time to think of you now. . . . I'm tired, my dear, too tired even to talk. . . . His Majesty is detained in conference with General Araktcheief, Madame, he regrets he cannot dine with you this evening. . . .'

The voices in her mind receded; they had been running through it while she dined, when she came upstairs to the bedroom and took the only revenge on Alexander Pavlovitch that she could.

Things she hadn't realized had wounded her so deeply came out in an endless repetition; excuses, evasions, the innumerable hints that after all these years their love affair was dying.

" Is it true? " her lover questioned.

" Aphrodite, rising from the waves. Yes, it's true. But I wasn't wearing these," she said, touching the big jewels in her ears.

The man laughed. " The Czar has the portrait, but I have the original," he said. " Madame, I adore you."

*   *   *

On August 16th the battle for Smolensk began.

Barclay de Tolly's army had occupied the ancient city and prepared to defend it, while the forces under Prince Bagration guarded their line of retreat; this at least Barclay had demanded, for he had no hope of holding out against the French. He had been in his headquarters for forty-eight hours, receiving reports from scouts who told of the huge army being assembled on the low hills which ringed Smolensk from the south.

Batteries of cannon were being brought up, men and supplies had been pouring over the bridge which the French Marshal Davoust had managed to build over the Dnieper below the city, and the core of the French Army was gathering in reserve. Marshal Ney, Davoust, the Polish Prince Poniatowsky and the flamboyant Murat himself were in command of the reserves, ready to sweep forward and decide the issue as they had done so often in the great campaigns of the past. Barclay identified each corps and its commander from these reports, and discovered to his relief that Napoleon had not attempted to cut the lines of communication with Moscow or make any effort to bar a possible retreat of his enemies out of the city.

" He's certain of victory," explained Colonel Ouvarov, and Barclay nodded, scowling down at the maps spread in front of him.

" Intelligence says he believes Bagration's army are joined with us; this is to be the decisive battle, my friend, ending with our annihilation. If I'd given way to the hot-heads completely, that's just what it would be." He yawned and pinched out the candles which dripped at his elbow. The dawn light was streaming in through the windows. Barclay looked up and suddenly put his hand on Ouvarov's arm.

"Listen," he said. Both men heard a dull rumbling like approaching thunder; the glass in the window-panes shook slightly.

"Cannon," Barclay said. "It's the beginning of the bombardment. Get the word to our batteries, keep calm and hold your fire till you see the infantry. And send a message to the commanders of the city outposts. Not an inch of Russian soil must be yielded while one man lives to defend it; those are the Czar's orders! Go now, and hurry!"

While the sun rose slowly, the French bombardment of the outer defences thundered on; buildings collapsed in a roar of masonry and blinding dust, the red finger of fire poked through the ruins and was hurriedly put out; behind the city walls crowds of civilians huddled in cellars, shivering and weeping with terror; they were mostly women and children who had not been forcibly evacuated, the men were with Barclay's troops, armed with ancient firing pieces, knives, pitchforks and even stones. Others, guarding piles of straw, pitch and vitriol, were stationed in buildings at points throughout the city.

By midday the shelling slackened and the Russians in the exposed surburbs of Smolensk crept out of the ruins and took up their posts. The order came through to the Russian batteries. Stand by to fire. Scouts posted in trees and buildings watched the ground before Smolensk through field-glasses, among them Barclay de Tolly himself, whose own headquarters had been hit. There was a series of shouts from each watcher, and then a bugle blew clearly across from the French lines, sounding the Advance. At that moment the host of French infantry began moving across the open ground, their gilt eagle standards shining in the sunlight. "Ah," breathed Barclay, squinting through his field-telescope. They were coming nearer, shouts of "*Vive L'Empereur*" could be heard from the front ranks who were marching steadily towards the muzzles of the Russian guns.

Barclay beckoned one of his aides, still staring out across the advancing French columns. "Give the order, Open Fire!"

Within minutes an inferno of shot and cannon blazed out from the defenders, thinning the French ranks like mown grass. The rifles of hundreds concealed in the suburbs poured a fusillade of fire into the enemy; Russian gunners fought and sweated, charging, loading, firing. The approaches to Smolensk were black with French casualties, but still the infantry came on. Wave after wave were flattened and thrown back; the sun was high and blazing down before the first stragglers reached the outer suburbs and hand-to-hand fighting began. Slowly, by means of savage fighting, the first line of the Russian defence was dented, then breached, while a mass of reinforcements poured through the gap. Gunners abandoned their batteries to attack the invading troops who leapt down on them; some of the bloodiest engagements of that day were fought out in the gun emplacements, until gradually the Russian front-line fire subsided.

It was late afternoon before the French occupied the southern suburbs, and Alexander's orders had been obeyed with fanatical obedience, only the wounded and dying remained. For a period there was silence, the lull in a battle which Barclay knew preceded a new assault.

"Can I get you some wine, Sir?" The General looked up into the face of a very young officer with artillery insignia on his uniform. The boy was trembling from head to foot with nerves.

"Where have you been most of the day?" he asked.

"In the southern sector, Sir."

"This is your first bombardment?"

The young officer nodded; he was still shaking while he stood at attention.

"Hm. You're lucky to be out of there alive."

"I was sent back, Sir, with a message. My commander

and the battery crews were wiped out; I couldn't get back to them."

The boy's lips trembled for a moment and he bit them.

'Eighteen at the most,' Barclay decided.

"Go and get me some wine before the next assault begins—and something to eat. Get something for yourself as well."

"Thank you, Sir," he swallowed. "I couldn't . . ."

"Then go and ask Count Ouvarov for some brandy. Tell him I sent you. And drink it, boy; that's an order!"

He had only just finished his meal when the first cannonade burst in the centre of Smolensk behind the captured outer lines. Napoleon's batteries had moved up and were shelling the walls and heart of the city before taking it by assault.

It was dusk by then, but the sky was red rimmed with gun flashes; later it became redder still above Smolensk where fire had broken out. The streets were blocked by piles of rubble; above the roar and crash of the bombardment people ran screaming out of blazing wooden buildings. By nightfall Barclay gathered his staff in their temporary headquarters and showed them a map of the city.

His eyes were swollen with tiredness, his uniform covered in dust. His short forefinger stabbed at the map.

"Gentlemen. In another few hours Smolensk will be taken. Our army can stay here and be blown to pieces in the ruins before the French overwhelm us. We've shown them that Russians can fight, and fight to the death this day. But I say now that we withdraw towards Moscow and meet Prince Bagration with our forces intact. Gentlemen, I give the order. Set fire to every house in Smolensk, and then retreat!"

In the French encampment Napoleon was also studying maps. His headquarters was a big tent, lit by dozens of candles; two torches flamed at the entrance where a soldier of the Imperial Guard did sentry duty, and the French standard fluttered overhead. Inside the tent the Emperor ate, slept on a narrow canvas bed, and held conferences with his Marshals. Davoust was by his side, the fierce taciturn man whom nobody liked and everyone respected, Davoust who had built the bridge and set up ovens to make bread for the soldiers of the French Army. Opposite him stood Murat, dressed in one of his elaborate uniforms, glittering with orders and gold embroidery, Murat who had married Caroline Bonaparte, Napoleon's sister, and been made King of Naples. He was also the finest cavalry officer in the Imperial Army. Beside these two the Emperor seemed smaller than ever as he bent over the table on which his campaign maps were spread.

"Smolensk will fall before dawn," he announced. "The city walls are breached. It will be the end of the war! "

"They certainly fight," Murat remarked, curling the long hair of his sideburns round his finger. "God knows how many men they must have lost with their whole army cooped up in that inferno."

"Our own losses are not light," Davoust said shortly. "We've more than ten thousand casualties so far."

Napoleon was not listening; men had fallen in thousands that day, he didn't need Davoust to estimate their numbers, he had done so himself and put the figure higher.

He raised his head and looked round him, seeing Murat fiddling with his scented hair, his lips compressed for a moment and then almost smiled. Blustering vulgarian, as vain as a woman where his appearance was concerned, Murat often irritated him. But Napoleon had seen him lead a cavalry charge; for that he forgave him everything.

"Order our troops to go in," he snapped suddenly. "If we take the place now we can use it for shelter and save some of the stores. Davoust! " The Marshal stiffened to attention.

"Transmit this order to the army. 'We will advance and capture Smolensk, God and French valour have given us the victory.' Go! "

Davout saluted. *"Vive L'Empereur,"* he said, and went out.

"When do you think the Czar will make peace, Sire? "

Murat asked. Napoleon shrugged. "After this, as soon as he can."

"Shall we occupy Moscow?" Murat smiled, it was a rakish schoolboy's grin; some of his troopers swore that when the Marshal led them he was laughing. . . .

"Certainly, we'll occupy Moscow. I intend to dictate peace terms from the Kremlin." Napoleon looked up at Murat. "So far I've treated conquered nations gently, but I'll teach friend Alexander a lesson the whole world will never forget."

Later he left the tent and rode to a vantage point where he watched his troops storming the walls of Smolensk. He watched in silence, and the silence spread to his Marshals and aides who watched with him. The sounds of battle had died down; only a tremendous crackling roar filled the air and a brilliant red glow spread up into the night sky from the inferno that was Smolensk, the ancient City of Holy Russia. A courier galloped back to the Emperor, his face blackened with smoke, to report that the French Army were advancing into the blazing city without opposition; Smolensk was empty; the bulk of the Russian forces had retreated after setting fire to the town.

CHAPTER SIX

"EITHER we stand and fight, Sire, or we make peace with Napoleon. The temper of the army and the Court won't stand another retreat."

Araktcheief stood stiffly when he had said this, and for once his pale eyes looked straight at Alexander. He loved Alexander, if it were possible for the term to be applied to such a creature's feelings, and it gave him the courage to speak as he did.

Alexander was in double danger, danger from internal

intrigue which was growing every day; if he resisted this last warning and allowed the foreigner Barclay de Tolly to keep running from the French, he would certainly lose his throne. This was what Araktcheief had just told him. He forbore to mention that the obvious focal point for any traitor was the Grand Duchess Catherine Pavlovna.

She was the fiercest advocate of meeting Napoleon in open battle. Smolensk was lost, a smoking ruin, Russian soldiers had withdrawn again, and to what purpose? Was Alexander going to allow Barclay to abandon Moscow!

Alexander turned to Araktcheief. " You advise this too? " he asked.

" I do, Sire. And I advise something else. Dismiss Barclay and put a Russian in command of the army. It's the only thing you can do now. If we lose Moscow . . ." He left the sentence unfinished.

"Then everyone is against me," Alexander remarked quietly. " My mother, my sister, Constantine, my generals, and even you, Alexei. Very well. If I dismiss Barclay the command must go to Kutuzov. Do you believe that he can beat Napoleon? "

" I don't believe anyone can beat him," Araktcheief answered. "At the moment the danger is here in St. Petersburg, not on the battlefield. If Moscow falls," he repeated, " God knows what may happen."

Alexander turned away from him and stared out of the window. The sun was setting behind the Palace roofs, turning the waters of the Neva red. The air was very still.

" Sire, I beg of you," Araktcheief whispered.

Alexander didn't answer; he walked slowly to his desk, sat down and began to write. Araktcheief stood in silence, waiting.

" This is an order to Barclay to give his command to General Kutuzov. See that it is sent at once. And inform the Court that I have decided to meet the invader in open battle."

He handed the paper to Araktcheief and looked up at him.

" You may also tell them that if Kutuzov is defeated and Moscow is lost, I shall still continue the war."

When Araktcheief left him, Alexander's head sank into his hands. He stayed at his desk with his eyes closed, unutterably weary; he had scarcely slept since the fall of Smolensk, studying reports from the battle area until the small hours plotting the advance of the French Army on a huge map hanging on his study wall.

Kutuzov. A prestige General who had participated in the muddles of Austerlitz, a lazy, fatalistic old man whose cunning and contempt for organization had won him the reputation of military brilliance. He was a jealous, cynical man, superstitious and intolerant of interference. He had been jeering at Barclay de Tolly throughout the campaign, waiting like a vindictive old turtle for public opinion to oust the foreigner.

So Kutuzov was to face Napoleon, Alexander thought bitterly. But it was done, and he had no alternative. He knew from all the things Araktcheief had not dared to say, how perilous his position was.

A week later he received a dispatch from the front. It was sent by General Kutuzov, accepting the Czar's gracious appointment to command the armies of Russia, and informing His Majesty that the site chosen for the defence of Moscow was the village of Borodino.

*   *   *

" This time," Napoleon said, " they are going to stand and fight."

The Emperor and his Marshals were dining in a large tent in their new camp a few miles outside the village of Borodino. Napoleon sat at the head of the long table with Murat and Marshal Ney on either side of him. Davoust sat farther down, eating steadily and saying little as usual, beside him Prince Poniatowsky, and opposite, Berthier the Chief of Staff with Marshal Grouchy on his left. The food was excellent; a raiding party had found fresh fruit in the neighbourhood for the Emperor's table, everyone had drunk a good deal and their spirits were high. Even Davoust was optimistic, for Napoleon's confidence was infectious that night.

The dragging frustration of the campaign had made considerable demands on all those men, men who excelled in the war of action and movement and had been pursuing an elusive enemy through a burning empty countryside until that time. Smolensk had yielded them nothing and cost them a great deal; there was trouble among the recruited element in the army, and difficulty in keeping the enormous numbers from straggling, losing their equipment and deserting during the march across Russia. Food supplies were short, the lines of communication stretched too far back; there was no time to establish proper base camps before greater distances were put between them and the advancing army every few days. But now it would soon be over; the enemy had stopped retreating, his entire forces were marshalled at Borodino, barring the way to Moscow, and Napoleon knew that he had caught up with them at last.

"They could hardly have gone on retreating," Murat remarked. "We'd have taken Moscow."

"I counted on that," Napoleon said. He emptied his wineglass and held it out to an orderly to be refilled. "I knew they'd lose their heads after Smolensk. Our brave Alexander, so far from the battle himself, would have to defend Moscow."

"It's a pity he didn't direct the armies himself, Sire," Ney said. "We should enjoy another Austerlitz."

Napoleon shook his head. "He's not that great a fool, my dear Ney. He's no soldier and he knows it; he's clever enough to stay away and let his Generals take the blame. Besides, Kutuzov was at Austerlitz."

Murat laughed. "Hé! there should be some action at Borodino! I can hardly restrain the cavalry, Sire. Can you, Ney? They think they'll never get at the Cossacks."

"Don't underestimate them, your Majesty," Ney answered.

He disliked Murat, and only addressed him by his Royal title when he wished to be sarcastic. Both men laid claim to be the foremost Marshal in the French Army, and their exploits were about equal. But Murat was tall and very handsome in his flamboyant way, while Ney was unobtrusive. Murat looked at his rival and grinned mockingly; before he could answer Napoleon interrupted.

"Ney is right," he said sharply. "Don't underestimate them. They're good soldiers; whether Kutuzov is an old goat or not, his men fight well."

He looked round the table and slowly he began to smile, his eyes searching each face, seeing the smile returned and the devotion behind it; even the dour Davoust looked at him with the eyes of a dog for his master. They loved him, all of them, the bravest and most brilliant soldiers in his king-dom, men who had risen with him in the struggle for power in France and continued it with him across half the world. He was the Emperor, but the bond of their common begin-ning and their tremendous victories transcended everything. He had seized supreme power for himself, but he had been equally generous to all of them. Money, titles, honours and lands had followed every campaign, and in every campaign he shared the dangers with them.

Only two of his old comrades were missing from the table that night; Lannes, whom he had loved and held in his arms before he died after the battle of Essling in the second war with Austria, and Bernadotte, the elected Crown Prince of Sweden, who had turned against him. A third absentee was the new Marshal Marmont, who had just been beaten by the English Commander Wellington in Spain, where the war still continued as fiercely as before. Napoleon banished the thought of Lannes, of Bernadotte and of Marmont. None of them was important enough to cloud his triumph or the moment of unity with his beloved comrades.

'Allies and politicians, I trust none of them,' he thought. 'But I trust these, my Marshals. . . .'

"We shall be victorious, my friends," he said. "I know it. Kutuzov has made one mistake already." He paused and they stared towards him; Poniatowsky, handsome and incredibly brave, Murat, Ney, Davoust caught with his mouth full, and Berthier half smiling, because he had studied the position with the Emperor earlier that day.

"The Russian lines extend north of the River Kolochá," Napoleon explained. "The general position at Borodino is excellent for a defensive battle; only a fool in a hurry would have disposed his army in such a wide half-circle, assuming that an even greater fool would attempt to attack on the whole front. But as I think you know, gentlemen, I am not a fool. Our full force of a quarter of a million men shall attack the centre and left flank of the position. The Russians to the north will have an excellent view of the battle."

"They're on a slope," Davoust said. "Casualties will be heavy."

Napoleon smiled at him and shook his head in reproof.

"Bah, you old pessimist," he said. "We meet to-morrow morning, Gentlemen, to discuss final details. I give you a toast." He stood and raised his glass. "To Borodino!"

*   *   *

Marie Naryshkin was walking up and down the little ante-room of Alexander's bedroom in the Palace. After a silence lasting three weeks he had sent for her, and she had immediately forgotten her resolve not to see him again and left her house on the islands to come to him.

It was already half an hour after the time appointed, and she was burning with restlessness. The story of her amour with the Polish admirer was now supplanted by fresh scandal and new names; everyone in Petersburg delighted in repeating the rumours, it helped them to forget the war and their own terror of Napoleon.

Alexander's mistress was unfaithful to him, openly and at every opportunity; any young and personable man who wasn't at the front was invited into her bed, and the Czar either didn't know or didn't care.

She was thinner, her lovely face colourless, the lips painted a vivid red; she was more beautiful than at any time in her life, though her body ached with debauch. Through it all there had been a hope that Alexander would show some sign that he had heard what she was doing; any reaction, even punishment, would have proved that he was not indifferent, that it was still possible for her to touch him. But there was nothing. No letter, no angry summons, nothing.

She had shut herself up in the house on the islands where they had spent so many hours of happiness together and cried hysterically. She had debased herself in the attempt to hurt him, and he had not even noticed. 'This is impossible,' she told herself at last. 'He can't have meant this much to me. He was unfaithful and I knew it, for the first few years he wasn't even in love with me. . . . I've lived with him for nearly thirteen years. I can't still love him. I can't, I can't. . . .'

Nobody continued to care for one man, she insisted, it was ridiculous, it was bourgeois. She was a fool to come to the islands, a sentimental snivelling woman sitting alone in a place full of memories. Even sleeping in the bed they once shared.

She had laughed suddenly and then stopped. That night she slept with a young footman; it was not a success, he was much too frightened of her.

The following day she received a note from Alexander. He was lonely for her, it said gently. Would she come and spend the evening with him?

Always the unexpected, she thought as she waited; would he mention anything; he must know, of course he knew. . . . But he was late, which was unusual; punctual and courteous and unpredictable, that was Alexander, so gentle and kind, so utterly immovable when he didn't wish to be moved. And yet tender and loving and gay; laughing with her as they sat by the fire in the white drawing-room in her house, cut off from the world by the Neva; wandering through the garden with his arm round her shoulders; dancing with her at a Court Ball, whispering things to make her giggle when she should have been grave; talking of problems and affairs of State she didn't understand because he trusted her.

The clock on a buhl table struck the hour and she started. "Oh, God," she said aloud. "Please, God, let him come! I'll go on my knees to him, I'll do anything, put up with anything just to be near him again. If he doesn't want me any more then I'll accept it, I'll be his friend. Please, please, God. . . ."

At a quarter-past the hour she opened the door and ordered the lackey on duty to find Alexander's Chamberlain.

It was not the Chamberlain but only his secretary who finally came to her.

"Where is His Majesty?" she asked him. "He sent for me. I have been waiting for more than an hour."

He opened his arms in a gesture of apology.

"I'm sorry, Your Highness. Someone should have come to you. We have received terrible news. Our army has been defeated at Borodino."

"Oh."

Marie felt for the back of a chair and held on to it. For a moment the full meaning of what she heard over-rode the sick disappointment, the knowledge that it might be hours before she saw Alexander now. Borodino . . . the road to Moscow was open. . . .

"Where is the Emperor?" she asked.

"I'm sorry, Your Highness. He has left the Palace. He has gone to his sister, the Grand Duchess Catherine."

* * *

Catherine and her husband George of Oldenburg were dining when the Czar was announced. Husband and wife were alone together, seated at opposite ends of the long table, so far apart that if George wanted to speak to her he had to shout. The situation always amused Catherine; she used to mimic George leaning towards her, blinking and clearing his throat, and Bagration used to sit back and roar with laughter.

" Why keep the poor fellow at such a distance? " he used to ask, having learnt of the ridiculous isolation in which they took their meals alone. And Catherine would laugh back at him.

" Because he bores me, my beloved. I assure you, I've reduced conversation to a minimum, and really he doesn't mind. He'd much sooner eat in peace and so would I."

She was thinking of Bagration during the meal, smiling to herself at the memory of all the laughter they had shared. He could manage her; she thought, of all the men he was the only one . . . and, oh, how she loved him. She looked up at her husband. Poor George, so small and ugly and forlorn. Bagration didn't really like her to torment him. Perhaps she would have their places set together the next time. . . .

At that moment the Controller of her Household came to her elbow and announced the Czar.

" The Czar? " She stared up at him. " George, did you hear that? Alexander's here! "

" He wishes to see you at once, Your Imperial Highness. And alone," her Controller whispered.

" Very well." She rose and waved George of Oldenburg back into his chair. " Finish your dinner. He only wants to see me."

Alexander was waiting for her in her private drawing-room. It was a charming room, elegantly furnished with the frail chairs and ebony tables of the new ' Empire ' style. A fire burned in the marble grate, for the September air was cold.

She came towards him and curtsied.

" Alexander. What a surprise to see you. And what a pleasure. Alexander, what's the matter, why are you looking like that? . . ."

He stood before the fireplace, his hands behind his back.

" Catherine," he said slowly. " Catherine, we've lost at Borodino. Kutuzov was beaten. We've lost 40,000 men."

She stepped forward quickly. "Oh, my God," she said. "My God, that old fool. . . . Alexander, have him shot!"

"It's no use. I should never have put him in command."

"I know I urged you," she retorted. "What have you come here for, to blame me?"

"No." He looked away from her then. "No, I didn't come for that."

There was silence for a moment, and Catherine's hand suddenly flew to the pearl locket she wore round her neck. Alexander saw the movement and knew that it held a miniature of her lover.

"It's Bagration," he said at last. She opened her eyes very wide and shook her head once, violently.

"No," she exclaimed. "No. What are you trying to tell me? . . . He's hurt. . . ."

"He's dead," Alexander said. "He died of wounds after Borodino."

She swung round and stood with her back to him. He had never heard her cry before. It was a harsh, agonized sound, muffled by the fingers pressed over her mouth; she bent forward as if she were going to fall and he moved towards her.

"Don't," she spat at him. "Don't touch me, leave me alone."

He walked away from her and stood staring down into the fire, listening to the terrible weeping of a woman who doesn't know how to cry.

"I never thought he'd be killed," she was saying. "All the time I was urging you to let our army fight, and I never thought of this. . . . I never thought he could die. It's all right, my brother, I'm not crying any more, you can turn round."

She pulled a bell-cord, and when the lackey opened her door she ordered him to bring some brandy. "Bagration liked it," she explained with terrible restraint. "He taught me to like it too. It's a good brandy, don't you think?"

" Yes."

He sipped out of his glass; he was tired and strained to the limit. Borodino, he was thinking, Borodino lost and Moscow defenceless. . . . But I have to make sure of Catherine first. . . .

" I can't believe it," she said tonelessly. " I shall never be able to believe that I'm not going to see him again."

She swallowed the glass of brandy and poured herself another; her movements were stiff and measured as if she were suddenly blind.

" It was good of you to come and tell me, Alexander. I'm grateful to you. Some more brandy? "

She filled his glass for him and he watched her face. It was sallow, as expressionless as a mask; only her lips trembled.

" I suppose we've lost the war," she said.

Alexander put his glass down. " *I* have lost nothing. I'll retreat to Tobolsk and fight Napoleon there if I have to. Moscow will fall now, there's nothing to stop it. But he can take every capital city in Russia and I won't make peace."

She stared at him without answering, thinking dully that she was seeing her brother properly for the first time. The intriguers had approached her again, murmuring that he was a weakling and a bungler who would deliver them all to Napoleon unless she agreed to overthrow him. And she had listened then as she had always done, the old envy and power lust rising in her. As she looked into his eyes she saw that he knew.

" There's a conspiracy against me," he said quietly, still staring at her. " There are people who think I should be deposed in favour of you."

He paused, and saw a flush rise in her face and die away.

" That's all Napoleon needs now; a Palace Revolution in Petersburg, that's what he's hoping for. Then he'll emancipate the serfs in the occupied areas, and that will be the signal for a general rising all over Russia. The day that

happens, what was done to the Bourbons in '92 will be
repeated here. If the conspiracy succeeds and you take my
place, you won't last a month on the throne."

"I know of no conspiracy," she said coldly. She was in
danger and she knew it, but her brain was numbed to any
impression but the one that Bagration was dead. There was
a plot in which she was implicated; Alexander had found
out, and Alexander was most dangerous when he was calm
like that; he was capable of anything. She'd need all her
wits to save herself, but all the time her attention kept
wandering; she listened to him almost vaguely, her head
throbbing with one sentence. 'Bagration is dead. . . . I'll
never see him again. He's dead. . . .'

"All my life I've tried to avoid hurting you, Catherine,"
he was saying. "Papa's death always saved you until now.
But now even that won't stop me. I'll have you imprisoned
and I'll have you put to death if necessary. Listen to me,
I mean what I say. Nothing matters to me now but to save
Russia and defeat Napoleon. Compared with that your life
isn't worth a kopeck. Unless you swear to me that from
this moment you'll be loyal. Give me your oath, Catherine,
and save yourself. Bagration died for Russia; he died in
agony," he said brutally. "Remember that, remember that
40,000 of our people died with him to protect Moscow from
Napoleon."

He caught her by the shoulder and suddenly shook her.
She was staring up at him, the mocking mouth a little open,
her eyes filling with tears.

"In agony," she repeated.

"He lived for days," Alexander told her. "You've never
seen a battlefield, but I have. You've never seen men dying
of wounds, rotting with gangrene, screaming for someone
to shoot them and put them out of their pain. . . ."

She wrenched herself free of him and shrieked. "Stop,
stop for God's sake! He didn't die like that . . . he
didn't . . ."

"He did," Alexander said mercilessly. "He fought and
died while you were plotting treason. But you'll be loyal

now, Catherine. He was brave and honourable and he loved you. He'd tell you to swear that oath to me."

She was crying with terrible abandon, sobbing and choking with her hands covering her face. Slowly he went back to her and held her against him, thinking that the grief of this arrogant and evil woman was the most painful thing he had ever seen in his life. She had no resources, neither religion nor self-control to help her; for once that implacable nature had weakened and admitted human love; the result for her was mortal. He had won and he knew it. "Stop now," he said gently. "You'll make yourself ill."

She drew away from him and sat on one of the spindle-legged ebony sofas.

"He always said I underestimated you," she said at last. "And he was right. It was a damnable habit he had of always being right."

She leant back and closed her eyes, utterly exhausted; her face was yellow and drawn like a death mask.

"He was a very great soldier and a great patriot," Alexander said. "He will never be forgotten." He came and sat beside her and she opened her eyes to look at him.

"You have won, my brother," she said. "I want nothing now but revenge on Napoleon. He slighted me years ago, and he took from me the only person I've ever cared for in my life. From now on, my aim is yours; to drive Napoleon out of Russia!"

Alexander clasped his hands and looked at them.

"My aim is to drive him out of France," he amended.

She half smiled as she glanced at him; she was outwardly quite calm again, only her hands betrayed her, for they were pulling her lace handkerchief to pieces.

"I believe you'll be as ruthless as I would like to be in your place. And now I believe something else; I believe you'll win."

He nodded gravely.

"I know I shall win," he answered. "Will you help me, Catherine?"

She lifted his right hand with the enormous Royal sapphire on it and kissed the ring.

"From now on, your sister is your subject. I swear it."

"And my friend and counsellor," he insisted.

"That too, if you wish."

"I wish it," he answered. He bent and kissed her cheek. "Good night, my sister. God comfort you."

He left her and the lackey escorted him to his bedroom, where a fire blazed and everything had been prepared. His valet dozed in a corner, and the Czar called him to undress him. Within half an hour he lay in the big bed, the brocade curtains drawn, shutting out the firelight. He closed his eyes and fell asleep immediately for the first time since the fall of Smolensk. He woke at dawn and sent for his secretary who followed him everywhere, and dictated a brief order to Count Feodor Rostopchine, the Governor of Moscow.

*   *   *

The slopes and woods round Borodino had been the scene of the bloodiest battle fought for a hundred years. At dawn on September 7th the French Army was drawn up for the attack; officers and men were ordered to wear their best uniform, a roll of drums preceded the Emperor's special proclamation.

They would be victorious, it said, and each man would be able to declare with pride, 'I was in that great battle before Moscow.'

Overhead the sky was very blue, the sun rose, shining in the face of the attack, and on the six-mile front of Kutuzov's defence line, men waited in the redoubts, by the gun batteries, in the entrenchments and pine woods of the Utitza Forest for that attack to begin.

It began with a fierce barrage, and then the French line began to move forward. Ney's corps was posted in the central position; his guns opened a terrific fire as the men advanced towards the outer Russian defences on the plain;

to the right Davoust pushed towards the high slope of the
Great Redoubt with its massed batteries of cannon, protect-
ing the army of Prince Bagration, while Prince Poniatowsky
led his men into the Utitza woods.

In the face of murderous fire and a most obstinate defence,
the redoubts on the plain were overwhelmed, and Ney turned
to help Davoust and Murat in the attack on Bagration's
position.

Again and again they advanced, captured the smaller
redoubts and were driven back; a great mass of infantry
struggled on the sloping ground and fought hand-to-hand
in the woods. Davoust's horse was killed under him, Murat
directed his infantry as well as the cavalry while the Marshal
lay unconscious. By noon they were being fiercely counter-
attacked by the Russians. A very hot sun blazed down on
the dark masses of men, and a thick column of smoke rose
up from a burning village, set alight by French artillery
fire.

An urgent message was sent to Napoleon. "Bring up the
Imperial Guard!" Ney, fighting desperately near the Great
Redoubt, bellowed with rage at the Emperor's refusal. The
infantry were exhausted, they were in danger of losing all
the ground so dearly won.

It was late afternoon when the defenders saw an extraordinary sight. Below the Great Redoubt a glittering mass
of cavalry appeared. The Cuirassiers, their breastplates
gleaming, magnificent in their uniforms of scarlet, gold and
blue.

They began to approach at the trot, led by Murat, King
of Naples; as the defenders' guns opened fire, the trot became
a gallop; line after line of horses went down, but the rest
burst through into the outer defences, sabreing the gunners
and riding down the Russian infantry.

While the issue was still undecided, the cavalry of Marshal
Grouchy followed up that bloody slope and the Great
Redoubt was taken.

Cossacks engaged them and were driven back after the
most savage cavalry fighting of the war; no quarter was given

to prisoners or wounded in that desperate fight to drive the French back down the slope, but Bagration's troops couldn't stop the impetus begun by the Cuirassiers, their ranks blasted by terrible casualties. During the battle Marshal Grouchy fell, severely wounded; after hours of bitter fighting, the Cossacks were driven back in confusion and the order was given to retreat.

Under a shelter of heavy gunfire, the Russian lines began to withdraw, leaving the Eagle standards of France to be carried into the heart of the Russian defences. By the end of the day the battle was over, and Napoleon sent for his Marshals.

They were dirty and exhausted, Murat's magnificent uniform was spattered with blood and torn in several places, and Ney, whose personal valour that day earned him the title of Prince of Moscow, was hatless, filthy with dust and sweat, too tired and sickened after the carnage he had seen to resent Murat's perpetual grin. When they entered Napoleon's tent he embraced them. He radiated energy; in spite of a heavy cold, his whole manner was charged with fanatical excitement. He looked at them and laughed.

"Ah, my children," he exulted. "We've won, we've won! Ney, Murat, I saw what you did to-day, and my good Grouchy. We've won," he repeated. "Do you remember our dinner before this battle? I gave you a toast then, Borodino. I'll give you another. Orderly! Bring wine for the Marshals, hurry!"

"Sire, there is hardly room to walk for all the dead," Ney said slowly. "Ours and theirs."

Bonaparte glanced at him. "I know," he answered. "You're tired, Ney. Take your wine." He lifted his own glass and addressed them. The candles blazed up as a sudden draught caught them from the tent flap; the shadow of Napoleon rushed up the canvas wall with the proportions of a giant.

"Gentlemen," he said. "I give you a second toast. Moscow, and the end of the war!"

" Moscow! "

" When shall we reach it, Sire? " Marshal Murat asked.

Napoleon put his glass down. " Within seven days. We march to-morrow morning."

*   *   *

Early on the 14th of September the leading French columns reached the top of the Hill of the Sparrows. Immediately a shout went up, and an officer of the Imperial Guard turned and galloped back to where the Emperor rode with a large suite.

" Your Majesty, Your Majesty, Moscow! You can see it from the hill-tops! "

Napoleon urged his horse forward and came galloping up between lines of cheering troops.

" *Vive L'Empereur! Vive L'Empereur!* "

Word had flown from mouth to mouth. ' Moscow, we've reached Moscow. . . .'

He had kept his promise to them, given them victory as he had always done, and now at last they would have proper quarters, warmth, shelter and food. The cavalry reined in and the infantry stood cheering as he rode among them and then suddenly drew up on the crest of the hill.

It was another cloudless day, brilliant with cold sunshine, and below the Hill of the Sparrows the Holy City of Moscow lay before him like a multi-coloured jewel.

The hundreds of gold-painted cupolas shone against the background of blue sky; the delicate oriental towers, the red and yellow buildings, the dark crimson walls, and the minaret towers of the Kremlin itself were perfectly clear. He shaded his eyes with his hand and stayed on the hill crest looking down for several minutes, thinking that the enormous building with its fantastic design of nine cupolas must be the famous Church of St. Basil, whose architect had been blinded by the Czar Ivan IV so that he could never build another like it.

Moscow.

Napoleon said it aloud. That moment on the hill-top was the greatest in his life and he knew it; the triumphal entry into the city, the Banquet in the Kremlin, all the means he had devised to humiliate his enemies would never match that first sight of Moscow from the top of the hill. It was over; he had won the war. He had never admitted even to himself that the Russian campaign had been the most strenuous and anxious of his career. He hated the easy victories, the occupation of one burnt-out town after another, pursuing a phantom army who occasionally turned, fought like demons and then disappeared again.

The whole affair was almost eerie, even the country itself had begun to get on his nerves; the poverty, the miserable peasants who fled before them, more like animals than men with their tangled hair and beards, the women muffled in ragged shawls with their blank faces and cowed eyes; everywhere silence and suspicion, and the sickening smell of smoke drifting to meet them, the smoke of hovels and great houses set alight with the same purpose.

He hated the queer poetic place names, the orientalism which obtruded everywhere. Remembering the cultured, elegant Alexander, it seemed impossible to reconcile his rule with such a country.

' But that,' he thought, ' was my mistake. He looks like a European, he *is* a European by blood, but in his own country the traditions of Europe might belong to another planet. He has the mind of an Eastern potentate, and I persisted in treating him as a European monarch.

' Only now, seeing the capital of his country, do I realize that neither he nor his people belong to Europe at all. . . .'

He turned his horse's head and rode back among his men, acknowledging their cheers. The faces along that road were burnt brown by months of sun and wind, but they were thin from hunger; some of the men wore dirty bandages, and many of the infantry were already barefoot.

They cheered and waved their muskets; hungry and dirty and tired out, their spirits bounded at the sight of the little figure on the grey horse, the Emperor who rode and fought amongst them and had brought them to victory again.

Murat came galloping up to meet him; he reined in sharply, pulling his horse on to its haunches; he swept off his plumed hat and bowed low from the saddle.

" I have just heard," he said. " *Vive L'Empereur!* Moscow at last! "

" At last," Napoleon repeated. " As my brother-in-law and King of Naples, you will take the first detachment of troops and enter the city. I'll make my entry to-morrow, unless they show signs of resistance."

Murat and his troops approached the city walls late that afternoon. They rode down the long road, raising clouds of dust, and as they approached the bridge over the Moscova there was no sound except the clatter and jingle of their own progress. It was quite warm by then, and Murat wiped his sweating face with a flowing lace handkerchief. He had been told what to say to the deputation of nobles which Napoleon confidently expected to be there to meet the invaders. Murat was to send them back to the French camp where the Emperor would address them and promise to respect their city. Murat, who was indifferently educated where any foreign language was concerned, had brought an interpreter with him.

Still they rode on and he glanced up at the high walls for some sign of life. " *Sacré Dieu*," he said to himself, " a cannonade would be better than this damned quiet."

At four o'clock he entered Moscow.

The streets were empty except for a few frightened peasants who ran away as the cavalcade approached. Some had been looting the houses which were also empty. Murat sent scouts into the centre of the city and they reported a few shots fired from behind the red walls of the Kremlin, but the defenders had scattered after the first French volley. The signs of a mass flight were everywhere; the gates leading out of Moscow had been jammed with troops, civilians and transport within an hour or two of Napoleon's advance; there had been chaos at bridges where the traffic had become hopelessly jammed. This was the story told by those they caught and questioned. It appeared that the remnants of Kutuzov's army had evacuated Moscow, taking the nobles and administration with them, leaving a few thousand peasants to run through the deserted city, looting.

As he listened to the reports of his scouts Murat heard the sudden discordant pealing of the Kremlin bells ringing for vespers; a cannon pounded the Kutafyev Gate of the Kremlin, where some peasants had barricaded themselves in and were sniping at the invaders as they surrounded the Palace. The noise was a feeble echo in the silence that enveloped Moscow; the shouts of the soldiers who were entering the houses were reedy and unreal; the majestic churches towered above them, shining like buildings in a mirage, and the bells pealed out the prayer of many centuries to a city that was empty except for the stream of invading troops who were pouring into it. Murat spurred his horse forward and rode towards the Kremlin; he was frowning, and shouted angrily to one of his aides to ride ahead and stop the troops despoiling any of the State rooms before the Emperor's arrival.

Messengers went back to the French camp and informed Napoleon that the enemy had abandoned their capital; there would be no deputation, no triumphal entry. Moscow was empty.

The following day Napoleon rode into the city. He crossed the bridge over the Moscova river and passed through the outskirts, watched by a straggling crowd of gaping peasants. He entered by the ancient Spassky Gate, glancing up at the Ikon of Christ which the Muscovy Czar Alexis had placed there in 1626. Murat and a large escort received him; he dismounted and walked slowly into the Kremlin buildings.

He was oddly silent while Murat talked. He passed from room to room, looking round at the tapestries, the priceless furniture and ornaments, even the velvet and gold throne under its canopy, which had all been left intact.

" They're a religious people," he remarked. " Every other

building was a church and this place is like a church too. Where are the Czar's apartments?"

It was explained to him that there were two Royal suites in the Kremlin; one in the newer part built by the Empress Elizabeth in the eighteenth century, and the traditional rooms in the old wooden buildings built by the first Czars. The later quarters were far more suitable.

"I will go to the old Palace," Napoleon said. "Take me there."

He entered the old Granovitia Palata, followed by a crowd of officers all staring at the small proportions of the old State dining-room, the frescoed walls, Byzantine representations of the life of Christ and Biblical scenes, the old oak benches round the walls, the throne where every newly crowned Czar received his subjects' homage.

Few among them were impressed; it was gloomy and small, a dim light was diffused through the old talc windows, and several officers began contrasting it with the glories of Versailles and The Tuilleries.

Napoleon said nothing. They returned and mounted the staircase leading to the Terem Palace, built by Michael, the first of the Romanovs, in the seventeenth century.

Here the Emperor's silence spread to his entourage as they walked from one low, frescoed room to another, their footsteps echoing. They crossed the red-walled Throne room, and Napoleon paused before the crude chair in which Michael Romanov had sat to hold audience.

"The State bedroom is through here, Sire," his Grand Marshal Duroc whispered, and then wondered why he had lowered his voice. He coughed and said firmly, "The room is not suitable. I understand these quarters are never used except on very important State occasions. I assure you, Sire, you would be much more comfortable in the other building."

Napoleon looked at him. "There will never be a State occasion in Moscow's history more important than this one."

They were standing on the threshold of the Czar's bed-

room. It was a small room, sparsely furnished, the gilded
walls and ikons gleamed in the dim light. An old, carved,
four-poster bed stood in the centre of the room.

"I shall make my quarters here, Gentlemen," Napoleon
said. He looked round at them and smiled. Immediately
the tension broke. They were no longer aware of the sound
of their own footsteps, whispering when they spoke; laughter
and talk and noise echoed through the old building. Duroc
went over to inspect the bed when his master's back was
turned, and then wrinkled his nose in disgust. It was as
hard as a board.

The army bivouacked in Moscow that night; it came into
the city like a hungry flood and dispersed like a flood, form-
ing rivulets of men searching the houses for loot, food, shelter
and women.

There was little violence to the few inhabitants they
found; it was a good-natured occupation, achieved without
the bloodshed that makes a conquering army so savage to
the people who have withstood them. The troops were
mildly destructive, especially where they discovered well-
stocked cellars. One officer received a report that three of
his men had died as a result of rifling a cellar, where they
had swallowed the contents of some bottles they found hidden
there. The bottles contained vitriol. The officer shrugged,
and wondered why anyone kept vitriol in a cellar instead of
wine. Then he repeated the Emperor's order forbidding
looting, and forgot about it.

By the 16th Napoleon had taken up residence in the
modern Kremlin apartments; the army was settled in; fed,
refreshed and assured of proper shelter. The Emperor had
made a tour of the city; one of the first places he visited was
the Church of St. Basil, the church he had seen from the top
of the hill. It was magnificent, he said. Magnificent. But
they were short of space and could not afford to be sentimental. The church was stripped of its ornaments and
put to use as a stable. Even then Napoleon didn't admit
that his motive was neither expediency nor sacrilege, but
jealousy.

He had begun to feel tired, a real sign that he was confident and felt he could afford to relax. He went to his bedroom and took out the portrait of his son, the little King of Rome. In the privacy of Alexander's old room the Emperor kissed the picture.

" For you, my son," he said. " When I've made peace with Russia, you shall be Emperor of France, ruler of Europe. Your mother and I shall live as private persons. God knows, I'm nearly tired of war. . . ."

His exhilaration over the fall of Moscow was comparatively calm; the strain had been greater than anyone realized, even himself. He had won and he was thankful, as thankful as he was triumphant, though he still clung to the atheism of his revolutionary youth. He owed a debt of gratitude to himself first and then to the men who had fought with him. To that splendid coxcomb Murat, whose vanity was only equalled by his courage, to the incomparable Ney, to the tenacious Davoust, Berthier the organizer, Poniatowsky, the Marshals and soldiers of France.

He repressed an impulse to thank the God in whom he didn't believe, and began thinking of the man he had beaten, the former ally who had dared to challenge him to war. He remembered a particularly offensive phrase which had been repeated to him: " The Emperor of All the Russias will be formidable at Moscow, terrible at Kazan and invincible at Tobolsk." Rostopchine, Governor of Moscow had written that, and the words had become a slogan. Brave words indeed, Napoleon thought, from the man who had fled and left his city intact for the invader.

A few patriots had tried setting light to some of the wooden buildings and been shot; most of them seemed to be convicts that the Russians had allowed to escape from jail during the evacuation.

He turned over in bed and yawned, missing Marie Louise. There wasn't a woman in the place fit for his bed. A strong wind rattled the windows of his room and outside the night was very dark; a pale half-moon hung in the sky. Napoleon pulled the covers over himself and fell asleep.

He woke with someone shaking him and shouting in his
ear. Blurred by sleep he pulled himself upright; one of his
aides was standing by his bed. The first thing Napoleon
realized was that he could see the man's face, the room was
full of light.

"Your Majesty! Sire, for God's sake get up!" he was
shouting. "The whole of Moscow's on fire!"

CHAPTER SEVEN

ALEXANDER had gone to his palace on an island in
the Neva, and lay there ill. He was feverish and
erysipelas had broken out on his leg. He stayed in his own
room reading dispatches and writing to his sister.

Moscow, where he had been crowned, where the inhabitants had come to offer their property and their lives to him
in the first days of the war, was a flaming hell. Rostopchine
had transmitted his orders and the incendiaries left behind
had carried them out. Napoleon had only just escaped the
blazing Kremlin with his life; the French had been forced
to evacuate the city after four days of fighting the fires which
swept through the wooden buildings, fanned by a strong
wind. They had dynamited parts of the Kremlin and many
ancient buildings before they withdrew, while the stores and
shelter they needed for the winter burnt in front of them.
The news was received with horror in St. Petersburg, and
Alexander had promptly blamed the disaster on the French.

Constantine and the Dowager Empress had besieged him
to make peace. His brother had stamped up to him in the
Winter Palace and shaken his fist in his face.

"This is your doing," he had yelled. "You would have
war! Moscow is lost, next he'll march on Petersburg and
murder us all! Make peace, I tell you, make peace or what
happened to Papa can happen to you ..."

He had defied them. Without Catherine none of them would do anything, and Catherine had kept her word. She wrote to him every day, reminding him of his promise never to capitulate, begging him to get back the love letters she had written to Bagration and which must not fall into other hands. . . . He could guess the kind of letters Catherine Pavlovna had written to her lover and he sent for them at once.

Even Catherine hadn't guessed what he had done. She wrote abusing the French for their destruction of Moscow and berated her own family like a tigress for wanting an armistice.

Alexander left for the peace of Kamenoi Ostrow on the islands, and sent for Marie Naryshkin to come with him.

He never accused her of anything, though he knew of every infidelity she had committed; he needed comfort and companionship, and whether Marie amused herself with a few lovers was of no importance to him. He had neglected her, she was a very sensual woman—what did it matter. . . .

For the first few hours she was strained with him, talking trivialities. He watched her, puzzled and disappointed.

" Marie, what's the matter with you? Didn't you wish to come here? "

She paused and looked at him.

" Of course, Sire, I was only trying to amuse you . . . if you're bored. . . ."

" I'm in no mood to quarrel," he said wearily. She never called him Sire except when she was angry. She sat down in a chair and then got up again and began walking up and down.

" I'm sorry," she said. " It's so long since I've seen you I feel like a stranger."

She realized that she was weakening; he was in the wrong, but once again she couldn't keep her bitterness alive when he was with her. She wanted to be reconciled; she wanted to go to him because he looked tired and white and ten years older. She still loved him hopelessly, and at that moment the knowledge that she would never mean very much to him again hardly seemed to matter.

He didn't answer, so she said, "I know what an anxious time you've had. I only wanted to be near to help you."

"You can help me now," he said. "I told you once you could do what you pleased as long as you never left me; it was years ago, here on the islands, do you remember?"

"I remember. But I never thought you meant it. I've taken you at your word, Alexander, you know that?"

"My dear Marie, I'm not angry. God knows you must have been lonely and I don't blame you."

She laughed unhappily. "Do you know, I only did it to make you jealous! Isn't that ridiculous? Oh, what's happened to us? We used to be so happy together. I know you're out of love with me, but can you just tell me why? Is it my fault?"

He held out his hand to her; she came over to him and caught hold of it, kneeling beside his chair.

"Too much has happened, Marie," he said slowly. "We're all changing."

"Not me," she interrupted, "I haven't changed, I'll never change towards you. . . ." But he went on without listening.

"We've all changed through this war. Even Catherine, my sister. Falling in love with Bagration and losing him . . . she's standing by me now, Marie, when she could over-throw me to-morrow if she wanted to. Not that she'd last long," he added.

"She's changed and so have I. It began when I saw them burning the villages on the way back from Vilna. Do you know how it feels to destroy your own country, and condemn your own people to starvation and death? And now Moscow. . . ."

"That's not your fault," she pleaded. "You couldn't help what happened."

He held her hand against his cheek, and after a moment he said, "I ordered it. It was nothing to do with the French."

"What! Oh, my God. . . ."

"I ordered Rostopchine to set fire to it," he said, looking at her. "Napoleon will have no winter quarters now."

He stood up suddenly and winced.

"My legs hurts," he said. "I came here to forget all this for a few days. I wanted to be happy with you as we used to be, just for a little while."

She rose and came close to him and shook her head.

"Our happiness wasn't something you had for a few days and then forgot," she said. "It was always there, Alexander, because we loved each other. That's gone now. Not from me, never, but from you. But if you want me, I'll do my best to please you."

She reached up and kissed him on the mouth. At the same moment his arms closed round her, and she remembered that this was all familiar, this was the first years of their relationship before Tilsit. This was the man she had known then, a man making love to a woman he was not in love with.

'And yet it's not the same,' she thought. 'Because even his passion isn't quite real; this resurgence of sex is only an escape—it won't last.'

The next morning he was feverish and the erysipelas rash covered his leg.

Within a few days he returned to St. Petersburg for treatment, and it was several weeks before Marie Naryshkin saw him again.

*   *   *

Napoleon stayed within a few miles of Moscow for five weeks, quartered in a country estate at Peterskoie. The flight from the Kremlin made a far deeper impression on him than anyone suspected; in his long experience of battle and horror, nothing approached the terror of that night when the orderly woke him and he looked out of his window to see a blinding glare thrown off by hundreds of fires. The streets were walled in by flame, the whole sky glowed, a horrible roaring interspersed by the crash of blazing buildings deafened him as he hurried out of the Palace, part of which had already caught alight. The heat and smoke were suffocating; he remembered the frightful beauty of millions of fiery sparks whirling above his head in the current of the wind.

Men were running through the streets, cursing because the city's fire engines had all been partially put out of order and there was no way of fighting the fires. Some formed lines passing water in buckets and helmets; the contents were flung into the flames with an ineffectual hiss. Others tried isolating the burning buildings, clearing the streets and roof-tops of everything inflammable. A few were intelligent enough to dynamite in the path of the fire, but the measures were totally inadequate to the problem.

The Emperor's staff had the greatest difficulty in getting him out of the city; he tried rallying his troops, shouting orders above the roar and thunder of the flames, blinded by smoke, coughing and roasted by waves of heat.

The officer who had woken him seized him by one arm and began urging him towards a carriage. "For God's sake, Sire," he shouted, "do you want to be killed here? For God's sake . . ."

He was almost pushed inside, and the terrified horses bounded forward and began racing out of the city and across the bridge.

He saw a big building burning as he passed it, and heard the high whinny of horses and the shouts of men; it was a converted stable, and his troopers were trying to coax and drag the horses out. Already the roof and upper floor were seething with flames. With a splintering crash that rocked the carriage, part of the building collapsed, burying horses and men in a tomb of fire.

Outside the walls he ordered the carriage to stop, and alighted. Within minutes, members of his staff joined him, and the little group waited by the banks of the Moscova, watching the sprawling mass of flame leap higher as a strong wind whipped it from one district to another, their faces scorched by the heat even at that distance.

At dawn the whole of Moscow was burning or in blackened ruins, and the fires continued for the next three days.

A lot of equipment and most of the stores vital to feed the army had been destroyed; though the peak of incendiarism had been reached, fresh fires still erupted as the old ones died, lit by the reprieved convicts and partisans whom Rostopchine had ordered to stay behind.

The French Army spread out over the surrounding countryside, pillaging and suffering daily losses from bands of Cossacks who swept down on stragglers.

At his headquarters at Peterskoie, Napoleon waited, obstinately refusing to advance on St. Petersburg or begin retreating to the south before the winter came. Alexander would give in, he insisted, and there was a ferocity in his manner that forbade contradiction.

The Russian Army was defeated, their Capital captured and burnt to the ground. They would have to make peace! And to prove it, he sent emissaries to the Czar proposing an armistice.

They had been friends, and the memory of that friendship prompted him to offer them reasonable terms. His promise to leave Turkey to Russia still held good.

The wording was conciliatory and yet proud. Alexander answered that he would never make peace while a French soldier remained on Russian soil. He also ordered his General Kutozov not to negotiate with any envoy from the enemy.

There was consternation at Peterskoie; Napoleon raged and swore, his staff stood round in an awkward silence, waiting for him to calm down. The situation was much too dangerous to waste time abusing Alexander, who was safe in St. Petersburg. Thanks to the attempt to secure a truce, it was too late to march on the Northern Capital.

It was Ney who approached the Emperor.

"Sire, we can't stay here any longer. There's no food and only canvas shelter for the army. We've got to move back."

"The weather's quite mild," Napoleon snapped. "We have time enough."

"We should still move, Sire," Ney insisted. Napoleon looked at the other Marshals and they nodded.

"Very well then. We'll confer here within an hour. I want to study our position."

When they came to the meeting the Emperor was good humoured and full of confidence. He showed them the map, tracing a line with his finger from the Moscow area southwards towards Lithuania.

"We'll retire through here. The weather is milder there and we'll be in our winter quarters before the cold sets in. And in the spring, gentlemen, we will return!"

On the 19th of October he left Peterskoie, and the Grand Armée, now numbering 115,000 men, began retiring towards Malo-Jaroslavitz, a town some fifty miles from Moscow. And at Malo-Jaroslavitz the French vanguard found a Russian army waiting for them.

Napoleon's stepson, Eugène Beauharnais, was in command of an Italian corps; they were imprudent enough to engage Kutuzov's forces, and the old General struck like a tiger. The corps suffered terrible casualties, and Josephine's son returned to fling himself at the Emperor's feet and implore him not to risk a battle.

"They're too strong, Sire," he insisted. "God knows we fought well enough, but we hadn't a chance! I've lost most of my men. . . ." He was almost in tears.

"What do I care what you've lost," Napoleon shouted, suddenly.

"Am I to run from a pack of mujiks led by that old idiot who didn't even know how to dispose his forces at Borodino? Don't risk a battle! You incompetent fool, snivelling over a few casualties—get out of my way, do you hear! Maps, Berthier, get me my maps, don't stand there idling!"

Berthier did as he was told; the big table was cleared and the shabby campaign maps spread over it. Murat, Ney and Poniatowsky crowded round the Emperor. He glared down and struck the table with his fist.

"We've got to engage them," he said. "How else are we going to get out by the route I showed you?"

"We can't, Sire," Ney said, quietly. "We're in no condition to take on a large army. Eugène here says the Russians are well equipped with cavalry and artillery. They've been waiting for us; they're fresh and well fed. Our men are hungry and worn out. If we have to fight Kutuzov now, we'll leave our army at Malo-Jaroslavitz. There'll be no return in the spring then."

Napoleon's face was white; he tore at his uniform collar as if it were choking him.

"Berthier!" he demanded. "Well?"

His Chief of Staff nodded. "I agree with Ney, Sire."

The Emperor swung round on Poniatowsky. "And you?"

"I wouldn't answer for my men in a heavy engagement, Sire. Ney is right."

Napoleon's voice cracked with anger. "Murat! What do you say?"

Murat straightened and the old reckless grin appeared. "I say, fight!" he said. "We've never run before."

After a pause the Emperor looked round. "The rest of you still counsel retreat?"

As he asked them, he knew he had made a mistake. He was right, and so was Murat; the same leonine courage and daring was in them both, the same dislike of taking the prudent course. Fight, fight, his instincts urged. Don't listen to them, fight!

But Berthier and Ney and Poniatowsky were shaking their heads; so was Marshal Bessière who had joined the discussion.

"Avoid them, Sire. It's the only way till we get our forces properly organized.

He turned from them without answering, staring down at the map; there was a long silence. Then he spoke.

"As you insist, Gentlemen. We retreat. Back over the way we came."

*   *   *

They smelt Borodino before they saw it. A strong wind carried the sickening stench of putrefaction over the country-side; the advance guard of the French Army marched through the old battlefield, pressing the ragged sleeves of their uniforms against their faces to keep out the smell rising from over 70,000 unburied corpses strewn over the slopes and in the woods. Cannon rusted, sinking into the grass, the bodies of French and Russian soldiers rotting by them. There were dead horses, surrounded by black clouds of evil flies; hundreds of weapons were scattered over the ground, and everywhere bundles of rags proclaimed the remains of the men who had fallen or died of wounds. The horror of the place was increased by the gentle twittering of many birds. The French marched slowly, not a voice was raised above a whisper; for some reason the sight paralysed them, even the veterans of many wars, so that while each man wished to get out of the place as quickly as possible, the general marching tempo slackened. Ney muttered to one of his officers as they rode.

"This will do more to lower morale than a major defeat. . . . Give the order none of the men should water their horses or drink from that stream. It's poisonous. . . . And post extra pickets to-night."

"Surely the Russians won't attack here, Sir," the officer said. He grimaced and immediately buried his nose in a large handkerchief again.

"Not the Russians," Ney replied. "Deserters. We'll have hundreds after this."

Slowly the huge cavalcade of men, horses and wagons passed through the green sloping ground of Borodino, cross-ing the polluted stream, seeing the blaze and thunder of the battlefield transformed into a silent stinking graveyard, where the long grass stirred and the trees gave shelter to the remains of brothers, comrades and the enemy. Many of the young recruits fell out during that march and vomited.

The Emperor rode at walking pace, staring ahead of him. He was familiar with the aftermath of battle and it no longer moved him. Death meant nothing to him, less for himself than anyone else; he realized the effect it must have on his troops, and made a mental note to enforce the death penalty for any man found abandoning his weapons or lowering the general morale. As he rode his head sank lower; he might have been asleep. Those who knew him well recognized it as his only indication of despair.

*　　*　　*

"It's snowing again," Catherine exclaimed. "No messenger will be able to get through to-night."

She was at Tver with Alexander; they were sitting together in the same drawing-room where she had heard the news of Bagration's death. She got up and walked towards the window.

"It's no use, the glass is coated, I can't see outside."

"He'll come," Alexander said. "But you needn't wait up with me if you're tired."

"I'm not tired! I'm as anxious as you are. It's just that I've always hated waiting."

She moved round the room, restlessly touching the ornaments, her long velvet skirts swishing after her. The large room was warmed by two log fires that burnt in grates at each end; the Czar sat in an old French armchair before one of them, looking into the flames.

Suspense and the atmosphere of the Court at Petersburg had driven him to Tver and Catherine. The rest of his family were uncomfortable and strained with him, remembering their disloyalty during the worst phase of the war; now when victory seemed near, they were fawning and anxious; he hated them all, fled the stiffness and etiquette of Palace life and came to Tver. Catherine's company was a stimulant; the knife-edge relationship which had grown up between them was a challenge and a comfort. He needed her, and now she needed him.

They were both alone; he had chosen isolation by leaving Marie, and it had overtaken her when Bagration died. It was rumoured that he spent his nights praying and reading the Bible in his room, and known that his sister occupied hers with debauch; but in effect they were equally lonely. Consequently they turned to each other, driven by anxiety and by grief. It was a grotesque alliance, for they had only the will to win in common; but each had the fascination of brilliance and each succumbed to it, little by little, without understanding why. Neither of them was capable of family affection for the other; it seemed ridiculous that any blood tie united them.

They were strangers and enemies and friends at the same time. At any moment one tendency might emerge above the others.

"You're sure he'll come to-night?" she asked.

"Kutuzov's never failed to keep me informed so far. And the weather has been much worse than this."

She laughed spitefully. "I wonder how His Majesty of France enjoys our winter! I wonder how they like frost-bite and starvation. If they last out much longer they'll be eating each other next instead of their horses!"

"They won't last much longer," Alexander said. "We've set a trap for them."

"A trap?" She swung round and hurried to the fire-place.

"What trap, where?"

"That's what the messenger will tell me. Kutuzov has a plan, a plan to capture Napoleon himself and wipe out the whole French Army—what's left of it. I've warned him to be careful though. He underestimated Bonaparte at Borodino; I don't want him to forget it. But this time, we may succeed. You always wanted to see Napoleon, didn't you, Catherine? I'll have him brought to St. Petersburg for your inspection!"

"Oh, how I pray God we get him! How I should like to have the custody of him, just for a few hours! I'd brand the word Bagration across his face. . . ."

"You are a savage, my dear sister. I said you could look at him if he's caught. I'm not going to behave like Ghengis Khan."

She shrugged and half smiled. "No, I suppose I can trust you to deal with him. Oh, Alexander, think of it! Napoleon a prisoner! What a triumph. We'll be the greatest nation in the world. . . ."

"We'll be that anyway, when he makes peace. What we've done, we've done alone, and we'll finish it. I'll follow him out of Russia across Europe, if he doesn't fall into Kutuzov's hands."

She sat down in a chair opposite to him. After a time he closed his eyes and she watched him, thinking he was asleep.

He was better looking, she thought suddenly, in spite of the tiredness, the thinning fair hair; it was a hard face even in repose, and she preferred it. His character was showing through the charm, and it increased his attraction. How odd that this religious phase had taken hold of him. He had even tried making *her* read the Bible till she threw it aside and laughed at him. If he didn't want Marie, he should find someone else, or if not one woman, then several. All this abstinence and praying was unhealthy, she thought. A different lover every night had kept her sane after Bagration's death, but her handsome, virile brother was leading the life of a penitent monk when he wasn't governing Russia. It was all very strange and very typical. One thing she had noticed. Like most conscientious despots, Alexander's harshness increased with his morality. Her thoughts drifted away from him and returned to Napoleon marching across the frozen wastes so many thousands of miles away. A trap was being set for him. A trap to destroy him and take him prisoner. . . .

At three in the morning a lackey awoke them with the news that the army messenger had arrived. His dispatches were brought to the Czar, who broke the seals and read them while Catherine strained to look over his shoulder.

"Well, tell me! What does he say?"

"The French are almost finished. Our Cossacks have been harrying them, and Kutuzov says he's mustering the main army to finish them and take Napoleon."

She caught at his sleeve and her voice trembled with excitement.

"Where, where?" she said.

"Directly ahead of them," Alexander answered. "At the River Beresina."

*   *   *

The weather was still mild when the French Army left Borodino. As they retrod the devastated ground of their former advance, the army straggled, marching with less discipline every day. Many carried bundles of loot stolen from Moscow; silks, dresses, jewellery, silver and gold plate, anything they had been able to grab up and take out of the blazing city. These marched more slowly than the rest; round the camp fires men fought each other over thefts, real and imagined, of the useless treasures, and the outposts reported attacks by marauding enemy units.

Soon the line of march was infested by Cossacks; the nights became more terrible than the days, when men who were miserable with hunger and fatigue slept fitfully between attacks.

The attackers grew bolder, inflicting greater casualties; they hid in the woods, behind every rise in the ground, and a new ally had joined them.

When Napoleon advanced into Russia, the mass of the people were apathetic; villages were burnt and evacuated by their own troops on their own Emperor's order, and many thousands died as a result. The wretched serf accepted his miseries as part of his lot in life; there was fear of the invader, as there was fear of the landlord and the Imperial troops; fear was an integral part of peasant life, but until Moscow burned, the fear hadn't become hatred. To the great mass of the Russian people, the infidel French had burnt Holy Moscow. The peasants rose in their wrath to attack the blasphemers.

They crept up on French stragglers and murdered them; sentries were knifed, often horribly mutilated; the women killed as ferociously as their men. That dread word, first used in Spain where so many of Napoleon's troops had died, was murmured among the soldiers of the Grand Armée. Guerrilla. The little war of the people. It was no longer safe to desert; it was better to keep together, to be hungry and sleepless from fighting the Cossacks in one ambush after another, than to venture into that silent country and fall into the hands of the mujiks.

They were about a hundred miles from Smolensk when the Russian forces attacked in numbers at Viasma. Again the brilliance of Napoleon repulsed them, in spite of his troops' weakness and their exposed position, and again Kutuzov blundered by not pressing forward with reinforcements which the French couldn't have withstood.

The French gathered their wounded—God forbid any should be left behind now—and set out for the shelter of Smolensk. Smolensk could be defended; they had left a garrison there and a good supply of stores. Forward! Napoleon ordered, forward to Smolensk as fast as possible!

Overhead the skies were still blue, but on the 4th and 5th of November a biting wind sprang up. Men turned up their coat collars and huddled round the fires. In his tent, the Emperor sat round a stove with Ney and Murat, holding his hands out to the heat. It was Ney who expressed everyone's dread.

"It's getting colder," he said. "The temperature is dropping suddenly."

Neither Murat nor Napoleon answered him.

That night the icy wind became a snowstorm and the thermometer fell to eighteen degrees below zero.

It was almost impossible to tell when day dawned. A blizzard howled with hurricane force over the whole countryside, and a smothering torrent of snow covered everything. Tents were swept away, horses froze to death, the supply wagons sank in deep drifts of snow; frozen, blinded men cursed and struggled to get them moving, but most of the wagons had be abandoned, and with them the shelter afforded the wounded.

The army began to crawl forward through an uncharted sea of snow, where columns wandered off the route, were lost and perished in a few hours. There were no roads, no landmarks, nothing.

Infantry, artillery and cavalry merged in hopeless confusion, struggling against the blizzard, and as the cold reached its peak, men began falling as they marched. Those too weak to go on were left to freeze to death. There was no room for pity; the spirit of comradeship died in that dreadful desert of snow and all discipline died with it. Only the Old Guard tried to maintain some kind of order, but they were helpless to control the savagery, the despair and the folly of the rest of the army. Rank was forgotten, officers and men dragged along side by side, groups formed which provided shelter and what scraps of food there were for themselves only; an intruder was driven away with blows. The miserable horses, once the pride of the world's foremost cavalry, faltered and fell, to be surrounded by fighting ravenous men who cut the meat from the living animal and tried to eat it raw. Thousands died of frostbite; men staggered forward, knee deep in snow, half blind from the glare, infested with vermin and ravaged by hunger. Many threw themselves down and died rather than go farther, and many went mad.

Seventy thousand horsemen had crossed the Niemen into Russia; only six hundred were left to form an escort for Napoleon. Murat, gaunt and unrecognizable, was in command of this battalion.

At night they bivouacked in woods or on the site of villages burnt out during the advance, and the sparks of many fires glowed wherever there was shelter, and the evening meal of flour soup, flavoured with gunpowder and horseflesh, was cooked and distributed. The strongest shelter was allotted to the Emperor and the tenderest meat reserved for him; men who had exhausted themselves searching for a few sticks for their own fire offered them gladly so that Napoleon might be warm. In the indescribable horror of that march the love of the starving, suffering multitude for Napoleon

Bonaparte transcended their agony and their indifference to each other. Men died gasping the old battle cry, "*Vive L'Empereur*"; at the sight of the little figure, wrapped in a shabby greatcoat with a fur hat pulled low over the eyes, every head raised with hope. He had brought them into Russia; he would get them out. The Emperor never failed.

He walked with the help of a strong stick, his head always lowered to the ground; the blizzard had spent itself but the savage cold continued. He seldom spoke and his escorts were silent also.

Once only, Ney surprised him; a crowd of bearded scarecrows had divided to let the Emperor pass, and some of them managed a quavering cheer. A boy in the filthy remains of a Cuirassier's uniform had lost a leg, and was standing on one foot, his crutch lifted in salute.

The Cuirassiers, so magnificently equipped and mounted, charging the Russian batteries at Borodino. . . . The dead Cuirassiers, rotting on the quiet battlefield, and the boy without a leg, his chafed armpits bleeding through his uniform, saluting his Emperor with a crutch. . . .

A terrible anger surged up in Ney, as he turned to look at the man who had caused so much suffering and whom no one had blamed. Then he saw his face; the plump cheeks were sunken, the dark eyes stared from side to side, and slowly, one hand lifted to return the salute. In all the years he had known him, Ney had never seen what he saw then. Napoleon was weeping.

It was still freezing hard when the vanguard reached Smolensk, to find the shattered city occupied by a garrison nearly as hungry as themselves. The stores left behind were exhausted; there was practically nothing to succour the main army.

They halted at Smolensk until the 14th of November, and Napoleon sent for his staff to assess their position.

By the light of a few candles they gathered round the stained campaign maps, to plot their route out of Russia with what was left of the army. Scouts reported the advance of Kutuzov with the bulk of his forces; Smolensk was not provisioned for more than a few days, much less a siege, and in those few days miracles of reorganization had taken place. If they marched at once there was a chance of missing Kutuzov, crossing the Dnieper and destroying the pontoons before the Russians came up. That would give them time to reach the Beresina, where a corps under the command of Marshal Oudinot had been left behind to protect the bridge at Borisoff.

"At the Beresina we will be safe, Gentlemen," Napoleon declared. On the 14th they evacuated Smolensk.

Ney commanded the rear-guard, and the Russians caught up with him at Krasnoe. The Emperor and the rest of the army were crossing the Dnieper ahead when the Marshal turned to give battle and allow them time to escape.

It was incredible that his men could fight at all, but they gathered under the Eagle standards as they had done so often and so gloriously in the past, starved and decimated by disease, to hold off the Russians till Napoleon got away. At Krasnoe they fought as bravely and fiercely as at any time during the campaign, led by Ney, whom the Emperor himself described as the bravest of the brave.

When the French buglers sounded the retreat he led them through a host of Cossacks in a desperate attempt to reach the pontoons and escape over the Dnieper. A salvo of artillery told Napoleon that Ney and his troops had crossed the river, and moments before the first Cossacks galloped up, the bridges were dynamited.

The army marched onwards, its numbers dwindling from cold, hunger and sickness, buoyed up by hope that Oudinot waited for them at the River Beresina, and after the crossing they would reach the shelter of Vilna and be on the frontier of Russia again.

On November the 24th they halted and began pitching camp, using the remaining supply wagons and a few ragged tents for shelter; it was a freezing night, but mercifully still. Thousands lay huddled on the ground, wrapped in rags, scratching, and groaning with hunger; others wandered off into the white wilderness in a mad search for food and better shelter, never to return.

In his own tent Napoleon dozed on a camp-bed, watched over by his orderly. The Emperor had eaten practically nothing; when they pressed him he cried out that his men were starving and he wished to starve with them. Then he lay down in his clothes and the orderly covered him while he slept.

In the small hours the orderly woke from an uneasy dream, to find someone bending over him, shaking him roughly.

It was the Chief of Staff, Marshal Berthier.

" Wake the Emperor!   Wake him at once! "

But Napoleon was already sitting up, looking as if he had never slept at all. He recognized his Marshal by the light of one candle guttering on a table in the middle of the floor.

" What is it, Berthier? " he said.

Berthier saluted. " News from Oudinot, Sire.   Terrible news." He paused and his face twitched. " The Russians have·attacked them.   They've burnt the bridge at Borisoff. There's no way across."

" Bring the messenger to me." Napoleon got up and turned to the orderly. " Go to Duroc, wake him and request the other Marshals to come here."

One by one they gathered in the tent; more candles were lit and chairs set round the table; at the Emperor's order a decanter of wine was served. Murat yawned, pulling at his long side-whiskers; it was bitterly cold, though he still wore his fur-lined greatcoat, the walk from his own tent to the Emperor's had chilled him. Ney was there, impassive as ever; his excessive calmness was a bad sign, as ominous as Berthier's nervous cough. Davoust stood by the table, his bald head bent, swilling the wine round in his glass.

The Emperor stood at the head of the table; he was pale and drawn with fatigue.

" Gentlemen, let us sit down."

The chairs scraped back, and when there was silence he

spoke again. "You've heard the news. Oudinot has lost the bridge across the Beresina."

The words were staccato; he glanced round at them and then suddenly stabbed at the map with his finger.

"We are here, and Kutuzov is coming up behind us as fast as he can. If he catches us, he'll drive us *into* the Beresina."

Murat was staring at the map, seeing the thin line as a swollen torrent of water and half melted ice, thinking that he was probably going to die without crossing it now. Their chances of escape had vanished as the burning timbers of the Borisoff Bridge collapsed; he would never see Naples again, or his wife Caroline. He had served a Bonaparte and married a Bonaparte, and loved them both. Not many rankers became Kings, he thought, and the impish grin appeared for a second. He had lived well; it was a pity to die in that freezing hell; he had always hoped to die in Naples, in the big sunny bedroom of the Palace which looked out over the Bay. . . .

"We can't fight Kutuzov," Davoust said. "The men are almost at the end of their strength."

Napoleon looked up. "We could surrender, Gentlemen," he said quietly.

"Never!" Ney exclaimed. "Surrender, let them take you prisoner, Sire! The men'd fight with their bare hands before they let that happen!"

The Emperor smiled wistfully, and Ney thought suddenly that Napoleon could summon pathos and wring the last sacrifice out of the men who followed him. He'd said the men would defend their Emperor with their fists, and it was true. It was also true that he would do the same.

"There is no question of surrender, Sire." Murat and Davoust spoke together. Napoleon smiled, his pale face had flushed with emotion.

"As you will not abandon me, Gentlemen, we must consider how to escape this trap," he said. "I've been studying the position while I waited for you. I believe we have a chance."

"My God, Sire, how?" Berthier cried out.

"Oudinot sent a further message," Napoleon answered. "Three leagues above Borisoff the river is fordable. We shall build pontoons and cross there."

"Kutuzov will catch up with us before we've time to build anything," Davoust objected. "There can never be another rear-guard action; Ney fought the last."

"I'll fight again," Ney said quickly. "If you need time to get the pontoons across, Sire, I'll stay here with my men and hold the Russians back. Just give the word!"

"I nearly sacrificed you once before, Ney," Napoleon answered. "No, we'll cross together or we'll perish together. I have another plan." He held out his glass and the orderly filled it.

"Berthier!" he said briskly. "How many camp followers have we?"

"Hundreds, Sire. Perhaps thousands," was the reply.

"Good, then we'll put them to use. Round up as many of the women as you can; detach two regiments and send them southwards in daylight. That should confuse friend Kutuzov into thinking we've changed direction. By night we'll march to join Oudinot while sappers go on ahead to build the pontoons."

"It's a perfect plan," Murat exclaimed. "Perfect. They'll follow them southwards while we reach the Beresina!"

"I'm confident they will," Napoleon said grimly. "It was a clever trap, Gentlemen, but I believe we've escaped it. I suggest we dispense with sleep for to-night. There isn't a moment to lose!"

*   *   *

Scouts came into the Russian headquarters with the news that a large column of French troops was moving southwards. Kutuzov raised his head and blinked; he looked exactly like an old tortoise as the brown eyes opened and shut under their wrinkled lids; he was seventy and often very tired. But he'd chased the enemy from Moscow to the Beresina, and the trap in which he had such confidence was about to be sprung. In it, he meant to catch Napoleon Bonaparte himself.

Grunting, he bent over his maps, and then gave the order to patrol the river to the south. When the French arrived there, they would find his army waiting.

He wrote a long dispatch to Alexander and then fell asleep over his desk.

*   *   *

The French sappers had built two light bridges over the river. The word had travelled from man to man as he worked: "To save the Emperor!" and they plunged into the icy waters of the Beresina, often submerged to the neck, and built the frail pontoons. Those who weren't drowned died of cold afterwards.

On the 26th of November the Corps of Marshal Oudinot was reunited with the rest of the army and the Emperor; by that evening 7,000 men had crossed the river, and the next day Napoleon himself rode across. The plan had worked perfectly; by the next night the whole army would be safe on the opposite bank. A feeling of relief invaded officers and men; they gave way to aching tiredness and fell down and slept; only a few straggled across the pontoons. The wounded and a miscellany of women who had followed the army, and somehow survived, remained in a confused mass on the wrong side of the river.

They woke to the sound of gunfire. Kutuzov had discovered the trick and the Russians had caught up.

CHAPTER EIGHT

"IT was the most terrible thing I've ever seen in my life, Sire."

Kutuzov shifted from one foot to the other as he stood in front of the Czar.

His old legs were aching and he longed to sit down.

Alexander said kindly, "It must be a long story as well as a distressing one, General. You have my permission to sit down."

Kutuzov accepted, and the Czar prompted him. "Go on, General. What happened then?"

"When we caught up with them there was a stiff fight. Napoleon had left Marshal Victor behind, and he tried to hold us off while the rest of the army got across. They fought very well, though God knows how. Then at one time we overwhelmed them and took one of the higher approaches to the river bank; we brought up artillery and began shelling the ground and the bridges. As I said, it was the most terrible thing I've ever seen. It was the wounded and the women, Sire. They panicked; there was a rush for the bridges. We were firing right into the middle of them, and there must have been thousands, fighting and screaming like wild beasts. One of the bridges gave way; they had cannon on it and the weight was too much; it was jammed with dead and people struggling to get over, and suddenly it gave way and the whole lot fell into the Beresina. There was a terrible cry then; it seemed like one cry, though it must have been hundreds screaming. God knows what Bonaparte must have felt when he heard it.

"Victor's men retook that height to stop the artillery fire, but it was too late. The French were trampling each other to death on the last bridge; I heard that dozens tried swimming the river and were drowned in a few minutes.

"We captured a division of the French, and at dawn on the 29th their rear-guard fired the last bridge to prevent our following. That was the end for the ones left behind. They were mostly wounded, hundreds of them, and before God, they began throwing themselves into the Beresina rather than be captured. With your permission, Sire." Kutuzov took out a handkerchief and wiped the perspiration from his face.

"All great victories are horrible, General," Alexander said. "And we're not at the end of it even now."

Kutuzov looked up at him quickly. "We've driven him out of Russia. He's gone back to Paris without an army. Only 20,000 survived to cross the Niemen out of half a million men, and they're mostly diseased and falling from hunger. Napoleon's routed, Sire."

"Napoleon's in Paris raising another army," Alexander said stonily. "And Austria hasn't taken up arms against him. No one has moved, Kutuzov. It's been left to us to complete our victory alone. And we shall complete it. Europe has trembled at Napoleon's name long enough. Now she shall tremble at mine."

He rose to end the interview, and the General bowed and backed out of the room. The Russian Army was back at Vilna and Alexander had left Petersburg to join it. It was curious, he thought, how patterns repeated themselves; again his presence was the signal for a ghastly gaiety, an echo of the elegant gatherings of those first months of 1812, when he stayed in the same town and heard the news that his enemy had crossed the Niemen with the greatest army of all time.

The remains of that army were in the woods and fields round Vilna, scattered in a terrible harvest of death and misery over the countryside from Moscow to the bridge at Kovno, where they had crossed to invade Russia on the 25th of June.

The host was obliterated, but Napoleon had escaped; Kutuzov's trap had closed over the miserable thousands who perished at the Beresina, but the real object of it was in Paris, and the French Senate had just promised him a conscript army of 300,000 men. Austria and Prussia were still honouring their treaties with Napoleon; everyone was waiting, too terrified of his power to exploit Alexander's victory. And his own staff urged him to overrun Poland and then stop. They argued that Russia's armies were decimated by continued fighting and by the diseases spread everywhere by the French. The country was stripped and burnt bare. The first need was peace. No one wanted to advance into Europe except himself and Catherine Pavlovna. No one trusted the Prussians or believed that the Austrians would rise later when they hadn't done so already. To go into Europe would be challenging Bonaparte on his own ground. Alexander listened and then gave the order to march through Poland and into Prussia as if no one had said a word.

If Prussia wouldn't support him of her own volition, he would invade her.

In the first weeks of 1813 the Russian armies entered Prussia. But a famous exile went ahead of them, the patriot Von Stein, entrusted with the task of rousing his country against Napoleon. It was a brilliantly clever move; Stein organized a militia at Königsberg, and the idea spread to Breslau and Berlin itself, where the student class rose in a mass to take up arms against the hated French. The sparks of German independence which Napoleon extinguished after Wagram erupted violently all over Prussia. On March 17th Prussia and Russia agreed to deliver the nation from the French, and the first side of the triangle of Napoleon's alliance collapsed.

In April the Austrian Ambassador to Paris went to see Napoleon. The Ambassador was the same Count Schwarzenberg who had been so popular in St. Petersburg. His considerable charm and talent were to be used to soften Napoleon and persuade him to agree with Austria's proposals. Metternich of Austria had been waiting and watch-

ing very carefully, and he disliked what he saw from every
point of view.

His decision not to attack France immediately had been
a wise one, for less than six months after the end of 1812,
Napoleon had mustered an army of nearly half a million
men. He had drawn troops from Spain to do it, and the
untried youth of France had rushed to arms, roused by the
unquenchable enthusiasm Napoleon's name inspired.

The homes and fields of France were emptied of young
men; the factories worked night and day making uniforms,
producing weapons and equipping this new army, the off-
spring of the vanished host of 1812. He had left Russia a
ruined man, and fled across Europe to save his throne in
Paris. A few months later he surveyed his enemies with an
army nearly as big as the one he had lost.

Nearly as big, but not the same, Metternich thought. The
veterans had perished in their tens of thousands. It was
unlikely that even Napoleon could replace their quality as
he had done their numbers.

But Metternich knew his opponent; the man had achieved
the impossible already; it would be wisest to wait. The
hordes of Russia pouring into Europe, ostensibly to pursue
Napoleon and swallowing Poland at the same time, didn't
please Metternich either. He dismissed the Czar's guise of a
Crusader as a piece of hypocrisy, and evaded all attempts to
embroil Austria openly against France. Then Prussia suddenly deserted her ally and joined Alexander. Metternich
liked this even less. There was going to be a major war,
fought out over Europe; whoever won would be supremely
powerful, too powerful for the safety of Austria. He sent
Schwarzenberg to Napoleon to offer Austrian mediation and
prevent the war. Austria's reward would be a share in the
lands parcelled out in the negotiations.

Bonaparte listened to the Count. He liked him, he liked
Austrians in general; he had once liked Metternich, who
used to be Ambassador to Paris himself, but he had measured
Metternich, and he remined him of Talleyrand, whom he
had used but always hated.

Peace, the Count explained, was the only sensible course for all sides. Austria was willing to secure it for France and for Russia and Prussia; her support to either side, he murmured gently, could be the deciding factor in any war. . . .

"In other words," Napoleon interrupted, "Austria is now as frightened of Alexander of Russia as she is of Napoleon of France. She prefers us not to fight so that neither can win! Tell Monsieur le Comte I appreciate his point of view. For myself I have no wish for war. If the Russians want peace they must ask for it; I'll always listen. But the real obstacle to any lasting settlement in Europe is England.

"Good evening, Count Schwarzenberg. My compliments to your excellent Foreign Minister; he could have found no better replacement for himself than he has done in you."

The audience was over, and Napoleon went to the apartments of his little son, where he took the child on his knee and played with him.

"I must not make an enemy of Austria," he was thinking. 'Even if I fall, Austria will protect my son: . . ."

In the same months Austria's envoy to London was received by Lord Castlereagh, and informed coldly that there could never be peace with France as long as Napoleon occupied Spain and refused to make greater concessions to his enemies' demands. England had no intention of embarrassing Russia and Prussia at such a moment.

At Vienna, Metternich considered. He had two alternatives, the latest was an offer by Napoleon to dismember Prussia and give the rich province of Silesia to Austria in return for 100,000 men in the coming campaign. It was an outrageous and very tempting bribe. But the combined might of Russia, Prussia and England were gathering against the tempter. Metternich thought for a long time and then decided. The odds were too much, even for Napoleon.

Austria had better abandon him and join his enemies.

*   *   *

Alexander's first meeting with Metternich took place at Opotschna. Each approached the other with deep suspicion and disguised it with fulsome words of friendship. Alexander received the Austrian informally; it was a ruse he employed to put his opponents at their ease and off their guard at the same time. When Count Metternich was announced he came forward and held out his hand. The Count kissed it and bowed, and the two men looked at each other. Metternich was tall, very slim and graceful and extremely handsome; he smiled at the Czar, thinking him older and more forbidding than he had expected.

This, then, was the victor of 1812, the man who had tricked Napoleon in the sphere of diplomacy and destroyed him on the field of battle. This grave, good-looking man with the gentle expression. Most dangerous, Metternich decided; we can't exchange Napoleon for you. . . .

They sat down and spent some minutes discussing the campaign which had been fought in Saxony.

"It is amazing, Sire, what Napoleon has been able to do with an army of recruits," Metternich remarked.

It was amazing; Alexander, whose troops had been defeated at Bautzen, flushed, and said suddenly, "Austrian support would have been welcomed by the King of Prussia and myself. We expected it long ago."

"You have our support," Metternich protested.

"We have your neutrality, Count, and that is not enough."

"My position is difficult, Sire," he said smoothly. "The Empress Marie-Louise is a Hapsburg. We must have an excuse to declare war."

"Prussia found one," Alexander answered.

"I believe we have too," the Count said. "No one can provoke a quarrel like a mediator." He glanced up at the Czar and smiled. "If he refuses a truce, then the war begins again and we enter it as your allies. And I am sure that if the terms are presented to him in the right way, he will reject the most generous offer!"

*　　　*　　　*

At Reichenbach Austria signed a secret treaty. If Napoleon had not reached a settlement by the expiration of the truce, she would join Russia, Prussia and England in making war on him.

Metternich went to see Napoleon, who was then quartered in the Marcolini Palace at Dresden, and there offered him terms. As he had said to Alexander, no one could provoke a quarrel as quickly as the mediator; Bonaparte lost his temper, swore and shouted at him, promising the most awful vengeance for the perfidy of Austria when he most needed her.

Metternich waited calmly until the outburst ceased, then he looked at the pale, sweating little man who had held them all in subjection for so many years. His hard eyes held the furious glare of the Emperor for some moments, then he said coldly, " You are lost, Sire. I had the presentiment of it when I came. Now, in going, I have the certainty."

In the ante-room an anxious crowd surrounded him, hoping for news of peace. They all wanted peace, even the Marshals whose fortunes were built on war wanted peace; only Napoleon refused to give way, obstinate and savage in the face of danger, sure that if he yielded an inch, his enemies would end by destroying him. Especially the main enemy, the man who had followed him out of Russia and had engaged him in Saxony. Alexander wouldn't be content with any treaty. He would attack again, there could never be peace while he remained undefeated. Marshal Berthier escorted Metternich to his carriage, and asked him whether he were satisfied with the interview. He must have confidence in the Emperor now, Berthier urged. Metternich turned on the coach step and looked at him as he had looked at Napoleon a little while before.

" Yes, he has explained everything to me," he said. " It is all over with the man."

Then he entered the carriage and drove away. Berthier turned back and walked slowly into the Palace.

In the worst days of the Retreat from Moscow he had never had such a presentiment of disaster as he did then with

Metternich's judgment sounding in his ears. "It is all over with the man."

On June 22nd Wellington inflicted a crushing defeat on the French troops in Vittoria, and Joseph Bonaparte abandoned the Spanish throne and fled into France.

It was the signal for which Europe had been waiting.

On July 12th the treacherous Bernadotte of Sweden signed a treaty with the Allied Powers to fight France at the end of the armistice, and at midnight on the 10th August Alexander received the news that bonfires were blazing along the heights of the Riesengebirge. The truce had expired; the beacons proclaimed war against Napoleon.

*　　　*　　　*

In the first days of February, 1814, Alexander sat in his headquarters at Bar-sur-Seine writing a long letter to his sister Catherine.

"I miss you," he wrote truthfully. "I know how much every triumph would have meant to you, how you would have rejoiced with me when you saw the first Russian troops cross into France. The last six months seem like as many years; he has fought like a man possessed of the devil, and everywhere he commanded he won. But elsewhere his Marshals lost. It is the hand of God, Catherine. Without Napoleon the rest made one blunder after another; MacDonald at Katzbach, Vandamme at Kulm, and Ney himself at Dennewitz. The Prussian Generals are magnificent; especially Blücher; he's old but he has the energy of twenty men.

"We defeated Napoleon himself at Leipzig; the retreat was nearly as horrible as the Beresina. You remember they found twelve thousand corpses there when the floods abated. There was another panic at Leipzig, and his Polish Marshal Poniatowsky was drowned. He has lost many friends, they betray him one by one as he retreats. Murat left him in November; we've promised to let him stay in Naples, and he's ready to turn on Napoleon. Ney remains with him, still fighting. Blücher is advancing on Paris now, but I do not intend to let him get there.

" I must reach Paris first, my dear sister, for I find we have other enemies besides Bonaparte. The Austrians want a Regency for the Empress Marie-Louise and Napoleon's son. As I fight the French I am also forced to fight Metternich. He betrayed Napoleon and he is quite capable of betraying us if it suits him. I will not have either a Bonaparte or a Hapsburg on the French throne. Neither will England. More and more I miss you, and my one comfort is your letters. But I promise you this, as soon as the war is over, I shall send for you. It seems impossible that peace is near, that he is really going to be beaten. God guide you, Catherine. The next time I write I shall be in The Tuilleries."

* * *

Alexander entered Paris on the 1st of April. He rode in with the King of Prussia on his right and the Austrian Commander on his left, leading a procession of Russian and Prussian Guards.

The streets were lined with silent crowds, the windows overlooking the route crowded with people who wanted to see the almost legendary Czar of Russia. It was the women who first began cheering him; he was dressed in a dazzling uniform of white, covered in gold braid and decorations. The idol of Napoleon had fallen from his pedestal; only the good sense of his timorous brother Joseph had saved Paris from the madness of a siege when the Allies approached. The Parisians, quaking for their lives and property surrendered with indecent haste while their Emperor fought overwhelming odds, struggling even then to turn back the invaders and almost succeeding. But Paris surrendered, and led by a few hysterical women, the people began cheering and pressing round their conqueror. The Liberator, they shrieked, the Republican Czar who had promised a free vote for the country, whose savage Cossacks had been ordered to remain in their quarters and spare the city the horrors of plunder and rapine inflicted on less lucky parts of France. . . . They had nothing to fear from that handsome, gallant enemy; they'd had enough of war, enough of Napoleon Bonaparte, Long live the Czar!

Alexander smiled and saluted. One year and seven months before, the Emperor of the French had ridden into Moscow; now his opponent entered his Capital in triumph, acclaimed by the crowds as a liberator and a protector. He thought how his sister Catherine would laugh when she heard of it; how her laughter would change to anger at the order to Russian troops not to molest or loot. He thought of Moscow, burning, and shaken by explosions as Napoleon's men dynamited, determined to destroy what the fire had spared. He could have taken the same vengeance, he thought; the Prussians were mounting cannon on the heights of Montmartre, ready to bombard the city at the first sign of insurrection; their troops and his were restless and longing to revenge the devastation their own countries had suffered.

Only his will stood between Paris and the full terrors of occupation by a vindictive and, in his case, half-civilized army. But his clemency to Paris was the debt he owed God for his victory; he paid it with rigid observance and forced his allies to do the same. That day the French Senate agreed to form a Provisional Government. It was the end of Napoleon's reign, and that night Alexander dined with the man who had addressed the Senate, the limping Prince of Benevento. It was the climax of Talleyrand's career; the cold aristocrat had finally triumphed over the parvenu. Seated at the table with Alexander that night, he drank a toast to the liberation of France from the tyranny he had helped to institute fifteen years ago, when he sided with the young General Bonaparte. He also drank a private toast at the same time. The insults and dangers of his service with Napoleon were finally avenged.

Alexander stayed in his great mansion facing the Place de la Concorde, where Louis XVI and Marie Antoinette had been guillotined. Now Talleyrand, who had helped Danton prepare the Terror, was proposing the return of the Bourbon dynasty to the throne of France. He was reverting to type, Alexander thought, realizing suddenly how much he disliked the man. But the Bourbons suited Prussia too, and England. Under their rule, France would never recover her power.

He lay awake until dawn in Talleyrand's luxurious bedroom, his hands clasped behind his head, thoughts rioting through his brain.

He had won; a Provisional Government ruled France, led by Talleyrand; Napoleon was at Fontainebleau Palace, less than ten miles away, with all that was left of his army. The Empress Marie-Louise was at Blois with the little King of Rome, preparing to desert her husband and go to her father, the Austrian Emperor; the whole Bonaparte family had fled Paris and were streaking for safety; everyone had abandoned the Emperor in his hour of defeat. It was a bitter lesson, Alexander reflected, and for the first time his hatred of Napoleon became tinged with pity. It would have broken a lesser man.

He lay back on the pillows frowning, thinking that he hated Talleyrand and could never trust him, or Metternich, or Castlereagh of England.

The pygmies had dragged down the giant; now they were turning against *him*, jealous of his power, his popularity with the French people. . . . Strange, that they should cheer him like that.

It had moved him till tears came into his eyes. He had beaten their idol, but been merciful to them, and they trusted him like children. It must be that they too recognized a man as great as the ruler they had lost, a man above the petty instincts of the other allies. A man whose cause was just, a man favoured by God. . . . He fell asleep at last.

He was dining alone with Talleyrand on the evening of the 4th of April. The Prince of Benevento was an excellent host; he had made every effort to amuse the Czar, relating one incident after another to Napoleon's detriment in the hope of pleasing him or provoking a smile. Usually silent and aloof, the Prince was unable to restrain his own good humour, in spite of the gravity and coldness of his guest. He watched Alexander carefully and then remarked: " I hope you have observed the number of white cockades being worn in the city streets, Sire. The people can hardly wait to welcome His Majesty King Louis XVIII."

Alexander stared at him; Talleyrand, a master of the art of disconcerting other people, became the victim of a much superior technique.

" I have seen some demonstrations, Monsieur le Prince, but not enough to convince me that the people of France wish for the Bourbons to return. It may be that they will want a Republic."

" A Republic? " Talleyrand's eyebrows lifted. " Surely, Sire, as an absolute monarch, you couldn't support that? "

" I have promised to honour the wishes of the French people," Alexander answered coldly. " My own country's constitution has nothing to do with it. And in your support for a Monarchy, are you not carrying your patriotism too far? "

A flush rose in Talleyrand's face and then died away.

" Your Majesty's meaning escapes me."

" I believe you had some part in the upheaval which removed the House of Bourbon from the throne of France, my dear Prince. Aren't you afraid that the new King might prove vindictive? "

Talleyrand regarded him with a smile of pure hatred.

" It is more likely he'll prove grateful, Sire. And my personal safety is small consideration beside the danger of a Republic which Bonaparte would probably be able to upset, or worse still a Regency for his son which he would undoubtedly usurp in a few months. The only safeguard against him is to give France a legitimate King. It is also the only way to restrain the influence of Austria," he added smoothly.

Alexander studied his hands.

"I hope for your support for King Louis, Sire," Talleyrand insisted. "Indeed, I have assured him he can rely on you."

"Your assurance will be honoured, Prince, if it agrees with the wishes of the French people."

"Of course, Sire."

Talleyrand smiled his crooked smile and his pale eyes flickered towards Alexander. The spectacle of the most absolute monarch in Europe upholding the rights of the people widened his smile into genuine amusement. It was curious how power affected different men, he thought. Napoleon . . . power and Napoleon seemed to fuse into an irresistible force, devoid of moral sense, mercy or human fear. Power had transformed the parvenu into an object of terror and personal hatred. Now he was broken and this barbarian might easily take his place; not a parvenu, Talleyrand thought, applying his vicious epithet for Napoleon, but an autocrat with a sense of God-given mission. He had read Alexander's dispatches, noting the increasing religious influence in them; since the Czar arrived in his house, the servants set to spy on him told Talleyrand that he spent hours praying in his room. And he had not availed himself of any of the women who clustered round him wherever he went in Paris.

It was odd, Talleyrand thought. Very odd. And it might be terribly dangerous. Once a man as powerful as Alexander of Russia claimed the Almighty as his ally, he might do anything. . . .

At that moment the door opened and one of the Prince's household came towards him, bowing low to the Czar.

"What is it? I gave orders we were not to be disturbed!"

"With His Majesty's permission, Monsieur le Prince, I have a message for him. I request his permission to speak," the man said. He was obviously very agitated.

"You have it," Alexander said quickly. "What is your message?"

"Sire, three gentlemen have come to the house and they beg you to grant them an audience."

Talleyrand turned round. "I must ask you to forgive this, Sire. I have no idea who would dare such a thing. . . . One moment and I will see."

"Who are these gentlemen?" Alexander asked.

The servant looked at him and mumbled.

"The one who requested the audience is Marshal Ney, Your Majesty."

*   *   *

Alexander and the most famous of Napoleon's Marshals came face to face a few minutes later. Ney walked towards him and then bowed.

"Your Majesty," he said. His voice was hoarse with fatigue and emotion. "May I present the Minister of Foreign Affairs, Monsieur Caulaincourt, and Marshal McDonald of the Imperial Army."

"Monsieur Caulaincourt and I are old friends," Alexander said, and nodded to the former Ambassador to St. Petersburg. He acknowledged the bow of the second Marshal with the peculiar name. Then he remembered; McDonald had been defeated at Katzbach in the Saxon campaign. He had written to Catherine about it. . . .

"Please sit down, Gentlemen. We shall not be disturbed. What have you to say to me?"

He had requested Talleyrand to wait in another room during the meeting, and been amused by the expression of dread on his face and the anxious warning not to listen to an emissary from Napoleon, it would only be a trap. . . .

"I come to you on behalf of the Emperor, Sire," Ney said. "I bring a message from him."

"Read it, if you please."

Ney cleared his throat and unfolded a paper; the eagle seal hung from it on a broad red ribbon.

"'The Allied Powers having proclaimed that the Emperor Napoleon was the sole obstacle to the re-establishment of peace in Europe, the Emperor Napoleon, faithful to his oaths, declares that he is ready to descend from the throne, to leave France, and even give up his life, for the good of the fatherland, inseparable from the rights of his son, of those of the Regency of the Empress and of the maintenance of the laws of the Empire.'"

Ney lowered the paper and then offered it to Alexander. " There is his signature, Sire."

Alexander read it through and looked at the angry sprawling word written at the end of it.

Then he stared straight at Ney.

" Tell me, Prince de la Moscova, do you believe he'll keep to this?"

Ney passed his hand across his face; it was a weary, despairing gesture.

" He has no choice, Sire. We held a conference with him to-day. He wanted to go on fighting, to attack Paris, but none of his Marshals would follow him. We forced his hand, Sire."

" I think he's gone mad, Your Majesty." It was Marshal MacDonald who spoke then. " He was ready to fight the whole allied armies with a force of less than 50,000 men. He has the Guards with him at Fontainebleau; they are as crazy as he is. It was our duty to save France while we could."

" And to save him," Ney said slowly. " He charged us to come to you, Sire. He doesn't trust anyone else's word."

" I am his bitterest enemy," Alexander said. " Why didn't he send you to the Austrians. His wife is an Arch-duchess."

" Because you have the final word, Sire." MacDonald answered him. " You've treated Paris honourably when the Prussians would have razed it to the ground. You've promised the people of France a free choice in their government."

" I beg of you, don't restore the Bourbons! " Ney burst out. " France doesn't want them. Appoint Marie-Louise Regent for the King of Rome. That's all Napoleon asks of you."

Alexander said nothing, and for several minutes the four men sat in silence. Ney wiped his face with a handkerchief, he looked old and exhausted; the other Marshal stared

Alexander attended a Ball given by the Empress Josephine at Malmaison. When she came forward to receive him he was astonished at her beauty; she curtsied to him with the grace of a young woman, and he bent over her hand and kissed it gallantly.

"Welcome to my house, Your Majesty."

She smiled, and the illusion of youth disappeared. Close to, he saw the fine lines under the make-up, the streaks of silver in the short curled hair.

Her large brown eyes smiled up at him in admiration, the old coquetry of her youth creeping into their expression.

How handsome, they said gaily, how tall and attractive.

She allowed her fingers to linger in his for a moment and then took his arm. "This is a great honour, Sire. I admit I have been dying to be presented to you."

"Madame, you overwhelm me. In Paris I saw everything and met everyone, and then they told me, 'If you wish to see France's most beautiful woman, you must go to Malmaison.'"

He smiled down at her. "I couldn't wait to come here, and I find I've been deceived. They should have said the most beautiful woman in Europe. It's unfair to confine you to France alone, Madame."

She laughed her pretty laugh. "You have an unfortunate effect upon me, Sire. You make me feel quite young again! Alas, I shall have to disillusion you. Come and let me present my daughter, Queen Hortense."

Napoleon's stepdaughter had married his brother Louis Bonaparte and been made Queen of Holland. She was waiting in the elegant salon, and Alexander's impression was of a young and not unattractive woman who carried herself well. He spoke to her with deliberate charm and she responded immediately; she was obviously in a state of emotional tension, because the few words brought tears to her eyes.

He escorted Josephine into dinner, and enjoyed himself in a woman's company for the first time in eighteen months.

The Empress was a born coquette; she talked amusing non-sense and made him laugh; the members of his entourage were flirting with several of her ladies. The conquest of France and the deposition of Napoleon might never have happened. He noticed how exquisitely she was dressed; her shoulders and arms were still smooth and beautiful. She was years older than he was, but he found himself laughing and paying her compliments for the pleasure of seeing her brown eyes shine up at him. After dinner they opened the Ball. It was a brilliant scene, and the Empress Josephine assured him he waltzed better than any man she knew.

Later she suggested a walk in the gardens.

"They're rather beautiful, Sire. My roses are quite famous." He sensed that she wanted to talk to him alone; they walked out on to the terrace and down to the lawns. A large moon hung overhead.

She slipped her hand through his arm and they walked in silence for some moments, he measuring his long steps to hers.

"How curious life is," she said suddenly. "I remember the first time he talked about you, when he'd come back from Tilsit. I was so bored, you know. Politics never interested me and he would discuss them with me. I suppose it was natural with one's wife, but I didn't think of it like that at the time. I remember distinctly what he said about you, Sire. He said, 'You would have liked him, my dear.' And in spite of everything, I do. Isn't that curious?"

She was not smiling when she looked up at him. She suddenly looked extremely tired and rather sad.

"I'm glad, Madame," he said gently. "I would be distressed if you disliked me. For myself, may I say one thing?"

"Of course. Shall we walk down here, you can see quite clearly the arrangement of the flower beds."

"I shall never be able to understand how he could part from you."

She shrugged and her gauze scarf slipped from her shoulders.

"I shall never be able to understand why he stayed with me for so long," she answered. "Is it true that wretched woman has run to her father and won't go to Elba with him?"

"I'm afraid so, Madame."

She said harshly, "That's curious too. A Hapsburg should have more sense of duty than to desert like Murat and Ney and all the others. She never loved him, I knew that, but she knows what the King of Rome means to him. He deserved better."

"Don't blame Ney and the Marshals, Madame," Alexander urged. "They had to make peace; France would have been laid in ruins if they had listened to Napoleon."

"Perhaps. You must forgive me, Sire; being only a woman I can't visualize such things, and being what was once termed a ci-devant aristo, I have that foolish, old-fashioned penchant for honour. . . . Public honour, I mean. One's private affairs are different. I wonder how he will manage at Elba?"

"It's a pleasant place," he comforted. "He's been allowed to keep the title of Emperor; we've given him the island to rule. He should find some happiness."

"It won't be quite the same as ruling Europe though. Tell me, Sire, is it true that he tried to commit suicide at Fontainebleau after the abdication? I heard some rumour of it." Her voice was unnaturally even.

"I think so," he said cautiously. "It was just a moment of despair. He had recovered his spirits by the next morning."

She laughed a little. "He would. I can imagine him. Always the optimist, always convincing other people he could work miracles because he was so sure of it himself. And now it's over and the Bourbons are back. That's a pity, I think. They really asked for the guillotine—they were so stupid. Look down there, Sire. See the little fountain; don't you think it's pretty?"

" I think it's charming, Madame."

She was standing close to him and he felt her shiver.

" It's cold for you. We should go in, or at least let me get you a wrap."

" No, thank you, Sire. After all, this is my most elegant dress, worn in your honour. Why should I cover it up under some old shawl? Let's walk through here."

The top of her curly head reached below the level of his shoulder, the diamonds in her head-dress sparkled in the moonlight as she turned.

Again they were silent until he said suddenly, " You said life was curious, Madame. Now I agree with you! In defeat Napoleon has more friends than he ever had in success; even you, Madame, whom he treated so shamefully. And I, the conqueror, find myself surrounded by people working against me! "

" Talleyrand, no doubt. He works against everyone; he's a horrible man. I really think his mind's as twisted as his foot. Who else, Sire? "

" The Austrians," he answered.

" They must be afraid of you," she said. " They were afraid of Napoleon, and now they're afraid of you because you've beaten him, I suppose. The hatred of mankind is the reward of greatness; I think he said something like that once; I certainly never thought of it myself! "

She smiled up at him, and impulsively he lifted the hand resting on his arm and kissed it. There was something unbearably moving in her loyalty to the man he had beaten. He saw that she was shivering.

" You are a very young man still, Sire," she said gently. " And now the world is yours, as it was his. . . . I never understood why men cared so much about such things. But now I'm old enough to have regrets. I missed the greatest opportunity ever given to a woman. I was loved by the greatest man of his age and I was too stupid to appreciate it. I lost him and I deserved to; but I can never quite forgive myself. Ah, it *is* cold! We'd better turn back."

"Madame," he said urgently. "Let me offer you my protection. I would like to guarantee your allowance and also the Queen of Holland and her children. I don't like to think that His Majesty King Louis might not be generous. Please allow me."

She smiled and nodded her head. "No wonder the French people look to you," she said simply. "You're a very good man, Sire. Far, far better than the Emperor ever could be. He used to be furious over my extravagance. I'm heavily in debt again, I'm afraid."

"Not from this moment," Alexander said. "You will leave all those affairs to me, Madame, and don't worry about them. There's the house now, we haven't far to go. You should have let me get a wrap for you. I'm afraid you may catch cold."

They walked indoors and sat with Hortense of Holland talking for some time. Josephine was herself again, smiling up at Alexander; the tinkling laugh, the pretty gestures had returned, there was no trace of the woman in the garden whose heart was bitter with grief and regret.

He rose at last and, bending, kissed her hand. He was surprised to find it icy cold.

She wished him good night, and her daughter curtsied to him, her eyes lowered; she had said very little during the evening. He was conducted to his suite and went to bed, to find his mind occupied with thoughts of Marie Naryshkin, of all sorts of women who had made love with him in the past. He was young, Josephine had said, and he was healthy and lonely again now that the strain of winning was passed. He turned in the big bed and lay still; his door had opened. He saw a woman standing on the threshold and couldn't recognize her; slowly he sat up. She came towards him, and he saw that under her long robe her legs were bare. She came to the edge and looked down at him. The pale face of Hortense Bonaparte softened as she smiled.

"Have I disturbed Your Majesty?" she whispered.

Alexander looked at her; the hand holding her robe together fell to her side and the covering parted.

"No, Madame," he said softly.

This woman was Napoleon's stepdaughter, once married to his brother Louis. They said she had been in love with Napoleon himself for years and was bitterly jealous of her own mother. This was the ultimate triumph. He smiled at her and held out his hand.

* * *

On May 28th Josephine, Empress of the French, died of the chill she had caught while walking in the gardens with the Czar. It was a fitting end for a woman whose career had been feckless and indiscreet; the gossips repeated it, adding details to the story, while Alexander was in Paris and the ex-Queen of Holland tried to put her mother's riotous affairs in order. She was as cold and silent then as she had been the night of Alexander's visit; when she heard the rumours that Josephine had betrayed Napoleon with his enemy, she only smiled. It was her own idea to go to his room. When she heard he had already promised money and protection to the household she burst out laughing. But it was worth it. Neither of them would ever forget that night; it was her revenge and his triumph, the revenge for the years she had loved Napoleon Bonaparte while he was fawning on her mother, and for her miserable marriage with a man she had detested. It was viler still, because she imagined Josephine to have designs on the Russian Emperor, and she meant to thwart her mother and get there first. It was worth it. Even if Josephine, dying of pneumonia a few days afterwards, looked at her as if she knew.

* * *

"Do you realize," the Grand Duchess Catherine said, "that we've hardly had a moment alone until now?"

Alexander smiled. "It's fortunate we're both good sailors and Frederick William isn't! I wonder what London will be like?"

"I'm longing to see it. They say it's black with fogs all the time." She leant over the rail of the ship which was carrying them to England on the State visit, and looked down at the dark water.

It was a still night, the Channel seas were calm, and brother and sister stood on deck, relieved of the King of Prussia's presence by a heavier motion of the ship.

The Prince Regent of England had invited Alexander, his sister and the King of Prussia to come to England before the Peace Congress opened in Vienna.

"I must admit," Catherine said, "I've never seen anyone more ridiculous than King Louis. And that Court! God's death, they might all have been embalmed since 1792! And I don't love them for their ingratitude to you. . . ."

"They're impossible," Alexander said angrily. "Apart from their insolence to me, which I shall never forgive, they're doing everything to antagonize the French people and infuriate the army already. We put that blockhead on the throne and now I suppose we'll have to keep him there. By God, it's as well Bonaparte's safe in Elba and the Austrians are guarding his son!"

"I heard the boy was delicate," Catherine said. "And the last thing Marie-Louise wants is to leave Austria and be Regent. No, they're safe enough as long as Napoleon's well guarded. Personally, I think he should have been put to death."

"In Russia, yes," Alexander answered, "but not in Europe. In Europe they have their own ways; we're only savages, my sister!" He spoke with bitterness.

"That was the attitude of that damned Bourbon who never fired a shot to get his throne; and Metternich, ah, how he hates me for making Louis King—and Talleyrand. A superior, treacherous snake. We fought Napoleon, we poured out our life-blood, destroyed Moscow, burnt our countryside, we chased him across Europe, and so did the Prussians. Oh, I could be relied on in war! But the peace is different. We might have some legitimate claims to make, and you can't have barbarians encroaching on Europe! But if they think they're going to deny me at the Congress, they're mistaken. The only one I trust is Friedrich Wilhelm."

"He's a fool," Catherine said contemptuously. "What of the English?"

He frowned. "I don't know yet. At least they struggled as hard as we did to beat France. They're ruthless people— look at their power! Bonaparte always said they were his one enemy, that as long as they remained he could never have peace. Or conquer the world, which is what he meant by peace. I don't know about England either . . . wait till we get to London. Oh, thank God for the fresh air. I felt I was stifling at times in the last few weeks!"

Catherine pinned back a wisp of hair which the breeze had blown across her face and smiled; the smile was mocking and reflected in the tilted eyes as she looked up at her brother.

"Success hasn't improved your temper," she remarked. "You're becoming quite the autocrat, my dear brother. I see that famous smile that used to irritate me so much less and less these days. God's death, at times you even frighten me! Don't be surprised our fond allies are not so fond of you now that the war is won. They're afraid of you."

He remembered the Empress Josephine saying the same thing, that night in the gardens at Malmaison. They were afraid of him. Afraid of his power.

"I only want Russia's due," he said angrily. "I want peace for the world. God gave me the victory; I know that. I know He wants me to secure the peace."

Catherine didn't answer. It was there again. 'God wants me . . . God gave me . . .' His simmering anger, his insistence that God was guiding him, that the men who resisted him were resisting the Almighty.

She glanced at him quickly, at the set expression, the lines cut into his forehead and at each corner of his mouth. There was a time during the war of 1812 when she had wondered if her brother were going mad, a time when he did nothing but pray and invoke the God he had never believed in before. He had lived a life of chastity after years of indulgence, but that phase had passed now, and she was sure the religious mania had gone with it.

Every gossip in Europe was whispering that the Czar had slept with Josephine at Malmaison—it was affirmed even more strongly that he had slept with her daughter Hortense as well. Catherine listened and laughed and thought cynically that he had become himself again.

But he hadn't; the sexual lapses hadn't changed him; he seemed able to ignore them and resume his rôle of prophet and arbiter as soon as they were over.

" If you could match Bonaparte, you'll match Talleyrand and Metternich," she said. " I wonder how he's enjoying Elba."

" They says he's content," Alexander said gloomily. " Some of his Old Guards followed him into exile, he's organized the whole island like a military camp. The reports say he's well and in excellent spirits, and I tell you Catherine, more people love that man now he's defeated than are grateful to me."

She shrugged. " Bah! " she said. " Twelve months from now he'll be forgotten as if he were dead. Let's go below and rest now. I want to look well before these English. Is it true the Prince Regent's mistresses are always old enough to be his mother? "

" I've been told so. We'll see soon and so shall they. They will see that a Czar and a Grand Duchess of Russia are a match for any Royal family in the world. I want you to look beautiful, Catherine. Wear Grandmother's rubies at the reception in London! Wear your most elegant dress! "

" Oh, I shall do you credit, Alexander," she promised. " I've no doubt they think it odd you brought me with you instead of Elizabeth."

" Their opinion doesn't interest me," he said stonily. " I do what I please. I'm allowing Elizabeth to come to Vienna for the Congress."

Catherine said nothing. She knew what had been said

about them in Paris; no doubt London would form the same
opinion. Her thwarted ambition derived a fierce pleasure
from the scandal her trip with Alexander was causing. He
had never let her have power on her own account, but shar-
ing his was almost as good.

She lifted his hand and kissed it, and he bent and kissed
her cheek.

"With your permission, I'll go below," she said.

"I'll follow in a few minutes. Go and rest, my sister."

When she had gone he leant against the ship's rail, staring
out to sea.

Alexander hated London. He hated the Prince Regent
and the members of the English Court, and his dislike was
brought to the point of explosion by his sister. Catherine
made enemies everywhere as soon as she arrived; the gloss of
the State visit was tarnished by her outrageous conduct to
the Regent's mistress, the middle aged Lady Hertford, her
sweeping arrogance and her unguarded tongue. She thought
London small, ugly and ridiculous compared to the splendours of St. Petersburg and the great Czarist Palaces; she
though the English cold and condescending to someone as
important as her brother, and the English ladies timid and
plain compared to herself; she disliked Castlereagh and
went out of her way to insult Metternich, who was also
visiting London at that time. And she aired her opinions
everywhere she went. Together brother and sister went
through the round of Balls and Banquets arranged in their
honour, causing comment by their intimate manner with
each other and offence by their disregard of protocol. The
Regent was polite to the Czar, but he conveyed the same
impressions as King Louis of France; he considered the
Russian a barbarian whom he was obliged to entertain, and
Alexander sensed it with increasing fury. He towered over
the fat little Prince, taller by a head than most of the English
courtiers, trying to hide his anger under the charm which
had once been so famous. As far as the younger and prettier
English ladies were concerned, he was successful, but
politically, the visit was a failure. His rage redoubled at

the sight of Metternich, always the polished courtier, making himself popular at the expense of the Czar and the Grand Duchess.

And Catherine, stung by the snubs she had invited, incensed him still further. " This miserable place," she said venomously, "dismal and cold even in June, with its ridiculous houses, small enough to fit into one floor of their own Palaces, and that gross idiot with his pomposity and his elderly frumps. Bah ! " She almost spat her contempt, and Alexander listened, his face reddening with anger and disappointment.

He had beaten Napoleon, he thought again and again, and this was his reward ! He left Dover on the 26th of June to return to Russia before the opening of the great Congress of Vienna which was to decide the peace of the world.

He arrived in Vienna in September, prepared to fight his former allies as bitterly as he had fought Napoleon.

CHAPTER NINE

THE Congress opened in Vienna on the 1st of October, 1814, in a setting of social brilliance reminiscent of Napoleon's zenith. Vienna was full; full of Kings, Princes, Royalties and nobles from every country in Europe; the crowded diplomatic staffs of the Allied Powers, attachés, equerries, secretaries, and spies and adventurers of both sexes. All fashionable European society poured into Vienna to watch the great world powers settling affairs, and to see men as famous as Alexander of Russia, Metternich and Talleyrand at close quarters.

Talleyrand was again Minister for Foreign Affairs, entrusted with the task of saving what he could for his defeated country by a King who disliked him and made the appointment to get him out of the Court. The Russians and Prussians were united in their demands. Poland for Russia and Saxony for Prussia.

Metternich and Castlereagh listened to these proposals and then decided they could have no better ally against the ambitions of their former allies than the Foreign Minister of France. Talleyrand made the utmost of the jealousy and dissension growing up between Austria and England and the bitter Autocrat of Russia, who was soon backing his demands with threats of war in language which was a warning echo of Napoleon.

A secret treaty was signed between England, Austria and France, promising mutual military aid if the Russo-Prussian claims were pressed too far. Talleyrand's place at the conference table had little relation to his country's defeat after a few sittings, and by the beginning of 1815 Alexander realized the extent of the barrier his allies had erected against his ambitions. The effect upon him was startling; the charm and gentleness disappeared completely; he shouted and raged, on one occasion threatening to throw Metternich out of the window after a particularly frustrating interview.

Only the Austrian Emperor's intervention prevented him forcing a duel on the Count. Metternich laughed at the uncivilized behaviour of the Czar behind his back and continued to avenge that broken promise not to restore the Bourbons. Alexander had smashed Austrian hopes of power, now he would smash Russia's; the Czar was proving himself nothing but a barbarian, he protested; he was claiming the victory over Napoleon for himself as if England and Austria had never taken part! It would be tragic indeed, he declared to the French and English Ministers, if their countries had made so many sacrifices to free Europe from Bonaparte's tyranny only to replace it by the domination of Alexander and his friends, the Prussians. Both nations were revealing themselves as aggressive and untrustworthy; their insolence was not only impertinent but unjustified. . . .

Napoleon's murderous victories were all conveniently forgotten, Metternich sneered; Jena, Friedland, Austerlitz, where the Czar himself had ridden for his life. . . . Austria had poured out men and money fighting Napoleon and never pressed the claims of the Empress Marie-Louise at the abdication. All Austria wanted was peace, and a just balance of power. Russia and Prussia would have to be checked.

Those first months of 1815 were restless and unhappy for Alexander. The Empress Elizabeth had joined him in Vienna; he hadn't seen her for nearly two years, and they met like strangers and immediately went their separate ways. Elizabeth avoided the Balls and Banquets as often as she could and stayed at her rooms in the Hofburg, while a round of gaiety and riotous spending engulfed the whole city. When she did accompany Alexander to an official function, they played their parts with dignity, the handsome Autocrat whose smile only warmed to women, and his stately wife whose marvellous jewels were the talk of Vienna. Afterwards they separated, and Elizabeth went to the arms of her old lover, Adam Czartorisky. Adam was on Alexander's staff at the Congress; it was years since he and Elizabeth had met, and neither had been faithful in the interval, but their passion for each other blazed up again, fanned more by sentiment than desire.

Both were unhappy, but Adam was becoming desperate as his hopes for Polish freedom faded with every word Alexander pronounced. His old friend had tricked him again, and he threw himself at the Czarina's feet, imploring her to forgive his desertion and take him back again.

Meanwhile Alexander alternated hours of prayer with fits of savage debauchery. His lapses in France were repeated in Vienna; the sensual fever raged in his blood, and it was only equalled by the turmoil of his mind. One of his first exploits was the seduction of Metternich's mistress, the haughty, beautiful Duchess of Sagan, who surrendered to him within a few hours, unaware that he was revenging himself on Metternich when he possessed her body, or that he left her to sink into a stupor of prayer that was almost a trance. He danced and dined and made love with the Viennese women of all classes, cynically judged them the most expert in the world, and then left them to agonize in wondering why God was allowing His servant to be treated so badly by the nations he had liberated.

In the last days of February he went to his wife's apartments in the Hofburg and asked one of her ladies, Mademoiselle Stourdza, to come to him. There was no lecherous intention; the Stourdza was a well-known mystic of unquestioned virtue.

Alexander received her alone; he had spoken to her before and found her simplicity refreshing.

"You must excuse this visit, Mademoiselle," he said. "I would be grateful for your company for a few minutes." His head fell forward into his hands and he stared gloomily at the carpet.

"I am tired and dispirited. Perhaps you can comfort me."

The young woman sat down and looked at him kindly.

"You need guidance, Sire," she said gently. "Would you like me to pray for you? I will pray now if you like."

He made a gesture of assent and closed his eyes; his head ached and his whole body felt paralysed by despair.

"God has abandoned me," he muttered to himself. "I destroyed Napoleon, all I want is to secure peace for the world, and everyone is trying to thwart me. I've told them it's not *my* will, but God's, but they don't listen!" His face flushed; he was beginning to get angry again.

He *should* have Poland, it was his due; it was God's reward to him for all he had achieved. . . .

The Stourdza had slipped to her knees; she was praying in whispers while he sat and watched her. The sight of her piety filled him with sickening shame; he thought of the hours he had spent with women of a different kind, and shuddered. He had tried to subdue that side of his nature, driven Marie away from him because he felt he must be worthy of the victory God would give him, and now, after that victory. . . . The Sagan, Princess Auesperg, Countess Orczy, and God knew how many more.

He was the grandson of Catherine the Great after all, the heir of the ' Messalina of the North '. He bowed his head again and began to follow Mademoiselle Stourdza's prayers. Later she asked if she might read him a letter she had received. He felt rested and calm for the first time in weeks, and he agreed at once. The writer was a Russian noblewoman of great prophetic powers; she had long foretold the Czar's victory and his selection by God to a wide circle of people, including Mademoiselle Stourdza, who was deeply impressed by her spirituality. This last letter mentioned Alexander in detail and foretold his triumph over the forces of the Devil.

" She is a most remarkable woman, Sire. I wish you would receive her; her powers of prophecy are really wonderful."

" She has just prophesied a victory for me over anti-Christ," Alexander said. " But I have already beaten him, Mademoiselle. He is at Elba. . . ."

Mademoiselle Stourdza rose and curtsied as he stood up to end the interview.

" Madame de Krudener is never wrong, Sire," she said calmly.

" I shall remember her name," he promised as he left.

*   *   *

On the night of the 6th of March the representatives of the five great powers met in the Austrian Foreign Minister's rooms, and after a long and angry meeting came to no conclusion. Alexander heard the report and then went to bed. He lay awake till dawn, slowly deciding that there was nothing for it but to take up arms against Austria and England. The peacemaker would have to unsheathe the sword again; the prospect filled him with fierce happiness and he smiled in his sleep.

He was drinking chocolate in his dressing-room, when his valet announced the Austrian Foreign Minister. Alexander looked at his watch; it was a quarter-past eight in the morning. He hesitated; last night he had been going to war; last night Metternich had managed to thwart his claims once again.

"What the devil does he want?" he exclaimed irritably.

"He says it's extremely urgent, Your Majesty. He has just left the Emperor Francis."

Could he have come to his senses at last? Was he going to agree to the Russian proposals? . . .

"Admit the Count," Alexander ordered.

Metternich was immaculately dressed as usual, but his face was expressionless and very pale. He bowed deeply to the Czar.

"My apologies for disturbing Your Majesty at this hour. Only the gravest development could excuse it. Unfortunately it does."

Alexander's eyes narrowed; in spite of the suave manner he knew that Metternich was shaken, and instinct prompted him to remain calm and prolong the other's suspense. Whatever had happened, they needed him again, he thought grimly.

"I believe you have just left the Emperor Francis," he remarked.

"I have, Sire, and he charged me to come straight to you."

Less than an hour earlier the ruler of Austria had stood trembling in his dressing-gown, wailing that if the Czar had been alienated too far by his treatment at the Congress, if he deserted them now, God help them all. . . . And for once Metternich respected his master's opinion. Without Alexander none of them had a hope of survival.

"Sit down, Count, and tell me of this grave development," Alexander said coolly.

Metternich remained standing, and one slim hand touched the satin stock at his throat.

"I received a dispatch from Genoa this morning," he said. "Napoleon has escaped from Elba."

*   *   *

The Emperor of the French landed at Cannes with a small following of his Guards who had travelled with him from Elba. Within a few hours their numbers were swelled by volunteers from every town and village within reach. The words flew ahead from mouth to mouth; "The Emperor's returned! *Vive L'Empereur!* To arms!"

Men rushed to join him; everywhere he went crowds cheered and wept with joy; the white cockade of the Bourbons was torn off and trampled underfoot, the tricolor of the Empire appeared in every hat and buttonhole. Everything was forgotten; the wars, the suffering, the acts of folly; they saw Napoleon and they rallied to him blindly. France was sick of the Bourbons already; she had recovered from the shock of defeat and decided her Emperor had been cruelly betrayed in favour of a gross old reactionary who was trying to reimpose the old régime as if the Revolution had never taken place.

Away with the Bourbons, who dared ignore the army which had made France so great. Away with them all! Thank God the little Emperor had returned, he'd smash the enemies of France, and bring her back to the forefront of the world!

Vive L'Empereur!

He rode among them, smiling and acknowledging one delirious reception after another, leading a growing army on the road to Paris. Wherever he stayed, crowds danced and sang under his windows, and the forces sent by King Louis to fight him simply arrested their Royalist officers and put themselves at his disposal. The veterans of his campaigns who'd been dismissed into civilian life, left fields and workshops, donned their old uniforms with tears of joy, and marched to join their General.

In Paris, Marshal Ney set out to capture him at the head of an army, swearing wild oaths against him to the King. As he advanced, he was met with the news of one Bonapartist victory after another; his men were murmuring, many deserted. Louis XVIII had pardoned him, but neither he nor the other Marshals were accepted by the old régime.

The Prince de La Moscova was still laughed at as the son
of a cooper, and the wife he adored was snubbed till she
refused with tears to come to Court. The sores of humiliation and neglect had been rubbed raw, and he missed the
presence of the Emperor in the stuffy Tuilleries as a prisoner
might miss the sun. Throughout the march he was gloomy
and quick tempered, fighting with all his strength against
the wild desire to break his word to the despicable King and
follow the beckoning drum-beat of the greatest soldier the
world had ever known.

Within a few miles of Napoleon's headquarters Ney
received a personal letter from him.

The two armies met at Besançon, and in scenes of
the wildest enthusiasm, Michel Ney flung himself into
Napoleon's arms. His entire force followed him.

Then Murat, who had gone over to the Allies in 1813,
declared for his Emperor and set out from Naples to conquer
Italy in his name. Everywhere men who had foresworn him
hurried to kneel and beg him to take them back. The
soldiers and politicians who had abandoned him because
they believed his ambition and obstinacy to be leading to
absolute ruin, forgot everything in the mad excitement which
greeted his return.

The old joy of battle and conquest surged up in them all;
released from the bondage of a feeble King and a reactionary
Government, the armies of Imperial France swept all before
them and bore Napoleon into Paris on the 20th of March.

Louis XVIII and his Court had fled into Belgium; the
Emperor was carried into The Tuilleries on the shoulders of
a hysterical crowd, and from there he issued a statement.

He was willing to honour the Treaty of Paris imposed
by the Allies after 1814, and he intended to reign peacefully
as a constitutional monarch, restored by the will of the
French people.

The powers at Vienna replied by declaring him an outlaw
and a public enemy, and ordered their armies to march into
France. Faced by the common danger, the allies solved their
differences in a few sittings; Alexander contented himself

with the Grand Duchy of Warsaw, Prussia accepted the Rhine provinces instead of Saxony, and a treaty was concluded by June 9th. But Alexander was not in Vienna on that date. He had left the capital and was at Heilbronn, waiting for his army. And at Heilbronn he met the woman who had prophesied his second battle with Bonaparte.

It was a night when he could not sleep; he had been pacing up and down his bedroom, unable to find his usual consolation in women or in prayer, when his aide-de-camp and confidant, Prince Volkonsky, knocked at his door.

" What is it? " Alexander asked irritably.

" Sire, there's a woman downstairs insisting on seeing you. I didn't like to send her away without your permission. . . ." Volkonsky paused; he had admitted so many ladies to the Czar during the past few months.

" I'm not expecting anyone," Alexander said. " Who the devil is she? "

" She says her name is Madame de Krudener, Sire."

De Krudener . . . the mystic who had foretold his victory over Bonaparte while Bonaparte was still at Elba. . . .

" Admit her at once! "

He tried to visualize her as he waited. She was middle-aged, he knew, a woman with a notorious past who had suddenly become religious after seeing one of her lovers drop dead in the street as he passed her window. But whatever she looked like she might bring him peace of mind; surely it was an act of God that she came just at that time, while the armies of Prussia and England were advancing on Napoleon's forces and his own troops were being rushed to join them.

The door opened again and Volkonsky appeared.

" The Baroness de Krudener, Sire."

A tall figure came slowly into the room; Volkonsky closed the door, and she threw back a long veil which covered her face. Even by the dim candlelight, Alexander could see his visitor was an extremely beautiful woman.

●　　　●　　　●

Madame de Krudener was singing to herself as she moved round the room. It was an elegant room, very well furnished, and it was full of flowers which she was arranging. She settled a large spray and stepped back to inspect the effect. It pleased her and she began filling another vase; the Czar liked flowers. He was coming to see her that evening and she prepared everything for him herself. Since that night at Heilbronn he visited her every day and had brought her to Heidelberg to be near him.

She sighed with contentment; he was paying all her expenses and had promised to take her to Paris with him after Napoleon's defeat. She knew Napoleon would be defeated, and she assured Alexander of it over and over again. They prayed a great deal; as soon as she knelt, the knowledge of her own beauty and eloquence affected her and enhanced her natural gift for acting. It was necessary, she admitted, to present prayer in an attractive way; so long as she saved souls for God the methods were not important, and since she had spent all her own fortune evangelizing, there was no harm in accepting money from someone as rich as Alexander. She had a large following of poor people whom she fed and clothed at her own expense, and later at the Czar's; her household was filled with reformed sinners like herself, and with some very unsavoury charlatans who made use of her name. Her gift for making vague predictions had won her a wide reputation and they were always nebulous enough to be made to fit any event of importance.

She told Alexander he was God's chosen among Europe's Kings, and roused his religious fervour to a pitch of frenzy; sometimes she took his hand while they knelt together and felt it trembling with emotion. She was fifty years old and more attractive than she had been at thirty.

She was blonde, with expressive blue eyes, a pale skin and a sensual mouth. Her figure was perfect and she dressed cleverly; the whole effect was sophisticated and yet simple; the woman of the world who had renounced the world. Emotional, passionate and a born exhibitionist, she believed in herself and her message for the world. The message was simple; brotherly love, peace, humility and constant recourse to the Scriptures. She also considered physical love the lawful result of close spiritual union, but she was shrewd enough not to mention that aspect to Alexander yet. It was necessary to attain a very high standard of mystical experience before the body completed the spirit's ecstasy. Some great event was needed, some overwhelming proof of her powers for the Czar. She had gone so far as to hint at a decisive battle within the next few days, while Alexander nodded; the armies of Wellington and Blücher must soon meet Napoleon in Belgium. . . .

She stood in front of a wall mirror and studied herself; at that moment she heard footsteps. Quickly she pulled the tiny muslin sleeves of her dress down, revealing her magnificent shoulders and the shadow between her breasts, then she ran to a sofa and lay down.

Alexander was not even preceded by a servant. He flung the door open and stood staring at her, his face flushed, too breathless with excitement to speak. She rose and hurried to him; he caught her hand as she tried to curtsy to him.

"Madame," he stammered, "Madame, your prophecy has been fulfilled! The news has just come through . . . he's been defeated, routed! We've won, Madame, we've won once and for all!"

"Oh, thank God!" She closed her eyes. "Glory to God! Where, Sire? No, no! Don't tell me . . . I know, I can see the place . . . Belgium. . . ."

"Waterloo!" he burst out. "You're quite right, it was at Waterloo!"

She caught both his hands in hers and pressed them eagerly.

"Kneel with me!" she urged. "Kneel and give thanks for your great victory."

It made no difference to him that Russian troops had taken no part in the battle. It was still his victory. The prophecy was fulfilled; he had beaten the anti-Christ again. Napoleon's army was scattered across the countryside; his

Old Guard were almost annihilated, fighting to the death to save their Emperor.

At the end, the traitor Ney and Napoleon himself had fled the battlefield for their lives.

He knelt, listening to the exultant tones of Madame de Krudener's voice; her words meant nothing to him, neither did his own when at last he joined her; it was a chant of triumph, the praise was for him, the glory of God was his glory. . . . The French defeated, the French who had ravaged his country, menaced his throne . . . the eagle standards which had once been carried into Moscow now lay in the dust, and Napoleon himself had ridden, as he himself had done at Austerlitz, in peril of his life from the victorious armies.

They looked at each other and began to rise at the same moment; they were still holding hands. Alexander's head was swimming, he felt superhumanly exalted, filled with the strength of ten men. For a moment they stood motionless, and Madame gazed up at him, her eyes brilliant with excitement, her full lips trembling. Neither knew who moved first, but the next instant they were in each other's arms, and the near-hysteria she had induced in him blazed up into furious passion. The borderline between religious ecstasy and eroticism was very narrow, as she knew from her own experience; weeks of emotional tension had brought the Czar to the edge of it, and the news of Waterloo had pushed him over. . . .

Outside the door one of Madame's penitents straightened up from the keyhole with a smile and pattered away to tell the rest of the household that Madame the Baroness had completed her conversion of the Czar and they would all be kept in comfort from then on.

*   *   *

" My Beloved Sister."

The words stared up at Alexander as he took up his pen for the third time to try and write the letter.

"I have a great deal to tell you and it is difficult to know where to begin. Firstly, Bonaparte has been exiled to an Island in the Atlantic called St. Helena. He placed himself under the protection of the English after Waterloo—truly God took away his wits, for they're more harsh towards him than anyone—and instead of giving him asylum in England they made him a prisoner when he boarded their ship the *Bellerophon*, and took him to this place. I have heard the island is very unhealthy and he is to be very strictly kept.

"Ney was arrested, and I regret to tell you that he was shot; so also was Murat. They were both brave men, and the executions have aroused great resentment among the people. The King returned to Paris after Waterloo, and the police are arresting so many Bonapartists it is being called the Bourbon Terror. Otherwise Paris is very gay and all the *émigrés* are back again."

He paused and dipped his pen into the gold inkwell. The King was in Paris, as he had said, but so was the English commander Wellington, and Wellington was the hero of Parisian society while the Czar of Russia was neglected. He couldn't bring himself to tell Catherine that; the humiliation stung too bitterly. He wrote about the review on the plain of Vertus instead.

"I held a military review on the 10th September at Vertus outside Chalons; one hundred and eighty thousand men and six hundred heavy guns. It was a most imposing and magnificent spectacle; if any of my allies feel inclined to underestimate my strength, they have only to remember Vertus!

"I ordered a Service of Thanksgiving for victory to be offered there the next day, and Madame de Krudener came with me."

He had taken a house for the Baroness in Paris, adjoining his own residence. After Heidelberg he found her indispensible, and she easily convinced him that their fiercely sensual relationship was lifted above the level of human sin by their spiritual condition. He prayed and read the Bible with her and discussed his plans for a world alliance based on Christian precepts. He gave her large sums of money for the support of her charities, and allowed her to rouse him and herself to that pitch of fervour which always ended in erotic excess. She began to speak of this aspect of their relationship as a rite in which she sacrificed herself, and for the first time Alexander's common sense was jarred. He was quite ready to believe he could reach peaks of spiritual experience through the senses, but there was nothing un-selfish about Madame's eager response. The pose irritated him, and then gradually Madame herself began to get on his nerves. He frowned as he wrote again.

" My proposals for World Peace were accepted and signed on September 26th. I have called it the Holy Alliance. Only England and the Pope have refused to sign. It is the finest achievement of my life, Catherine. Under its rules all nations can live at peace together, and if one commits aggression, the rest combine to punish it. All the disappoint-ment, the treachery and ingratitude I've experienced since I left Russia at the end of 1812 has been worthwhile, for this has passed my Allies' full approval. It is my plan and no one else's."

He underlined the last sentence heavily. That was Madame de Krudener's mistake; he had discussed the idea with her and she had promptly claimed the authorship. All over Paris the intellectuals who thronged her salon were saying that the Holy Alliance was her conception and not the Czar's original idea. The boast cost her his patronage. His pride, already outraged on so many points, was now hurt by this woman who owed everything to his generosity. She was making herself more and more ridiculous every day, and ridicule was catching; their relationship seemed to have quite unbalanced her, and his advisers were imploring him to get rid of her and her household.

The spell was broken, and he recognized the whole incident as eccentric and revolting; though he knew the Krudener to be as sincere as she was mad, her influence was at an end.

"You will have heard of Madame de Krudener," he continued. He could imagine Catherine and the pious Baroness. . . . "She is a good woman and her companionship has helped me a great deal. However I am leaving Paris tomorrow, my dear sister, and the lady is not coming with me, though I fear she expected to do so. I long to see you! Do you know, I shall be thirty-nine soon and I feel like an old man. . . . At last it is all over, my sister; I have accomplished what I promised you that night at Tver when we waited for word from Kutuzov. Do you remember that evening? I said I would drive Bonaparte out of France. Now he is driven out of Europe, out of the counsels of the world as if he had never been born. . . . It is done, and by December I shall be back in St. Petersburg."

*　　*　　*

Alexander returned to his Capital as the greatest conqueror in Russian history. The streets were packed tight with cheering crowds in spite of the bitter cold; lines of troops held them back as the Emperor passed, acknowledging the shouts and waving hands. A salute of cannon sounded as he entered the city and every church bell pealed. The procession halted at the Winter Palace and Alexander was met by his mother, his two younger brothers, his wife and his sister, waiting at the head of the whole Court.

"Ah, my son," the Empress Dowager cried, as she kissed his hand with tears of pride on her cheeks; he embraced her and paused to salute the Empress Elizabeth; for a moment their eyes met before he touched her cheek quickly with his lips and passed to Catherine Pavlovna.

They forgot protocol at that moment; she curtsied to him and then clung to both his hands as he kissed her warmly. Her mocking eyes were shining, she looked brilliantly beautiful with a high flush of excitement in her face.

"Hurry," she whispered, "I can't wait to hear everything. . . ."

He smiled and promised under his breath, thinking how

strange it was that they should once have been rivals, and that out of his conflict with Napoleon, this love for his irreligious, unprincipled sister should now be the strongest feeling in his life. He greeted his second brother, the Grand Duke Nicholas. Nicholas had grown even taller than he was himself, and he was good looking in a stiff way. Alexander remembered Catherine's jeering description of him as Nicholas bowed. 'I'll swear he's worked by clockwork!'

Then his youngest brother, the Grand Duke Michael; Michael had grown up in the last two years, he too was tall. Only the monstrous Constantine was absent; he had been given command of the new Polish Army and was adding to his reputation for committing atrocities in Warsaw. Alexander received his Ministers and Generals, foremost among them being Araktcheief in a magnificent uniform, so tight and heavy with gold braid that he bowed with difficulty. Everywhere, lines of Courtiers as he passed through the huge reception rooms, bowing, curtsying, watching him with pride. The atmosphere of popularity was so strong he flushed with pleasure. Thank God to be home again! Thank God he was out of Europe. At least his own people loved him and were grateful.

He went to his apartments to rest after the journey, and later joined his family for a State dinner. But he retired early, sent for his sister and gave orders they were not to be disturbed.

* * *

"When I heard of this Krudener creature, I couldn't believe it! Do you mean to say you did nothing but pray all the time?"

Alexander frowned. He had done his best to protect that damned woman's reputation and conceal their relationship while they were in Paris, but he had no hope of deceiving Catherine.

"Not all the time," he answered.

She laughed. "I thought not! Isn't it fortunate I'm a

pagan. Or perhaps it isn't, perhaps I miss something. . . .
You know, I've never considered kneeling in a seductive
posture; but in her case it was, is that it?"

"I suppose so," he said. "God knows! My intentions
were always good, but she made me feel uplifted,
excited. . . ." He stopped and passed his hands over his
eyes.

"I can imagine," Catherine said dryly. "I wish you were
an honest sensualist like me, it's so much simpler. Oh, I
can imagine what the Baroness was like! Thank God you
didn't bring her here." She looked at him narrowly. "Keep
away from those people, Alexander, they're dangerous.
You've always had a weakness for them. You need gaiety,
amusement, my brother. You look tired out."

"I am," he admitted. "I feel as if I'd lived my whole
life in the past three years. And it's not over yet; there are
more conferences to be held later on, and I·shall have to
go to them."

She glanced at him and then said quickly, "Then you'll
be visiting Europe again?"

"Oh, quite often I should think."

"Then if I were to marry again and live in Europe, we
could still see each other."

His head jerked up and he said sharply, "Marry? Live
in Europe? What do you mean?"

She met his angry look without flinching, only her hands
tightened on the arms of her chair.

"The King of Würtemburg wishes to marry me," she said.
"He's going to ask your permission and I want you to give
it." He sat rigid with anger and disbelief. Marry, leave
Russia . . . he had never for one moment imagined she
would want to leave him. His first impulse was to forbid
her to do anything of the kind. How dare she, he thought
furiously, how dare she want to marry Würtemburg as soon
as I've come home. . . .

"I have a right to re-marry, Alexander," she continued.
"I'm young and I made my first marriage with the man
you chose for me; he's dead and now I wish to choose for

myself. I've lived my whole life in your shadow and you
would never let me go; now I want to cast a shadow of my
own. I want to be Queen of Würtemburg."

He stared at her coldly. "Do you love him, is that it?
Why didn't you tell me?"

"I loved one man once." Her voice was harsh when she
answered him. "And *you* brought me the news of his
death. Do you remember? Würtemburg is a King. That's
why I want to marry him."

His anger was fading, giving way to surprise at his own
reaction. She was right; he'd forced George of Oldenburg
on her, and then told her Bagration had been killed on
the night he broke her heart and her spirit to save his
throne.

"Don't keep me here against my will," she said suddenly.

"You know I would never do that," he retorted. "I was
just selfish for a moment. I couldn't help thinking how
empty life will be without you here. Is there nothing I
can offer you to make you stay with me?"

The clock at her elbow chimed the hour; she turned to
watch the little golden figure of Cupid strike the bell with
his arrow; it was a French clock, brought back from France
by Alexander when he first entered Paris.

Then she looked at him and answered.

"Nothing society would allow. We should never have
been born brother and sister, Alexander. But we are, and
you had better let me go to Würtemburg."

It was said at last; the hints and scandals which had
followed them for so many years were acknowledged in
those few words. . . . 'We should never have been born
brother and sister. . . .'

Was that it? Was that the explanation for their hatred
and duelling for power in the beginning, for the queer
alliance which had grown up between them after Bagration's
death? . . . The letters he had written in the days when he
feared her, letters more fitting for a mistress than a sister.
. . . Did he say he adored her and thought her the most
fascinating creature alive because it placated her or because

he meant it in some terrible twisted way? . . . God knew!

He thought in horror: 'We played at this thing, she and I, for our own purposes, for reasons of deceit and power-lust, but though the world accused us, it's not true, it was never true! Of all the sins on my conscience, murder, concupiscence, treachery, infamy is not among them!'

She knelt beside his chair, looking up at him, and the flames from the fire shone on her face, highlighting the jutting cheekbones and the brilliant Kalmuck eyes. There was an expression in them that he had never seen before.

"You don't want me to go, do you?" she whispered. He was trembling; drops of sweat ran down his temples, he clung to the arms of his chair; he thought suddenly that his sister Catherine looked a little mad as she stared at him, her face a few inches from his own.

"You must let me go, Alexander . . ." her voice murmured. Something inside his head said clearly: this is damnation. Keep very still.

"I only want you to be happy," he said hoarsely. "You have my permission."

He sprang out of his chair and rushed from the room without looking back.

*   *   *

Catherine had left Russia when he went to see Marie Naryshkin. Marie had attended Court as usual, and at the State Ball given in his honour, he had asked her to waltz with him. He had noticed immediately her simple white dress, the clusters of flowers she wore in her hair and knew she had dressed to please him; he had always hated elaborate clothes. The implication touched and saddened him at the same time.

One afternoon he drove over to Dmitri Naryshkin's mansion to visit her. The lackey who admitted him, gaped, and then mumbled that the Princess was in the nursery, but if His Imperial Majesty would wait for one moment in the Gold Salon. The household was in a panic at the news of the Czar's arrival; the Naryshkin's Comptroller hurried forward, bowing and stammering apologies. "His Majesty was not expected . . . there had been no one to receive him properly . . . the Princess would be furious. . . ."

Alexander calmed him with a few words. It was a private visit, he insisted, and he wanted to be taken straight to the nursery; he would see the Princess there.

He was shown into a large sunny room, and kissed Marie's hand as she curtsied to him. A gaping nursemaid held a little girl on her knee; the child was wriggling and staring at the strange man with her mother.

"This is a great honour, Sire," Marie said. She had flushed and instinctively one hand flew to her hair; it was fluffed up and untidy, she wore a loose pink wrapper and house slippers.

"I had no idea you were coming or I would have been ready to receive you properly; you must forgive me. Won't you come downstairs, Sire?"

He smiled at her, but his eyes were on the child.

"In a moment, Madame; I find this domesticity quite charming. I believe you've forgotten to present Mademoiselle Naryshkin to me."

Marie signed to the nursemaid, who let her charge get down; she was frowning slightly. Alexander had never shown the slightest interest in her children till that moment.

"Sophie, come here!"

The little girl walked slowly towards them and her mother turned her to face Alexander.

"Curtsy to His Majesty," she ordered.

The child bobbed down, her face tilted up, her blue eyes open wide with curiosity. Gravely he took her hand and held it when she stood in front of him. Sophie. This was his daughter. He hadn't seen her since she was a tiny child, and there were two more reputed to be his; but there was no doubt about this child's paternity. For a moment they stood considering each other, and then Alexander smiled down at her.

"Good day, Mademoiselle."

Slowly the solemn face softened in an answering smile, the image of his own, and the small hand curled round his fingers.

"Good day, Monsieur."

"Sire!" corrected Marie.

"Sire," Sophie amended, and then laughed up at her father. He knelt and touched her cheek with his finger.

"How old are you, Sophie?"

"Nine, nearly ten, Monsieur." She paused and then asked sweetly, "How old are you?"

Alexander laughed and silenced Marie's reproof with a quick gesture.

"A great deal older than that, I'm afraid. What were you doing when I came in?"

"Playing with Mama," she said. "I have a new doll, Monsieur, would you like to see it?"

"I would indeed." He looked up at Marie and said, "Send the nursemaid away. I want to talk to you and Sophie alone."

The maid slipped out, walking backwards and curtsying; she fled to the servants' quarters with the news. The Czar himself, just like an angel out of Heaven, talking away to little Sophie! Oh, she would never forget that day as long as she lived!

When they were alone Alexander sat down and took his daughter on his knees; she showed him her doll and he admired it; when he kissed the top of her curly head she slipped one arm round his neck and squeezed him affectionately.

"Why have I never seen her?" he demanded of Marie, and she flushed.

"I see you so seldom myself, Sire, and I could hardly bring Sophie to Court!"

He was too absorbed with the child to notice her tone.

" Does she know who she is? "

" No," Marie answered. " I saw no reason to tell her yet. She wouldn't have remembered you and it would only have confused her. Why didn't you let me know you were coming; I could have made proper arrangements to receive you."

" I wanted to surprise you," he said. " And I'm very glad I did. I've made Mademoiselle Sophie's acquaintance, and that's very important."

" She'll be impossible after this," Marie said shortly. " God knows she's spoilt enough! "

He looked at her in surprise, and suddenly realized that she was jealous; he had found her carelessly dressed, playing in the nursery like any little *bourgeoise*, and he had given his whole attention to the child. No setting could be less romantic for a reunion between lovers. . . . He remembered the plain Court dress, the forget-me-nots in her hair; years before she had worn an identical costume during a State visit by the King and Queen of Prussia, and he had told her afterwards she was the most beautiful woman in the whole gathering. Poor Marie. And suddenly dear Marie, because she had given him this enchanting child.

" Let's go to your apartments," he suggested gently. " I should like some tea and we can talk."

He set Sophie down and she lifted her face to be kissed.

" Will you come and see me again, Monsieur? " she asked, and he promised that next time she should come and see him.

Then he took Marie downstairs and told her very kindly that he hoped she was happy and would allow him to be her friend. He also hoped he might see his daughter as often as he wished. She cried as he spoke of the happiness they'd known together in the past, and the necessity to keep it in a new relationship.

Friendship was a precious thing, he said, and kissed her lips like a brother, and she was not to weep, because he was still devoted to her. Only his mode of life had changed, not his affection or his gratitude, especially for the gift of Sophie.

She reminded him he had another daughter and a son, but he dismissed the mention of them.

"My father had a son," he said blankly. "A son can betray, he can covet. . . . I'm not concerned with my son. But take care of Sophie for me. You are both precious to me now."

CHAPTER TEN

FIVE years had passed since Waterloo, and the man Europe had entitled the Agamemon of Kings was sitting with Araktcheief in the Count's study at Gruzino.

Gruzino was the most efficiently run country estate in Russia, and the Czar had become a constant guest. It was peaceful and orderly; it gave him a feeling of secular calm that was the counterpart of the solace he found in monasteries. When he wasn't on a pilgrimage he often left St. Petersburg and stayed with the most powerful administrator in his kingdom, for that was what Araktcheief had become.

Alexander trusted the Count and admired him deeply; he confided everything to him, especially his urge to reform the Russian peasants' way of life. They were dirty and ignorant and hopelessly unmethodical; something should be done about it. He brooded on the memory of the clean Prussian towns and villages whose uniformity pleased him so much, and out of his talks with Araktcheief the horrible idea of the military colonies was born.

It was the answer! Alexander said excitedly; the answer to two pressing needs, the need to discipline the Russian and teach him the value of order, and the need to keep a large standing army ready for any emergency. The war with Napoleon had taught him that lesson. The plan was worked out and Araktcheief undertook to put it into effect.

All over Russia colonies were built where troops and

peasants were forcibly confined, all living and training under the harsh army discipline, their lives ruled down to the most intimate details of marriage and childbearing. The settlements were all identical, clean and inhuman; their wretched inhabitants combined the duties of labour and soldiering under ruthless supervision. Every contingency was covered by the rules, and when he read them Alexander couldn't imagine how their application could fail to make everyone under them happy.

But like Gruzino which he admired so much, the colonies were a hell of slave-driving and brutality, and Alexander knew as little about what really happened in them as he did about the methods used at Gruzino itself.

He spent hours kneeling in Araktcheief's private Chapel, where a marble bas-relief of his father was set into one wall with an inscription in letters of gold.

' My heart is pure and my spirit just, before You.'

Araktcheief was almost the only contemporary of Paul I who could truthfully claim that; if Alexander ever hoped to forget his own guilt and his servant's loyalty, he had only to enter that Chapel. . . . Only a man who knew how sick the Emperor was would ever have dared erect such a monument. But Araktcheief knew, and it was the secret of his power over Alexander.

They were discussing a revolt in the colonies that evening as they sat in the study. The room was an exact copy of the Czar's own study in the Winter Palace; every piece of furniture, every ornament was duplicated; he might have been in his own home. He was sitting in a high-backed chair before the fire, his head resting against his hand; he looked old and over-burdened.

"I can't understand why they should revolt," he said. "It's a perfect system; they're fed, housed, clothed, properly disciplined. Is there no sense in the human race? Do they prefer to live like dogs?"

Thousands of serfs penned up in the Chuguyev district had rebelled against the system and been put down after unspeakable cruelty.

Araktcheief raised his stiff shoulders.

"They will learn, Your Majesty," he promised.

They would indeed, after he had done with them, he thought. He would go to Chuguyev himself to supervise. . . . He might even take Anastasia with him; Anastasia would enjoy Chuguyev. She was a gipsy who had been his mistress for the past nineteen years; together they had organized the most revolting exhibitions of sadism Araktcheief could remember, but they had to be very careful not to go too far with the miserable serfs at Gruzino while the Czar was there. Anastasia was always kept out of Alexander's sight.

"I have done my best," he was saying. "Everything seems to end in failure."

Araktcheief began to comfort him; part of the man's horror was the fact that he was easily moved to tears, and they filled his eyes as he saw the Czar's distress.

"Ungrateful swine," he wept. "But what does one district matter? Everywhere else it's a great success. You haven't failed, Sire! Just leave this to me. I'll attend to it!"

That was what Alexander wanted him to say. Araktcheief would deal with it, as he dealt with most of his problems. It left him so much more time to pray for himself and for his sister Catherine.

Catherine. He stared into the fire, forgetting Araktcheief and the rebellion. He had to pray for Catherine. It seemed impossible even now that she was dead. She had died at the begining of 1819, but he still looked for a letter from her or thought he heard her voice or her quick step. It was an effort to remember there would be no letter, that her voice and footstep was only an echo in his own mind. She was dead and buried in Würtemburg, and he could do nothing now but pray to God that she might not be damned.

The idea of Catherine in hell had obsessed him for months after her death. He knew her, he cried, he knew how wicked she was, how jeering and unrepentant! Oh, God,

no one knew as well as he did! He remembered her face
the night of his triumphant return after 1815, and his own
blind panic to escape her and himself. He shuddered for
her and caught cold kneeling on the stone floor of his private
chapel praying for her soul.

He had given Araktcheief wide powers to govern in his
name; it was necessary since he travelled so much. Since
the end of the war he had journeyed all over Russia,
ostensibly inspecting his country, in reality fleeing from himself. He was alone. His sister was dead, he had no mistress,
his family were only interested in the succession; he had no
one in the world he could trust but Araktcheief and his
daughter by Marie Naryshkin, the child Sophie. He loved
Sophie. She was gentle and devoted to him; through her
he kept an affection for Marie alive, a feeling without passion
and almost without guilt. They were both older and life
had struck each of them down in different ways; Marie had
ruined her health and reputation, and he had come back
from France a sick, dispirited man.

Now when they met it was as Sophie's parents; Marie
had noticed that he seldom smiled except when he played
with his daughter.

He was thinking of Sophie then, half dozing by Araktcheief's fire. She loved him and looked up to him; God had
been merciful to let him have her; it eased the overwhelming sense of anti-climax that tormented him. He had beaten
Napoleon—by this time the other nations' contributions had
faded from his mind altogether—instituted the Holy
Alliance and restored hereditary monarchy to the world, and
his reward was this burden of personal despair. The strain
had broken him mentally; there were times when his mind
was fogged by religious mania, and his body was impotent
and worn out by self-imposed penances.

He still asserted his will with bursts of savagery and
then lapsed into apathy again or disappeared on a long
pilgrimage.

In the Europe he had liberated there was widespread
unrest; revolutionary parties in Spain, Italy and Germany

were clamouring for reform. And in Russia too. In Russia even the army was tainted. He scowled; Araktcheief would deal with that. How dare they presume to question his will when God had chosen him out of all the Kings as the instrument of His Divine purpose! But God was releasing him at last; he had felt for some time that his own soul's salvation was the first consideration now. . . .

Metternich had called another Congress to be held at Troppau; he must first attend it before he could make the initial moves in a plan known to no one. A plan which would mark him out for posterity as more than just the man who had beaten Napoleon. It had begun as a wish, become an idea, and developed into the goal of his life. The time had come to set the scenery in place for the last great act of his reign. After Troppau.

*　　　*　　　*

He was dining quietly one evening with the Empress Elizabeth, Araktcheief and Prince Volkonsky when he was told a courier had arrived in St. Petersburg with an urgent message. It was a dull meal, taken with the Empress for formality's sake, and Alexander welcomed the interruption; he had no idea what the news could be, unless another revolt had broken out in the military colonies. His face clouded with anger, and he said sharply, "Will you excuse me, Madame. A dispatch has arrived marked urgent, I'd better read it now."

He sent for the courier and opened the sealed letter at the table. Araktcheief, who watched everything he did, saw his colour change suddenly. He sat there holding the paper for some moments, until one by one the others looked up and saw that something had disturbed him so much his hands were trembling. Only Araktcheief dared to ask him.

"What is it, Sire? Bad news?"

Alexander lowered the letter and looked round the table. "News from St. Helena. Napoleon is dead."

The Empress Elizabeth was the first to speak.

"Oh, is that all! I was quite alarmed for a moment, Sir, you seemed so agitated. Well, thank heavens the world is rid of him."

Volkonsky and Araktcheief joined in the talk that followed; only Alexander was silent, still holding the letter, with his wife's casual words echoing in his ears. 'Is that all. . . .'

The Master of the World whose legions had been as invincible as the phalanxes of ancient Rome . . . the man he had engaged in the greatest struggle in history and finally overthrown.

Napoleon. His head was full of noises, thundering cannon, the tread of armies, their eagle standards shining in the sun, the clatter of great troops of cavalry. . . . The faint battle cry he'd heard for the first time at Austerlitz, "*Vive l'Empereur!*" as the hordes of French infantry advanced into battle. Bugles blew, French bugles, sounding out over the countryside on a sunny June morning, and a tiny figure in the uniform of his Old Guard stepped forward on the raft at Tilsit and shook hands with him. . . .

Erfurt, performances by the Comédie Française, State dinners, brilliant military reviews and the quiet talks with Talleyrand. . . . Talleyrand had fallen now. The King had dismissed him. . . .

Then in his mind he was back at Vilna, attending the Ball at Zakret when Balachov approached him, and he heard his whisper as distinctly as if he were at his elbow again.

"The French have crossed the Niemen, Sire. We are invaded!"

The smell of burning was in his nostrils; Russian towns and villages blazing under that hot summer sky of 1812 as he rode back with Barclay de Tolly's army; the smoking shell of Moscow, shaken by explosions as the invaders dynamited. The map in his study in the Winter Palace, pinpointed by lines of little flags marking the advance of the enemy and then turning back on themselves as the retreat began. The churches he had knelt in for hours, beseeching God's guidance; Catherine Pavlovna weeping for Bagration, leaning over his shoulder to study the maps with him, following the progress of the war with the intelligence of any man.

Names sounded like trumpet calls. Smolensk. Borodino. The bells of Moscow ringing the alarm for 'Fire'. Days and nights of blizzard, the worst winter for many years, and then the swollen waters of the Cresina and the voice of Kutuzov trembling as he described the shriek of terror that went up as the bridge collapsed and hundreds fell to death in the river. . . .

Kutuzov was dead; the brave Ney who had stood in Talleyrand's drawing-room pleading for the Emperor, Ney had fallen before an execution squad after Waterloo. So had Murat, who was almost a cavalry legend; Berthier, Napoleon's Chief of Staff, had thrown himself out of a window as he watched Russian troops crossing the frontier into France for the second time in 1815.

A British warship had sailed out across the Atlantic with Napoleon aboard, bound for an unhealthy little island which was to become the most famous prison in the world.

He suddenly remembered the face of Josephine, the pretty face of an old-young woman, as she looked up at him in the dusk of the rose garden at Malmaison.

" I was loved by the greatest man of his age and I was too stupid to appreciate it. . . ."

The thunder of those great wars dying down to a whisper in men's conversation, the veterans whom no one cared to listen to. . . . French eagles in the Russian Imperial Museum, cannon rusting in the countryside and children playing over them. A total of ten million dead.

The letter. . . . " General Bonaparte died at St. Helena after a painful illness. . . ."

General Bonaparte. That was the English. They forbade the members of his staff who followed him into exile to address him as anything else. General Bonaparte was dead.

" Oh, is that all! " his wife had said.

He pushed back his chair and left the room without a word.

* * *

Metternich had not seen the Czar since the last Congress at Aix-la-Chapelle two years before. When the Congress reassembled at Troppau he would hardly have recognized him. Alexander stooped, as if he carried an invisible load on his back; he was nearly bald, his splendid physique had gone. There was a distant expression in his eyes that startled Metternich; it gave the impression Alexander was not even listening to much of what was said. During one discussion the Austrian thought he saw the Emperor's lips moving as if he were praying, but he dismissed it as a trick played by his own eyes. But the change in Alexander was not only physical, he discovered that very quickly, and his shrewd brain saw endless possibilities.

His old adversary of Vienna was a sick man, impatient and lethargic by turns; he had become bitter and almost insanely suspicious; his great triumphs had turned sour and he was rapidly withdrawing from the world. The more he listened to Alexander, the more convinced Metternich became that his eyes had not deceived him when he suspected the Czar was praying at the conference table, for it was clear that the gay and brilliant idol of the Vienna salons had got religious mania. The influence of people like that humbug Madame de Krudener and the monks and mystics surrounding Alexander at home had culminated in this, the Count thought contemptuously; they had turned the Emperor into a crank and a tyrant as soon as he no longer had the common sense of his vixenish sister to protect him.

Metternich watched him carefully, and within a few days invited him to dine with him privately. He would be so grateful, he murmured; he was badly in need of the Czar's advice.

Much of the past still rankled where the Austrian was concerned, but Alexander accepted, reminding himself that it was Christian to forgive. Also he now found himself in general agreement with much of Metternich's policy.

The dinner was excellent, and the host exerted all his wit and conversational gifts to amuse the Czar, and gradually Alexander thawed. He laughed at Metternich's easy malicious comments on the other envoys, and accepted a good deal of courtly flattery without noticing how much trouble the Austrian was taking to gain him over. When they left the dining-room, brandy was served; the footman withdrew, and as soon as they were alone, Metternich began to discuss the problems which the Congress was debating.

"It's tragic to think this spirit of revolution is so widespread," he remarked. "After the miseries of Napoleon's wars and all our efforts for peace—especially yours, Sire— you'd think people would be grateful for stable government. I sometimes feel as if the system of monarchy has never been in greater danger!"

He glanced sideways at Alexander; he had heard about the revolts in the military colonies, the murmuring among even the nobility. Alexander shouldn't have let his officers mingle so freely in European society during the Napoleonic wars; they had developed a dangerous taste for freedom of expression.

"Why did the King of Spain give way?" the Czar demanded angrily. "Why did he give them a constitution and encourage every other malcontent to start making demands! Of course he's another damned Bourbon, and none of them are fit to rule!"

"The King of Naples also granted a constitution," Metternich pointed out. "If I hadn't been seriously alarmed over the situation, I wouldn't have suggested this Congress so soon after Aix-la-Chapelle. Secret Societies are spreading everywhere, Sire. We had to restore the Bourbons to their throne otherwise any adventurer could follow Bonaparte's example and make himself King." He leaned forward.

"We re-established them, and unless we support them

against this new Jacobinism, revolution will sweep Europe. And sweep more than the Spanish and Neapolitan monarchs off their thrones! "

Alexander understood his meaning only too well. Jacobinism, atheism, revolt . . . all revolutions began that way and culminated in the destruction of the monarchy. It was all the result of free-thinking, of this ignorant worship of liberty, of which he himself had been guilty in theory if not in practice when he was young. God, the folly of it, the bad example! That was another error he must purge. . . . Freedom is an evil, he thought violently, and startled Metternich by saying so.

" Even in Russia I've found these damnable tendencies," he admitted. " But I've done everything in my power to stop them, and I shall do even more! God makes a King responsible for the protection of his people. I've always guarded that trust; it's every sovereign's duty to stamp out this moral disease! "

" You've given the world the solution, Sire," Metternich said eagerly, " in the Holy Alliance! You said all nations should guarantee the rights of others and defend them if necessary. And I believe we have the right to protect the people of Spain and Naples from these revolutionary scum. I believe we should support their anointed rulers by force! "

He waited; this was the object of his invitation and his attempts to make friends with Alexander. He wanted him to authorize the invasion of any country which dared adopt a constitution.

The man who had protected the French people from the fury of their conquerors and interceded for political prisoners during the Bourbon Terror after 1815, now turned to the architect of reaction and said hotly: " Certainly, Count. The maintenance of Christian sovereignty is the prime purpose of the Holy Alliance! It's the plain duty of every Christian nation to protect religion and uphold the authority of Christ's anointed Kings. You can rely on as many Russian troops as you wish! "

Metternich bowed his head in acknowledgment and smiled. How easy it had been after all. . . . Prussia and France would follow the Czar's lead, and since he dictated Austrian policy himself, only England's reaction was in doubt.

"Russian troops won't be needed for Naples, Sire. We can deal with that. May I assume you support this idea, then?"

"With all my heart," Alexander answered.

"We might call the resolution something special . . . the Protocol of Troppau, perhaps?"

"An excellent suggestion, my dear Count. We shall call it that."

*   *   *

After Troppau, the Congress met again at Laibach. Austrian troops invaded Naples and Piedmont where a similar crisis had arisen; the constitutional Governments were abolished and full power restored to the Kings. The reformers were arrested and executed in hundreds. So, within six years of its inception, Alexander's plan for Christian rule in Europe had become the instrument of wholesale oppression

The only country who refused to join it and disposed of any idea that she might be bound by its terms, was England. And England was too powerful to be made to bend. By then Alexander had returned to Russia, and the misery and turmoil of unhappy Europe interested him less and less. His own country preoccupied him to such an extent that however opprobrious Metternich's suggestions for keeping the peace, he agreed almost without reading them. Let Metternich settle Europe's problems; he had his own to resolve, the dangerous and so often bloody issue of who should inherit the throne of Russia.

As early as 1819 he had made his choice; he merely began legalizing it. His younger brother Nicholas was to succeed him; Nicholas was obstinate and stupid, but he was reliable and married to a German Princess who was a model of wifely obedience. Sometimes Alexander laughed at the thought of the *bourgeois* respectability of the two people who would mount the thrones of his turbulent, bloody ancestors.

What a dull Court it would be after the splendours and catastrophes of his own reign! He had told Nicholas his intention and not been deceived by the humble pose adopted by the Grand Duke and Duchess. The more they protested their unworthiness the more certain he became of their delight.

But Constantine, Nicholas had asked, his rigid mind straining to overcome the obstacle of a succession which deviated from the rules. . . . Constantine was the rightful heir! On his way to Troppau Alexander saw his brother, and watched the grotesquely ugly features twist with fright when he mentioned the succession. " No. No! " he pleaded. He didn't want to be Czar, he had no ambition to follow his glorious brother . . . Nicholas was the one. . . . Alexander reassured him, knowing that behind his reluctance lay the memory of Paul's ghastly death. Weeping with relief the Grand Duke resumed his cruelties and debaucheries while his brother went on to the Congress. Later he was able to tell Nicholas it was settled; Constantine was only too eager to escape the awful destiny of ruling Russia. While he told the Grand Duke and Duchess, he thought how different it would have been had Catherine Pavlovna lived! Everything would have been hers; he could have made her a gift of the Crown she had coveted so fiercely, and then left Russia in the hands of a successor worthy of him. And what a reign hers would have been!

But she was dead and it was just a dream. . . . It must be Nicholas, as soon as affairs were put in order and his beloved daughter Sophie secured in a suitable marriage.

*   *   *

Alexander's spiritual adviser was then the famous visionary and ascetic monk Photius, head of the Yuriev Monastery in Novgorod. Photius was a wild-eyed fanatic, emaciated from fasting and self-discipline, who made prophecies and held conversations with God in his cell; he also had fits and hallucinations, and Araktcheief introduced him to the Czar. He was a mixture of charlatan and lunatic; his extraordinary personality and blistering denunciations of his sovereign as an idolater and a sinner brought the astonished Emperor to his knees at their first meeting. From that moment Photius's ascendancy was assured, and Araktcheief's power increased through the medium of his protégé. Whenever Alexander was troubled he sent for Photius or went to the monastery in Novgorod. There he knelt for hours without food or water, absorbed in passionate prayer, and Photius assured him that his daughter Sophie would be cured of her long illness.

He was sitting in her room in the first months of 1824, holding her hand and trying to convince himself that she was better. The active, high-spirited girl of a year before now lay all day on a couch by her window, coughing into a handkerchief. Alexander noticed the high flush on her cheeks and his heart lifted with hope.

"You're better, my dearest, aren't you?" he said eagerly. She looked up at him and squeezed his hand.

"Much better, Papa. I'm always better when I see you. Papa, I want to ask you something."

"Anything, my Sophie, anything!" he promised.

"Do you think I shall be able to go out for a drive soon? I haven't been out for so long, and it's spring now and quite warm. Will you ask Mama for me? She worries and fusses so much, but I'm sure she'll listen if you ask her!"

"I'll ask her," he said. "And you shall take your first drive with me! After the Guards Artillery Review we'll drive down to Tsarske Seloe. How would you like that?"

"Oh, I should love it! It's the most beautiful palace in the world! Let's do that, Papa; promise me we'll go to

Tsarske Seloe when I'm better. We might even stay there for a little while . . ."

"For as long as you like. It's your home too, my darling child; all these palaces are your homes. You're a Romanov, Sophie; never forget that."

"I don't," she said sweetly, "but it only really matters to me because it means that I'm related to you. Sometimes I feel selfish because I'm glad you don't love Emmanuel or Zinaida as much as me."

He shrugged at the mention of the other two children Marie had borne him. "I'm fond of them too, but you're my favourite."

She smiled up at him, and he thought how pretty she was, and how the Romanov blood had come out in her. It was there in the set of the little head and the vivid eyes; she had the sunny temperament of the Great Catherine herself, and the bodily beauty of Marie Naryshkin, before the disease ravaged through her. He noticed that the hair curling over her forehead was damp with perspiration; he wiped her brow with his own handkerchief. She must get well! She must! He'd given alms in her name, ordered prayers to be said for her in monasteries all over Russia; Photius himself had petitioned God. . . . Everything good in himself he saw personified in the purity and gentleness of the eighteen-year-old girl; she was his sole justification for the years of adultery with Marie, for the sin and passion of that long, ill-fated love affair. He had sinned more with Marie than with any other women, even the well-bred sluts of Viennese society, because with Marie he had experienced the most breathless and consistent pleasure. Sophie was the result of that early passion before indifference and misunderstanding embittered their relationship. If God took Sophie from him, it could only mean he had not yet been forgiven. . . .

He had planned a splendid marriage for her, a semi-royal marriage with a suitor worthy of the Czar's natural daughter, while the smiling child who had climbed on his knee in her nursery grew into an accomplished, lovely girl. Whatever

happened in Russia or the outside world, he could escape the
ugliness and disillusion of it all by going to see his daughter
and pretending for a few hours that he was not the Czar.
He used to sit with his eyes closed, listening while Sophie
played the piano and Marie sat on the opposite side, sewing,
and his thoughts turned again and again to the day Nicholas
would succeed him. How would he wear his great brother's
mantle?   Well, Alexander decided ruefully; imagination
would never lead Nicholas to make his mistakes. Russia
would be safe with him, he had been born an autocrat,
he would never need to learn. . . . When Nicholas was Czar
. . . after Sophie's marriage, of course.

But there would be no marriage for Sophie now.

" Dear Papa, please don't cry! "

She was looking up at him, one horribly frail hand reaching out to him.

" Really, I'm better. And we're going to Tsarske Seloe,
just as you promised. You mustn't cry for me," she pleaded,
and in her distress the high colour and big hollow eyes were
terrifying in the thin face. " I'm awfully happy, Papa. Even
if I don't get well, you mustn't cry. . . ."

She stopped and began coughing violently; he held her in
his arms, helpless and horrified until the spasm stopped.
Then he ran to the door and flung it open, shouting for
Marie. Slowly Sophie Naryshkin opened her eyes and
breathed deeply. She turned her head and looked out of
the window; it was May and the trees outside were flower-
ing. It would be warm in the spring sunshine, warmer still
at Tsarske Seloe where her mother had often taken her to
see her father. It *was* beautiful, so vast and full of lovely
things; strange to think the Czars and Czarinas who'd built
and furnished and altered it were her own ancestors, that
the Emperor himself was her father. She smiled as she
thought of him, and then bit her lip as it quivered. She
was a Romanov, and they were brave. . . . But she would
have liked so much to go to Tsarske Seloe with him. . . .

*   *   *

"Alexander."

Slowly he raised his head and saw his wife standing in the doorway of his study; she hesitated for a moment and then came towards him.

"Please don't be angry with me for intruding. I just wanted to tell you how sorry I am about Sophie."

He tried to speak normally; in all the years of a nominal marriage he had never shown his feelings to this woman, this stranger who came now at one of the most wretched hours of his life.

"Thank you, Elizabeth. It's good of you to come."

She shook her head. "I was afraid you might not want me, but I heard how upset you were. . . ." She shivered and said quickly, "It's so cold in here! Let me ring and have the fire built up. You'll be ill if you sit here like this."

"I wanted to be alone," he said. "When I saw her I couldn't believe she was dead, she looked asleep. . . . I can't stop thinking about it. It's God's judgment on me, Elizabeth!" He hid his face in his hands and burst into tears. The next moment she was on her knees beside him, her nervousness forgotten. Gently she laid her hand on his arm.

"She was very sick," she whispered. "Nothing could save her, and remember she's in Heaven now."

"That's what Photius tells me," he mumbled.

"You mustn't let anyone see you like this," she said. "I heard how brave you were when they told you, how you reviewed the Guards and gave no sign; you've got to be brave now. . . ."

Within a few minutes a fire was blazing and some brandy was brought to them on the Empress's order; she had taken control of the situation for the first time in their married life. When they were alone she made him sip the brandy, and drank a little herself; the candles were lit and the room grew very warm. He leaned back in his chair, and without speaking, took her hand in his; she sat with him quietly, glancing round the room she had seldom entered for more than a few minutes during the last years. It was a comfortable room, dominated by the huge desk, everything in it was heavy; the furniture, the deep-red curtains drawn across the tall windows, the ornaments, the massive silver candelabra which stood on his desk, and the portrait of Catherine the Great which hung the full length of one wall. Some of the most important hours of his life had been spent in that room, and he had taken refuge there after the death of his daughter.

"You're being very good to me," he said suddenly. "Few women would share my feelings over a child which wasn't theirs."

"She was a sweet child," Elizabeth answered him. "And you loved her. No one can understand better than I can what you're suffering. I too lost my daughter. . . ."

He struggled to remember, and then realized; the child born of her lover Okhotnikov, prematurely born and dead in so short a time, thanks to the shock of the cornet's murder. She had come to him once, asking him to protect her against Constantine, and he'd sent her away. . . .

How much she must have suffered in the years since he had married her! Parted before they ever had a chance to come together, driven to the Countess Golovine and then to Adam . . . paying for thirty years for his adolescent inexperience and the self-disgust of that first night with his grandmother's procuress. . . . May God forgive him! But how could He? His sins were numberless, his guilt beyond expiation. . . . He should have lived chastely with his wife, his good, gentle wife whose failings were nothing compared to his own. . . . He thought of Marie with loathing, a subconscious loathing which emerged the moment Sophie died. But for Marie and the fulfilment she had given him he might have treated Elizabeth less shamefully. . . .

"Life has been sad for us both," the Empress said. To her surprise he raised her hand to his lips and kissed it.

"Do you remember when we first married, Elizabeth?" She flushed at the question. In all her life she had been unable to forget.

"I remember, Alexander."

"We should have been happy," he said slowly. "Have you ever wondered what went wrong with us?"

"I spent many years of my life wondering that," she answered, and her voice shook.

"It was mostly my fault. I was selfish with you and you were very young. . . . We were foolish, Elizabeth, and had no one to guide us properly. But it's different now."

She stayed very still while he talked, her heart racing in the disturbing way it did lately if she became upset or excited. He was distressed and nostalgic, she told herself quickly, only a fool would interpret his words as anything more.

"We're not young any more," he was saying. "We've both made mistakes and wronged each other. . : ."

Adam. Thoughts flew through her mind; Adam and her desperate love for him and the brief reunion at Vienna after years of separation . . . the young Okhotnikov, the gentle lover who was murdered because she favoured him, the loneliness and humiliation of her life; her own reflection in the mirror, old and prematurely faded.

"Elizabeth, will you forgive me for making you unhappy?"

"I have nothing to forgive," she stammered. "You are the one . . ." The colour was rising in her face and neck; a tiny pain needled her heart, a pain of happiness, she thought hazily. Happiness and struggling hope.

"Then we forgive each other," he said eagerly. "The past is wiped out between us. Elizabeth Alexeievna, will you come back to me?"

For a moment she sat without moving or answering, feeling as if a bond which had become part of herself was suddenly splitting open. It parted then, and the full force of her love for him overwhelmed her, the love which had never died at all.

She was on her knees beside him, pressing his hand to her lips when he smiled down down at her. "Will you? I need you very much."

"Oh, Alexander! How I've prayed that one day you might ask me. . . . I always loved you, always. . . . And now I'll make you happy."

"My dear wife," he murmured, and for the first time in over twenty years he kissed her on the mouth.

Elizabeth's passion only slept; it woke then as he touched her, with the fever of the young girl whose inexperience and sensuality had once repulsed him. She was his wife and they were reconciled, but the man who held her in his arms and went to her room that night was a man in whom passion was dead; a sick, tired man, who laid his head on her breast and went to sleep. And in the darkness she submitted to this unspoken condition; her disappointment faded in gratitude for an end to the estrangement. Though he never indulged in sexual relations with her, she did her best to make him happy, and he seemed happy for the first time in ten years. They spent quiet evenings together, the Empress sewing while one of her ladies read to them aloud. Often she looked up and exchanged a smile of understanding with her husband, while the Court discussed the situation with amazement and giggled behind their backs. The hero of 1812, the fabulous sensualist who'd followed his grandmother so faithfully, was actually settling down to a stolid domestic life with his own Consort! It was almost indecent, the wits declared, until it became known that the idyll was platonic. The Court physician, Sir James Wylie, retorted that the Empress's heart was weak.

In the first months of 1825 she became very ill; she fainted and complained of an agonizing pain in her breast; in the same spot, she thought one night, which used to ache for Alexander when she was a young woman. . . .

He kept a long vigil by her bed, patting her cold hand, and his presence gave her strength.

"I need you," he insisted, and she struggled against death for his sake more than her own.

By summer she was convalescent at Tsarske Seloe, and Alexander returned from one of his inspections of the countryside to confer with Sir James Wylie.

"She's better, Sire," Sir James admitted. "I must say I
didn't expect her to recover, but she has great will power.
I believe her devotion to you really kept her alive."

"What do you recommend for her complete recovery, Sir
James?" the Emperor asked.

Wylie hesitated. He was a shrewd man who'd served the
Imperial family for many years, and was in no doubt about
who really cared for whom. "Poor lady," he used to mur-
mur, watching the Empress convulsed in one heart attack
after another, and he said it to himself at that moment as
he prepared to answer Alexander. "Poor lady, if he knows
the truth perhaps he'll be extra thoughtful to her. . . ."
Pity made him unusually abrupt when he spoke.

"There'll be no complete recovery," Wylie said. "Forgive
me for being blunt, Sire, but the Empress cannot live long.
With great care her life might be prolonged a little, that's the
most we can hope for. The first requirement is a change of
climate for the winter. She needs to go somewhere where
it's warm and mild. I can't answer for it if she spends
another winter in St. Petersburg."

Alexander had walked away and was looking out of the
window.

"I imagined you might advise a change, Sir James. I
shall certainly take the Empress out of the Capital this
winter. By September we shall be on our way to Taganrog."

"Taganrog!"   The word escaped Wylie like an oath.
"But Good God, Sire, Taganrog's on the Sea of Azov, it has
a vile winter climate! Why the winds alone will be enough
to kill . . ."

"Taganrog will be most suitable," Alexander interrupted,
and suddenly Wylie left his protest unfinished.

"We are going to Taganrog in September," the Czar continued. "I have already told the Empress and she is looking
forward to it. You may go now, Sir James."

CHAPTER ELEVEN

JUST before dawn on the 13th of September, a carriage drawn by three horses reined in at the barrier before the city of St. Petersburg. The hood was lowered, and a tall man dressed in a plain military uniform and greatcoat, stood upright and looked out over the scene.

The night was very still; the dark tide of the Neva lapped the stone parapets, a few lights twinkling in the houses along the bank were reflected in the black water; sentries stamped and marched along their beats under the city walls; the sharp spire of the church built on the St. Peter and Paul Fortress stood out in the sky, outlined against a faint glow where the night was fading.

Petersburg. The great Admiralty building, the splendid Nevsky prospect with its lovely mansions, the trees and parklands, the towering churches and the dazzling façade of the Winter Palace, rising like a cliff from the banks of the great river. Petersburg, the monument of a crazy, epileptic Czar who'd built it on a foundation of sinking marshland and the bones of thousands of serfs. Alexander Pavlovitch, Czar and descendant of Peter the Great, stood for some moments looking down on the city which had been the scene of so many of his triumphs, the city which stood in all her beauty, unscathed by the war which had destroyed Moscow. Petersburg, untouched and unoccupied; the monument to his victory and the defeat of the French.

He prayed for his Capital of the North, for God to protect it and its people, because God knew now that he would never see it again. In the monastery of St. Alexander Nevsky, he had just attended his own Requiem, and heard the monks sing a solemn Te Deum in thanksgiving for his glorious reign. He had knelt alone in the vast church, joining in the service for the repose of his own soul, with the doors bolted and the plain carriage waiting for him outside, and fervently offered his past life with all its imperfections to Almighty God.

The reign of Alexander I was coming to an end. He sat down and gave an order to his coachman. The hood was raised and the horses whipped; dawn was coming up behind St. Petersburg as the carriage turned on the road that led southwards to Taganrog.

"Whatever possessed them to come to this place!" Sir James Wylie exclaimed. "There's not even a proper house for them. These quarters are cramped and the winter winds will be enough to kill the Empress!"

The Russian Court Doctor, Tarasov, shrugged.

"The Czar likes informality," he explained. "They live a simple domestic life here, and the Empress and he seem very happy."

"Hmm," Wylie snorted. "The Empress isn't well again, and the Czar's leaving for this tour of the Crimea to-morrow; I'll admit *he's* taken a new hold on life, I've never seen a man so pleased with himself! Why the devil he's taking us on the tour with him when it's the Empress who needs attention, I can't imagine!"

"The Empress has her own physician here," Tarasov said quickly. He disliked the conversation and dreaded being overheard. Wylie had a loud voice and tactless opinions; he curbed neither, and Tarasov's long experience of the Czar warned him that he was planning something, and that he and Wylie and Taganrog were all part of that plan. He knew as well as the Scot that the Empress was a dangerously sick woman who needed more than one doctor to attend her, but he also knew better than to call attention to the fact.

"If you'll excuse me," he murmured, and hurried away.

Wylie stood looking after him. "Will ye look at him scuttling away like a scared rabbit!" he demanded aloud, lapsing into his native accent. "There's some damned mystery going on here!"

*   *   *

"Try not to be away too long, Alexander; you don't know how much I shall miss you."

Alexander bent over Elizabeth Alexeievna and kissed her.

"I won't be long, my dear. How are you feeling?"

"Much better," she smiled at him. He sat beside her and she slipped her arm through his. It was true; she felt almost well as long as he was with her and prolonged this platonic honeymoon which was happier than any other relationship she had ever known. She wanted so often to tell him she loved him, was indeed in love with him, but some instinct advised against it. He was a strange man, her husband; if anything upset him and things changed between them, she would never be able to bear it again. . . .

"What have you been doing to-day?"

"Walking through the town," he said. "You know, it's a wonderful feeling, Elizabeth, just to be able to walk down the streets like any ordinary person . . . nobody recognized me," he added in an odd voice. "Nobody. I could live here or anywhere far from Moscow or Petersburg and no one would ever know who I was."

"It wouldn't be possible," the Empress said. "People in our position often envy their subjects their private lives, but we couldn't exchange; I could never forget my birth and live in some miserable little town without an equal to speak to; neither could you."

He stared over her head.

"I suppose not," he answered. "As you say, my dear, it wouldn't be possible. It's just a dream, that's all. A King's dream. . . ."

"More like a nightmare if one did it," Elizabeth retorted. "Tell me, are you looking forward to this Crimea trip?"

"Very much," he said cheerfully. "Very much indeed. I hope I shan't ever have to make another."

*   *   *

He left Taganrog on November 1st, and made an extensive tour of the Crimea, reviewing his fleet at Sevastapol, visiting towns and villages, inspecting hospitals, churches and arsenals. The melancholy of the past years seemed to have left him; his carriage was upright and his old charm shone forth, recalling that splendid figure of repute, 'the autocrat of waltzes and of war' as Byron called him. This line was quoted all over Russia; the rest of the poem, a bitter attack on Alexander's suppression of liberty and the tyranny of the Holy Alliance, was not printed.

He found kind words for everyone, even the most pompous officials were received graciously. Nothing was too much trouble, no ceremony too long or journey too far; his temper, usually so capricious, was even and cheerful. He seemed a happy and contented man, determined to fulfil his duties as well as he could. He looked out on his fleet with tears of pride, saying a private farewell as he had done to his beloved St. Petersburg. He was leaving it all, and with it a tradition of glory which would live on long after he was dead. His great antagonist was dead, and legends were gathering like mourners round the grave at St. Helena. Now he too must die, the public death of a Czar of All the Russias.

Everyone who saw him agreed on one impression of him afterwards. He combined dignity and grace with the most striking humility.

When his duties were over for the day, he prayed with ecstatic concentration, and on the 15th of November God solved one vital problem for him. The courier, Maskov, who brought State papers from Petersburg, was killed when his carriage overturned on the road. The Emperor sent Tarasov to find out if the man were really dead; when the doctor confirmed it, the Czar wept for him, but not before

Tarasov had surprised an expression of excitement on his face.

The following day both Wylie and Tarasov were summoned to Alexander's apartments, where they found him tossing with fever; Wylie, who knew his tendencies to run high temperatures, forecast another outbreak of erysipelas on his leg and ordered him to stay in bed. But Alexander refused; he insisted on reaching Taganrog by the seventeenth. He had promised the Empress, he said, and they dared not oppose him. He travelled the last miles to Taganrog in a closed coach, wrapped in rugs, and lay back dozing against the cushions, complaining that he felt very ill. Behind him, the body of the humble courier took the same road.

* * *

"You really shouldn't talk, when you're not well," the Empress protested. She had been sent for, and was sitting by Alexander's bed; he had been back in Taganrog for several days; neither his wife's pleas nor the warnings of his doctors had prevented him from getting up each day and dealing with his papers. His fever continued and he complained of pain and sickness, but the erysipelas had not appeared and neither Wylie nor Tarasov could diagnose his illness.

"Elizabeth, sit down here beside me," he said gently. He noticed how tired she looked, and for a moment he hesitated. A shock, Wylie had warned him. . . . So he had to protect her as well as enlist her help.

"Sit down, my dear," he repeated. "I have something I must tell you."

At the end of an hour he had finished and they sat together, Alexander smiling and holding his wife's hand, the Empress white-faced and trembling. She looked at him once and seemed about to speak, but he said quietly, "Now send Volkonsky and Sir James to me. And you had better go and rest now."

Both men remained shut in with him for some time; then they left together and walked down the short corridor leading away from the Emperor's rooms. His lifelong friend, Volkonsky, spoke first.

"Where's Tarasov? Why wasn't he sent for?"

"Tarasov's busy," Sir James replied. "He's been busy since we came back to Taganrog. He's been embalming the body of that courier who was killed."

*   *   *

On November 21st the funeral of the courier, Maskov, took place in the local cemetery with military honours, and a large wreath with the Imperial Crown and the Emperor's initials was placed on the grave. Long afterwards the bearers remembered that the coffin was surprisingly light, for Maskov was a big man, as tall and of the same build as the Czar himself.

*   *   *

On the evening of the 26th a footman on duty outside the Czar's apartments saw the door of his room flung back with a crash. He recognized the figure of Prince Peter Volkonsky standing in the opening.

"The Emperor!" he shouted. "Get Sir James Wylie! Hurry, hurry, for God's sake!"

The terrified footman ran down the corridor and threw himself at the door of Sir James's suite, hammering on the panels with his fists. Within minutes the doctor had raced to the Emperor's apartments, followed by Tarasov, while members of the household gathered in groups, watching the Empress brought from her room and heard the door of Alexander's bedroom open and close every few minutes. Slowly the sounds of panic died away; the hurried footsteps ceased and the door remained shut, with a pale streak of light shining under it, blotted out by a shadow as someone moved in the room.

As dawn broke, a courier mounted in the courtyard and galloped out of Taganrog, taking the road to St. Petersburg. In less than half an hour another followed him, but turned off towards Poland. Word had spread through the town; already weeping crowds had gathered outside the little stone house, and they murmured as they watched the couriers go. St. Petersburg and the Dowager Empress Marie. . . . Mother of God, pity the mother in her grief! Warsaw, and the Grand Duke Constantine, the heir to his brother's throne.

Alexander Pavlovitch, Czar and Autocrat of All the Russias lay dying.

The morning of December 1st was cold and grey; Taganrog was empty, most of the population were attending Mass for the Emperor's recovery or standing outside his house watching the windows. There was only one ship in the bay; the rest had sailed before ice formations closed the entrance to the Sea of Azov. The lone ship was British, the private yacht of Earl Cathcart, who had been Ambassador to Petersburg and a friend of the Czar.

By half-past ten that morning a large crowd had gathered round the Royal residence; a door opened and someone posted a notice. There was a rush forward and someone who could read was pushed to the front. It was a few minutes before eleven, and suddenly a wail went up from the crowd. One old peasant lifted his voice above them. . . . "Far flies the Eagle to rest with God. . . ." The Czar was dead.

The Empress Elizabeth heard them as she stood by a window, looking down on the heads of the people, seeing them sink to their knees to pray for the flight of the White Eagle of legend and ballad, who had delivered his soul to God. It was the name his humble millions of subjects had given him after 1812. . . . She went to her dressing-table, opened her jewel-case and took out the miniature of Alexander in its frame of large diamonds. The painted face stared up at her, young, incredibly handsome; but it was a dead face; the artist had not been able to catch the

expression. Neither had anyone else who painted him. . . .
She fastened the miniature to her black dress and then
walked slowly out of the room; Prince Volkonsky and Sir
James Wylie were waiting to escort her to Alexander's suite,
where the body, its face swathed in bandages, was laid out
on the Emperor's bed.

On December the 26th the Grand Duke Nicholas ascended
the throne according to the terms of Alexander's will, and
Constantine renounced his claim for ever. The body of
the dead Czar remained in Taganrog until the funeral
procession to St. Petersburg started on January 10th. By
then there were no ships left in the harbour; Lord Cathcart's
yacht had sailed suddenly after December 1st and was on
its way to the Holy Land.

*   *   *

The candles were lit in the Czar's study in the Winter
Palace, the red curtains drawn across windows covered by a
crust of snow, and the portrait of Catherine the Great looked
down on a new Czar sitting at the desk she had used more
than fifty years before. The year was 1837, and the Czar
was Nicholas. He was reading a long report and frowning;
the room was very quiet except for the rustle of paper as
he turned a page; the silver candelabra shed their light at
his elbow, placed at the same angle as when his brother
read and worked in that room and at that same desk. He
put the report down and began to write a letter. It was
addressed to the Governor of a Siberian province which
included the penal colony of Bogoyavlensk. It was a terse
letter, for Nicholas wrote and spoke in parade ground
brevity.

'A saintly hermit known at Feodor Kusmitch, who lived
in Bogoyavlensk, came under the Imperial protection like
all religious pilgrims, and was on no account to be pressed
into labour gangs or supervised by the police. The Governor
himself would be held responsible. . . .

'Any person claiming to have seen the late Emperor

Alexander living in the Governor's district, or that the said Feodor Kusmitch resembled him, was to be flogged, irrespective of age or sex, and deported to the mines.'

*   *   *

Eighty years afterwards, the great-grandson of the Czar Nicholas I was marched down a flight of steps into a cellar in a house in Ekaterinburg, the town named by Potemkin in honour of Catherine the Great. The little cavalcade moved slowly down into the gloom, for the Czarevitch was scarcely able to walk. A few moments later the Czar, his Czarina, their daughters and the little sick Czarevitch were shot dead. The Emperor Nicholas II was the last to die, after being forced to watch the execution of his family.

The last fusillade of shots ended the Romanov dynasty. Lenin and the Bolsheviks were ruling Russia from the Kremlin.

The Revolutionaries had been in power for some time before they heard rumours that the tomb of one of the greatest of the Russian Czars was full of priceless jewellery and valuables which had been buried with him. The order was given to open the grave.

The tomb was in the vault of the church of the St. Peter and Paul Fortress; it was inscribed with the name Alexander the First, and the date, December 1st, 1825. It took the efforts of a squad of men working with picks to dislodge the monument; when the hollow beneath it was uncovered, a gust of foul air rose in the stuffy vault. Ropes and tackle were lowered into the pit by torchlight and round the shell of a coffin lying at the bottom. With great care it was hauled to the surface, edged on to the floor, and the ropes untied. There was a long pause, while the men who had brought the dead out of his grave hesitated, their lights shining on the old stained casket, with the remains of gilding still gleaming on the sides.

The tombs of other Czars made high shadows on the walls. Peter the Great, the Empresses Catherine I, Anna,

Elizabeth; the murdered Peter III and his wife, the Great Catherine . . . Paul I. The grave of the Empress Elizabeth Alexeievna, Consort of the Czar Alexander I with the date May 16th, 1826 . . . Nicholas I, Alexander II, the gentle Czar who liberated the serfs and was killed by a Nihilist bomb . . . the tyrant Alexander III. And the place where the last Nicholas should have lain. But his body, and those of his wife and their children had been burnt and thrown into a pit full of quicklime. . . .

"Open it!" The order echoed through the silent place. A blow from a pickaxe split the coffin lid. The Commissar in charge of the exhumation knelt by the casket and levered the lid off with a chisel; impatiently he pushed it aside and plunged his torch into the inside.

One of the men on the edge of the group stood on his toes to look, and then quickly made the gesture now forbidden by the new régime, the Sign of the Cross.

No one saw him; they were all staring at the coffin of the Czar Alexander. It was empty.

EVELYN ANTHONY

CURSE NOT THE KING

It is ten years since Catherine the Great ascended the Imperial Throne of All the Russias. Now she is locked in a bitter and deadly conflict with her hated son, Paul Petrovitch. His ugly twisted face, so like his father's, is a constant reminder of the bloody act that gave her the throne.

Although the hatred is mutual, Catherine cannot bring herself to give the order that would remove this thorn from her flesh. For twenty years they play cat and mouse but in the end Paul survives – only to go down in history as the Death's Head Czar . . .

'Evelyn Anthony is a master of the art of story-telling'
Woman and Home

Post·A·Book

A Royal Mail service in association with the Book Marketing Council & The Booksellers Association.
Post-A-Book is a Post Office trademark.

MORE TITLES AVAILABLE FROM
HODDER AND STOUGHTON PAPERBACKS

EVELYN ANTHONY

☐ 48762 3	Curse Not The King	£2.99
☐ 42092 8	Imperial Highness	£2.95

JOHN ATTENBOROUGH

☐ 42649 7	Destiny Our Choice	£2.95

NOEL BARBER

☐ 34709 0	A Farewell To France	£3.95
☐ 37772 0	A Woman Of Cairo	£3.95

All these books are available at your local bookshop or newsagent, or can be ordered direct from the publisher. Just tick the titles you want and fill in the form below.

Prices and availability subject to change without notice.

Hodder & Stoughton Paperbacks, P.O. Box 11, Falmouth, Cornwall.

Please send cheque or postal order, and allow the following for postage and packing:

U.K. – 55p for one book, plus 22p for the second book, and 14p for each additional book ordered up to a £1.75 maximum.

B.F.P.O. and EIRE – 55p for the first book, plus 22p for the second book, and 14p per copy for the next 7 books, 8p per book thereafter.

OTHER OVERSEAS CUSTOMERS – £1.00 for the first book, plus 25p per copy for each additional book.

Name ....

Address ....

....